W9-AYP-437

Seasons of Sun
A Novel

Paula Renee Burzawa

Hope you enjoy my Greek Story —

— Paula Burzawa

iUniverse, Inc.
New York   Bloomington

Seasons of Sun
A Novel

Copyright © 2010 by Paula Renee Burzawa

This is a work of fiction. All of the characters, names, incidents, organizations, and dialogue in this novel are either the products of the author's imagination or are used fictitiously.

iUniverse books may be ordered through booksellers or by contacting:

iUniverse
1663 Liberty Drive
Bloomington, IN 47403
www.iuniverse.com
1-800-Authors (1-800-288-4677)

Because of the dynamic nature of the Internet, any Web addresses or links contained in this book may have changed since publication and may no longer be valid. The views expressed in this work are solely those of the author and do not necessarily reflect the views of the publisher, and the publisher hereby disclaims any responsibility for them.

ISBN: 978-1-4502-5104-4 (sc)
ISBN: 978-1-4502-5105-1 (dj)
ISBN: 978-1-4502-5106-8 (ebook)

Library of Congress Control Number: 2010912024

Printed in the United States of America

iUniverse rev. date: 08/27/2010

For my mother:
Thank you for giving me Greece and teaching me how to live.

For my father:
Thank you for showing me the world, and the value of home.

For my Yiayia:
Thank you for your wisdom, for Magoula, and for surviving.

For my relatives in the village:
Thank you for your abundant love that brings me back.

For Elaine:
Thank you for your trueness. You are my rock star.

For John:
Thank you for helping me realize my dreams.

For John Michael and Athena:
Thank you for letting me show you the magic.
May you see the wonder and someday create your own story.

God bless you all.

Vassara is life. Vassara is love. Vassara is a miracle village. Vassara is a story worth telling.

Contents

Chapter I
Endings Before Beginnings

THEIR FACES ARE MINE. So is the smell of wood-burning ovens cooking afternoon feasts. The secluded road to Koulouri is mine, along with the view from its edge. The day of the Transfiguration, the courtyard of Brikakis' café, even the abandoned school belongs to me. Forgotten classrooms remain frozen in history behind locked doors. Walking the narrow, cobblestone roads, I see a shepherd, his wrinkled, leather grin aged by the sun. Radiant children sing with laughter, chasing a ball across the town square. Old widows wearing black kerchiefs ride sidesaddle atop sluggish donkeys to harvest fields of almond and olive trees. These are the faces of my villagers, and they belong to me.

They are mine as I have come to cherish them, summer after summer, growing from child to adult in the isolated mountain village of Vassara, located in Greece's Peloponnese. Originally called "Baccharas," Vassara was named in ancient times after the god of wine, since the best wine in the region came from these hills. Through time, Baccharas became Vassaras, and it is simply called Vassara today. Stories have long been told about this village, its traditions and uniqueness in the Greek countryside of Parnonas. Family history and folklore are passed down from generation to generation.

I first visited Vassara in the spring of 1984 after my mother's sister passed away from cancer. What grew from her death was life itself. My aunt was in her forties—too young to die. I took her death particularly hard, crumbling from heartbreak. Grieving for her sister, my mother decided to travel to Greece for the summer. Somehow, the trip would heal our pain. I was about to start high school, and like any preteen, I was utterly insecure. Sad, confused, and intimidated by the world, a vacation abroad seemed the perfect prescription.

Like any transatlantic flight, ours was long and boring, with small portions of bad food. Unfortunately, the ride to Mom's ancestral home outside Sparta wasn't much different. During the 1980s, the highway which connects Athens directly to the main cities in Southern Greece was still in the planning stages. We endured rugged, poorly maintained country roads, adding another six hours to our journey, winding up and down mountainous terrain in a cab lacking air-conditioning. By itself, the ride might have been tolerable if we hadn't just finished a nine-hour flight to Holland, a three-hour layover, and another four-hour trip to Athens. To make matters worse, this was long before the days of the CD Walkman or iPod. Tuning out this strange, new world was not an option.

I sat in the back of Spiro's cab, gazing out the window at a place I didn't recognize, speechless in my uncertainty. With a small, portable boom box on my lap, I played all of my American cassette tapes on the long ride, one after the other, trying to make out the lyrics over our cab driver's voice. His volume increased dramatically as he overemphasized political opinions to my unassuming mother in the front seat.

Mom spent most of the cab ride evading Spiro's questions regarding Greece's relationship with the United States while he took us around every mountain-edged curve at daring speeds. Gripping the backseat's center partition with intensity, I tried at one point to understand their Greek conversation, but to no avail. Despite my lessons at Greek school, Spiro spoke too fast for my elementary skills. Their discussion was above both my head and interest. At only fourteen, I had little desire or knowledge to debate my own country's politics, let alone the world at large. My friends and I back home talked about Madonna, not Milosevic. Boring banter between Spiro and my mother continued endlessly. Poor Mom seemed trapped in his questioning. She politely attempted to neutralize his hatred for the United States, Reagan, and the entire American way of life, but her efforts went unrewarded. The only thing he seemed to like was American tourist dollars.

Every now and then, Spiro, who actually lived next door to our house in Greece, looked back in the rearview mirror, flashing his decaying, yellowed teeth to ask if I was okay. I think "okay" was his only English word. Spiro had a wife of his own, and they had four kids, all under the age of six. Their farm, consisting of goats, chickens, and orange trees, was adjacent to our property in a town called Magoula, on the outskirts of Sparta in Southern Greece. We didn't see Spiro much during our visits, except for rides to and from the airport in Athens.

Spiro's wife, Stathoula, however, visited us early each day, eager to learn about our life in Chicago. She sat for hours chattering with Mom over a coffee cup in the morning sun. Stathoula's daily arrival into our courtyard was as timely as the rooster's crow at daybreak. She was friendly and spoke English well. She didn't hate Americans, which was helpful. Stathoula was also pretty, with long, dark hair and big, dark eyes. Her curiosity caught me off guard. Staring at every detail from our makeup to our shoes, Stathoula asked an endless list of probing questions. Her constant inquiries made me feel like an alien.

Our house in Magoula served as headquarters for our trips to Greece, allowing us to unpack our bags and have a central location for the season in my mother's childhood home. During the winter, the house was closed, but it was cared for by another nearby friend who lived on the other side of Spiro. Each May, my grandparents moved in for a six-month stay until they returned to Chicago the following October. Since they arrived in Magoula first, the house was filled with food, and the bedrooms were prepared for our stay. Equipped with a washing machine, two televisions, and a telephone, we had the basic amenities. Mom and I were comfortable in Magoula, and we were grateful that we had a place to leave our things. The Magoula house was like a second home, complete with mail from the Greek postman. Before I left Chicago, I handed out stacks of self-addressed envelopes to my friends with the hopes of staying in touch with girlfriends back home. Each afternoon, I eagerly awaited the mail for envelopes with my name written in familiar handwriting. Getting a letter from the States was gold.

Sparta's small suburb of Magoula is made up of homes set on properties abundant with lemon and orange groves. Some of the homes were gorgeously renovated and looked like estates. Others were left as farms from the 1940s, when Greeks fled to America during and after World War II in large numbers. The two-story, white house at the end of the street stood vacant for many years after my mother left in 1951 as a child, but reconstruction work began

3

on the place in the 1960s, and the house gradually became updated. My grandmother, or *Yiayia* as we say in Greek, made improvements each year on her visits to Greece. One year, she had the roof redone. Another year, she put in new windows. Whatever money Yiayia saved from her waitress job in Chicago, she put into her Greek home. The Magoula house was supposed to be the place where Yiayia would live for the rest of her life, but as fate played out, this never came to pass. After my biological grandfather was killed in World War II, Yiayia was left alone to care for her three small children. Unable to survive in a country torn apart by war, she closed up the house and went to live with relatives in America.

Standing outside the front gate in Magoula, I tried to imagine what went through Yiayia's mind when she returned home to Greece for the first time in the late 1960s. How did she feel seeing her home for the first time in almost two decades? Her courage to refurbish the place after all those years into a vacation home we came to love was remarkable. Later remarried to a friend from Magoula, Yiayia and her second husband were able to keep the house going, to our benefit. Even though he was not my biological grandfather, I still called him Pappou (grandfather). After seeing the house they resurrected together, I felt a sense of curiosity regarding the past and those who helped build our family home.

The Magoula house stood at the end of a dirt path, running parallel to a larger main road that connects downtown Sparta to the town of Mistras, making for constant traffic. One of the house's most noticeable details was the large, green entrance gate. Standing roughly eight feet high and twelve feet wide, the gate's large stature created an impressive entryway. Beautiful, bright orange climbing flowers cascaded across the archway atop the gate, but at the same time, they encouraged an infestation of bumblebees. Hundreds of them buzzed over the gate at all times. This made a peaceful entrance into or exit from our home impossible. Fearful of getting stung, I quickly came up with a "duck and run" method.

Past the main bee gate was a large courtyard of white marble flooring my uncle laid when the house was restored. Walking through the courtyard was like a florist's dream, as Yiayia filled the adjacent gardens on both sides with roses. She loved flowers. Soft fragrance filled the lower level. On the first floor of the house was the living room and kitchen. I spent little time in the living room area since my grandparents slept there on two pull-out beds. The room smelled like my grandparents' apartment back on Armitage Avenue in Chicago, and to be honest, the entire room grossed me out. Pappou's pajamas were always lying around, along with ashtrays filled with old cigarette butts.

Next to the living room was our kitchen, large and accommodating. We had a new refrigerator and a huge sink, making food easy to prepare. The floor was tiled black-and-white checked, and above the sink was a huge window that looked out unto the property. Past the kitchen stood a small tool room with a door that led out to the abandoned chicken coop. I liked to go back there every now and then and look at the decaying building, still untouched from the time my mother's father, Anastasios, was alive. I imagined him inside the tiny, white-stoned structure, collecting chicken eggs from the chickens and bringing his yield to Yiayia. For some reason, I felt his presence there more than anywhere else in our Magoula home. The chicken coop was the only edifice left alone since his death. Standing near the tattered, old shack was the closest I could feel to a man I never knew, in a place he left long ago.

The property beyond the chicken coop area was full of tall, dried grass, and it was not safe to walk around in it. Thorns, snakes, spiders, and who knows what else lurked in the tall, dry grass. I didn't dare explore. A chain-link fence sectioned off the orchards with our adjacent neighbor, and the rest of the property was thick with green citrus trees. Since we traveled to Greece in the summer, I never saw our fruit ready for picking. The oranges and lemons were still small, green, and hard. Like me, they had yet to ripen.

Connecting the main floor to the upstairs level of the house was a large, outdoor, marble staircase. The stairs were both wide and tall, with hard, sharp edges. I cautiously held on to the metal railings every time I ascended or descended. Atop the staircase was our home's greatest asset—the terrace. This was the most beautiful terrace I had ever seen. Our view overlooking the mountains was breathtaking. Most of all, our terrace gave a marvelous, perfect view of Mount Taygetos, the grandest mountain in Peloponnese's valley. Mount Taygetos is not only tall but quite wide, with a dimple in the middle. The mountain always reminded me of a giant letter *M*. From Mount Taygetos, locals gather the sweetest mountain tea, selling it at local markets and street corners. Taygetos, the timeless warrior, stands tall in pronounced glory, reaching the top of the Mediterranean sky, demanding attention. I loved to sit endlessly staring at the mountain to soak in its glory, imagining ancient Spartans using Taygetos as a protector from invading forces.

A huge, wrought iron railing bordered the terrace and reached the same heights as the treetops, offering a panoramic vision of green. What looked like an endless carpeting of emerald orange trees rolled foward into the distance. From the terrace, Magoula's orchards stretched out to a blue haze of mountains and created a horizon, making the view nothing less than majestic.

We kept two white, wooden chairs and a small, round table on the balcony to soak in the tranquility at sunset. Late at night, the terrace provided a different sense of wonder, a true astronomer's dream. The black sky, illuminated with thousands of stars, set off a mesmerizing glow. On nights of a full moon, the cosmic beauty was impossible to ignore. I would sit atop our Magoula balcony, entranced by the wonders of nature. Staring up at the sky on quiet evenings of solitude, I thought about who I was and what my future might bring. I confessed many personal dreams to the glistening stars and received a hundred answers back from the night sky.

The days in Magoula, however, passed with much less excitement. Within a week of arriving from Chicago, and without having gone anywhere else in the country except Yiayia's house in Magoula, I was soon bored out of my mind. Even though the scenery was amazing, after a while, I grew restless.

I can still recall the day that all changed. I was the last one in the house to wake up. Having stayed awake late into the night to look at stars, I was kept up for the rest of the night by a pack of wild dogs that ran through the streets, making sleep nearly impossible. As soon as the dogs settled down, roosters began to crow at daybreak. Still in bed well after 11:00 am, the summer heat blared. Warm air filled my bedroom. Sweat covered my body.

Unlike other mornings, when a foreign-sounding horn or my mother's voice woke me, this particular morning began with a shuffling of slippers clapping atop each marble step of the terrace outside my bedroom window. The giant metal door opened and then slammed shut, making a cruelly loud bang. I jumped from the crack. This door was the loudest in the universe, I decided. In walked Yiayia, calling out, *"Kimate akoma"* (Is she still sleeping)?

There was no use trying to fall back asleep. I was awake. Yiayia entered my bedroom carrying a tray with Greek coffee. She always carried a tray of something, always with a colorful apron tied around her waist. After placing the tray on the orange tablecloth-covered round table standing in the center of my room, she asked me, as she did every morning, what I wanted for breakfast. I replied, *"Tipota"* (Nothing), much to her dismay. Already a regular coffee drinker at fourteen, I cared little about nourishment besides my short cup of hot, semisweet Greek coffee. This would snap me out of a sleepy state.

Yiayia returned downstairs, clanging the big metal door again, off to clean or hang our clothes on the lines of string stretched across the terrace. This was so embarrassing. In Chicago, we had a dryer like everyone else, and no one knew the colors of our underwear or pajamas. Here, everything was on display for the entire town to see. Whenever one of the neighbors stopped by to visit Yiayia, they had to bend down or get hit in the head with pink and white flowered panties hanging from the line. To my mother and grandmother, there was no shame. Everything embarrassed me. I embarrassed me. My braces embarrassed me. My stupid hairstyle embarrassed me. I knew I was awkward and hated feeling this way. European girls I saw in Sparta looked confident, so easygoing, with free-flowing hair and little makeup. Feeling self-assured seemed easy for them.

By the time I awoke, my mother was already out of the house. Why didn't she wake me? Didn't she know going into downtown Sparta was the only highlight of my otherwise boring day? While I waited for Mom to return, I hit play to the cassette tape sitting in the travel boom box that sat on the nightstand. Playing one of the mixed cassettes I'd taped off of the radio in Chicago, I sang along to top-forty pop songs. Both the mailman and Stathoula asked if they could keep my American song tapes when I returned home. That first summer, however, I left them all with Stavros, hoping he would better understand me by listening to my music.

While Bananarama's "Cruel Summer" jammed through the upstairs level of our house, I drank the first sips of coffee, still half asleep. My bare feet shuffled across the wood-planked floors, and I sang along to the prophetic tune. Blasting American music always made me feel better. My collection of mixed tapes was one of the few connections to home and all that was normal. A few letters from my friends in Chicago sat on the chair next to my bed. I'd read and reread them at night when homesickness was in full swing. Summer was nowhere near over. In fact, it had just begun. I already felt like we had been in Greece forever.

At the age of fourteen, there was absolutely nothing cool about being with grandparents in a foreign country. I was anxious for action, especially in a land famous for world-class beaches, legendary islands, gorgeous Greek men, and fantastic nightclubs. The potential for excitement was immeasurable.

Meanwhile, Ben Gay permeated the upstairs, and granny-sized underpants hung to dry off the balcony's railing. I had no one to go with me to the beaches. I was too young to visit nightclubs in town. Stathoula, the nosy neighbor, was too old to be my girlfriend. Stuck in the house with Yiayia, my step-grandfather, and mother, I missed my friends. I missed air-conditioning. I missed Walgreens.

Down the hall and into the scary bathroom, I headed for a morning shower, where one never knew what creature lurked. It might be a lizard. It might be a new breed of spider. I was brave. The upstairs bathroom was like an alien planet. Although I tried like crazy, I was never able to completely remove the bugs. They were everywhere. Setting out my clean towel on the pedestal sink, I pulled the shower curtain back only to discover a chameleon on the bathtub wall. The lizardlike creature waited to scare me. Standing naked, I screamed my head off at the ugly monster stuck to the shower wall. Thoughts of *Psycho* came to mind. The memory of that chameleon was in my head every time I pulled back a shower curtain for the rest of the vacation.

Even though Yiayia and Pappou had their own bathroom downstairs, they still kept a lot of essentials upstairs. Half of the bathroom was littered with dried-up VO5 shampoo bottles, leaky Ben Gay tubes, and orange plastic denture containers. The other half of the sink contained Yiayia's rollers, dirty hairbrushes, and stacks upon stacks of hard washcloths. I made it my mission to do an entire bathroom sweep and get the bathroom clean. I needed something or someplace of my own, no matter how small.

After the bathroom was cleared of all creepy crawlers and my grandparents' things, I began what was a two-hour process of getting ready, perfecting both hair and makeup. I had nothing else to do that day, and I was still figuring out a beauty routine. I fantasized that a gorgeous Greek might miraculously drive down our forgotten road and take me to the beach. Realizing this was unlikely, I kept my attention on the green curling iron plugged into the outlet through an awkward-fitting converter.

By the time I was finally ready, Mom came back from town. The kitchen pumped in activity with the arrival of fresh fruits and vegetables. Smells of heated olive oil and tomato sauce permeated through the air, and I prayed something good was coming for lunch. I knew our meal wasn't going to be Kraft Macaroni & Cheese, but I hoped for something edible. Even though I enjoyed Greek food, I still found enjoying the local food challenging. Instead,

I consumed a lot of bread, salad, and ice cream. Only my obsession with Greek *tiropitas*, or cheese pies, tempted my palate. The flaky, buttery, phyllo pies filled with Greek cheeses and baked in local *fournos,* or bakeries, were sold hot each morning. I had to devour a *tiropita* every day.

Our meals were typical—a Greek village salad consisting of fresh tomatoes, cucumbers, green peppers, and Kalamata olives soaking in fresh olive oil with a huge chunk of fresh feta cheese. Heavily flavored with oregano and sea salt, even the french fries took on a Greek twist. Bread from the bakery down the road was irresistible. We also had freshly cooked green beans in a tomato sauce called *fasolia*. All of this was tolerable, with the exception of the main course. I found the meat category completely disgusting. No one ever gave me a straight answer as to what animal was being served. I simply couldn't eat what could only be termed as mystery meat. Looking at small, curvy bones on a platter clearly indicated that the meat was *not* chicken. Yiayia never owned up to the identity of the meat, and even Mom seemed unsure. She didn't eat it, either. I suppose this could have been rabbit or goat. I knew the meat wasn't lamb. In addition, the custom of eating a big meal in the middle of the day was never to my liking. I didn't want hot, heavily sauced food of any kind when it was one hundred degrees in the shade. A simple, sliced turkey sandwich on whole wheat with lettuce and tomato and a bag of chips would have been perfect, but that wasn't going to happen.

After lunchtime, boredom set in, and I was ready to do something. At the same time, the town shuts down for afternoon siesta like most cities in Greece. This meant that all of the stores and even the post office closed for several hours. I longed for a big swimming pool in which to pass the day away like the public pools back home. With rising temperatures making the outside unbearable, our only relief was to sleep or somehow get to the beach. The coastal down of Gythion was only a thirty-minute jaunt, but I was too young to drive. My world was a lot smaller. I could only pass the hot afternoons away sitting in the shade and reading two-month old copies of *Cosmopolitan.* My golden days in the sun were still around the corner.

That day after lunch, however, Mom said we were leaving Magoula to stay at her summer village home of Vassara, about twenty minutes away. She said the town was up in the mountains. I was glad to get out of Magoula, but I was unsure if this next place would be better or worse. Little did I know that this was the most important day of my life, and I would never be the same again.

Chapter 2
Out of the Hills of Parnonas

PAPPOU PACKED OUR OVERNIGHT bags into the Audi that he left parked in our makeshift garage in Greece each year. I'm not sure what year the car was, but the small, gray, compact car seemed in decent shape—if only Pappou knew how to drive. I was certain he was the world's worst driver, even though I had yet to obtain my own license. Every time he turned the key, the car screeched a horrific, bloodcurdling cry for help as he shifted gears. Pappou pounded his fist on the steering wheel, cursing in Greek, insulting the car as if it were an uncooperative donkey. Poor Pappou had no understanding of a manual transmission, although he loved to believe his difficulties were the car's fault. Since Mom wasn't comfortable driving through Greece's winding mountains with an absence of streetlights and speed limits, Pappou was unfortunately our only driver.

With the Audi finally moving, Pappou, Yiayia, Mom, and I passed through Sparta's city limits. I quickly realized that in order to reach the surrounding villages of Parnonas, where Vassara was located, we would have to endure steeply inclined roads. My stomach flipped over like a pancake looking at the rounded roads of oncoming mountains. Streets quickly changed from straight pavement to curvy, dirt roads that twisted and turned, winding up through the hills. The Audi made each bend against high cliffs. I tried not to look down, tightly squeezing the handle of my boom box with sweaty hands. Concentrating on lyrics from Van Halen's "Jump" was my only diversion.

Eventually, we came to a fork in the road that left us two choices: continue onward toward Tripoli, another large city in Greece's Peloponnese, or head further inland to Vassara, one of three small villages in the mountains. A large municipal sign at the fork announced Tripoli—68 Kilometers with a white arrow pointed to the left. A smaller, much older, hand-painted sign stood underneath reading Vassara, Verroia, Tsintzina with an arrow to the right but no indication of distance. The sign could have easily read Paradise: This Way. We turned right, and I grew nervous, wondering where in the world we were headed. This was my first trip through these hills, and the idea that anyone lived in them had me baffled. I thought our house in Magoula was meager, without air-conditioning or a washing machine, but at least we had the city of Sparta nearby. Now I would be roughing it even more—an unsettling thought to a suburbanite teen.

"How much farther is this place?" I asked my mother, who was sitting in the front seat.

"Oh, it's a ways. We have to go through these mountains first."

Everywhere I looked, I saw green. Green hills, green trees ... we were surrounded. How much more "through the mountains" was there? Turning up the volume on my boom box, I closed my eyes, hoping not to get carsick. After an eternity of winding, we came across a small creek with a red painted bridge. Mom became excited.

"Oh, look, Ma!" She turned around from the front seat and tapped Yiayia, who had fallen asleep next to me in the back. "The red bridge."

Yiayia opened her eyes and smiled. *"Eimaste konta"* (We're close).

I sat up in my seat and lowered the music.

"Look! Look! There it is!" Mom rolled down the window and pointed. I didn't see a thing.

"Where? What are you guys talking about?"

"Over there. See?" Mom pointed.

We were in a sea of green. Tall cypress trees and evergreens stretched high to the sky. The countryside was endless. I scanned the landscape but saw nothing. Then, very far off in the distance, a little, white speck appeared.

"That's Agia Triatha, the church that sits on top of Vassara. Now that we can see it, we will soon see the entire village," Mom exclaimed.

Mom was right. Out of nowhere, a tapestry of little houses visibly unfolded onto the mountainside ahead. With every turn, we saw more of the village.

The church of Agia Triatha sat like a watchdog atop the entire community. A small line that was the main road zigzagged through the town. Houses grew vivid as we approached. Each home was a clone of the one next to it—white stone walls with clay-shingled roofs. Like a fairytale land, Vassara came out of nowhere and looked ancient.

"This is where I was born, kiddo." Mom stretched her arm out the window.

I rolled my window down to take in a breath of cool mountain air and smelled the brick ovens burning. Someone was cooking dinner over an open fire. Vassara expanded far across the approaching hillside. The village was bigger than I'd imagined. We could see a school and a town square. Vassara's entire community was nestled away in Peloponnese's isolated mountains. Its location was like a secret, keeping the rest of the world away. Our car continued along the main road, which became paved again, marking our entrance into the village. We passed a shepherd directing his flock of sheep. His tattered clothing and wrinkled face made him look like he stepped out of a storybook written a hundred years ago. The shepherd stopped and smiled at us, holding his tall, wooden staff up in the air.

"*Yia*!" he called out to greet us.

"*Yia*!" Pappou answered with a smile.

We passed a clearing that had planted vegetables. Pappou slowed down as we drove next to a fenced-off area.

"*Kita to kipo kipera, Maria*" (Look at the garden up there, Maria). Yiayia pointed.

"That's Tatzaforo's garden, right, Ma?"

"*Nai*" (Yes).

Mom turned around and smiled. "Your uncle Tatzaforo keeps his garden on the outskirts of Vassara. Look at the tomatoes he's growing!"

"How come no one steals his stuff?" I asked. Everyone in the car laughed.

"What?"

"Not Tatzaforo," Pappou answered. "No one messes with *him*."

I didn't understand. "What's so intimidating about Tatzaforo?"

"The man was the sheriff around here," Pappou answered. "All of the villagers respect and fear him."

"Well, he's not a sheriff anymore," I persisted.

"Once a lawman, always a lawman. You'll see what we mean when you meet him."

"Will there be anyone for me to hang out with?" I asked.

"Your cousin Despina is just a year older than you, and your cousin Petro is eighteen. He's about to go into the army in September," Pappou explained.

"Why?"

"Because he has to," Pappou popped up again. "Greek government says so. All young men of eighteen must serve their country for two years."

"Great," I thought. "That means all the cute eighteen-year-olds won't be around. There goes my chance of meeting an older guy and having a summer romance." Fifteen-year-old boys didn't exactly thrill me, especially if they were dorks like those back home.

We finally stopped winding and traveled straight onto the main road.

Yiayia pointed and said, *"Eki inai o kambos"* (There's the lowland)!

"Huh?"

Mom translated. "That's the *cambo*. It's like an athletic area, see? There's a soccer field over there."

"Cool." I figured that if there was soccer, there would be kids. Things were looking up. I started becoming excited to meet my cousins.

Just then, Pappou suddenly pulled the car to the side of the road and turned the engine off.

"Why are we stopping?" I asked.

"Remember the special church I told you about?" Mom asked. I nodded. "Hopefully, Ourania is there, and you can meet her now." She smiled.

As I looked beyond the tall, green trees, a white cobblestone path led to a large gate with a circle-shaped icon of the Virgin Mary over the entrance. The attached buildings were new. A white church with a large bell tower stood beyond the gates. This was the monastery I had heard so much about.

The church and its entire complex was the result of an old woman named Ourania. As I had been told, Ourania had a vision one night where the Virgin Mary told her to build a church in Vassara. Initially, Ourania didn't grasp the meaning of her dream, but a series of miraculous events that subsequently followed persuaded her to continue. Shortly after, Ourania noticed a reflection of the Virgin Mary's image in a glass window on a windowpane. Everyone came to see the extraordinary sight. The face of the mother of Jesus clearly appeared on the glass. Villagers were astonished. Ourania was deeply moved, and many Vassareans believed. Although Ourania questioned how she would raise enough money to fund the construction, people from all over began to respond. Along with Vassareans living in America, Canada, and Australia, enough money was raised, and the church was successfully built. Together with many contributors, Ourania had answered the Virgin Mary's request. Then, a large icon of the Mother of God, or *Panayia*, as she is called in Greek, began to cry. Wet tears dripped down from the Virgin Mary's eyes to dampen the icon. Christian believers were amazed at this holy sight.

We walked up to the church and looked for Ourania but didn't find the nun. The place was quiet. I felt an aura of peace in the stillness of the air. Only the sound of wind blowing through the trees broke the undisturbed silence. This was a small monastery, different from the larger, more populated monasteries that become the destination of religious pilgrims worldwide. The only visitors to this holy place were local people and those like us who returned to Vassara for vacation. Without any nuns populating the ground, the only person living in the monastery was the old nun, Ourania.

Yiayia called, and a few minutes later, a small, delicate old lady appeared. Ourania was short, with gray hair pulled back in a bun and covered in a black kerchief. She wore a black gown like most Greek Orthodox nuns and shuffled her tiny feet across the courtyard in old dusty slippers. She greeted us with a gigantic smile. Her voice was raspy.

"*Kalosorisate, paithia* " (Welcome, children). Yiayia kissed her hands and cheeks, and they embraced. When we were introduced, Ourania reached up with both her hands, placing them on my cheeks. "Bless you, child," she said in Greek.

I felt awkward as I hugged her, not sure if I should be afraid. But something made me feel as if I had known her all my life. Fear quickly fell away. I was instantly comfortable in her presence and felt as if she somehow understood me. Without saying a word, she looked right through me and took my hands into hers. I knew she could sense the pain in my heart from my aunt's death, as if she were saying, "It's going to be okay, child. Her pain is over. Don't hang on to yours any longer." Ourania held my hands silently. The moment was surreal. Ourania was completely peaceful. Her warmth reached out and enveloped me as my eyes filled with tears. I smiled at her with glassy eyes. Her presence was enigmatic. As I looked at Ourania's face, I noticed her beautiful eyes were a mix of blue and green. They held a sparkle like I had never seen. As if this saintly lady beheld the light of God with her own eyes, Ourania glowed with faith, exuding love and serenity.

Yiayia lit a handful of beeswax candles and placed them in a silver tray full of white sand next to the church's altar. Mom directed me to the various icons of holy saints, translating Ourania's blessings. Our visit wasn't long, but it was full of impact. The nun's vision was just the beginning. The blessings and miracles bestowed upon Vassara emanating from this little woman's faith were beyond anyone's understanding that day.

We left the monastery, passed the *cambo,* and headed up the road that led to the town square, or *platia,* as the locals say. Like any of the villages dotting the mountains of Greece, Vassara's *platia* is located at the entrance to the village and has a large tavern. An old, cobblestone parkway stretches around the square with a few benches and trees offering shade to those passing the day away in this common area. The *platia* is the center of the village, where the old men play backgammon and the young kids come to buy ice cream. The town square is also the center stage for anyone entering or leaving Vassara. All major activities take place in the *platia.*

Our car turned through narrow streets where only one vehicle could pass at a time. Pappou beeped his horn loudly to avoid an oncoming collision. I sank low with embarrassment in the backseat and put my boom box up to hide my face. Pappou's driving was bad enough, but announcing our arrival into town was more than I could handle. When we reached the town square, I sat up to peek out the window. A large gathering of villagers enjoyed an evening stroll. Some small children chased a ball from one end of the square to the other. Several groups of old ladies dressed in black sat on park benches.

Everyone seemed to stop and look at us. We might as well have been on stage. A café stood at one end of the square with a middle-aged woman in the doorway. She wore a dirty apron over her modest housedress. Outside the café gathered a group of teenagers, playing cards at a small table and eating ice cream. A few of them looked American. I wondered if they were visiting Vassara for the summer, too. Pappou turned up a cobblestone road, heading to my aunt Vivi's house and then my mother's childhood home.

Mom was instantly a kid. After an absence of thirty-four years, not a face nor a building escaped her memory. She pointed and smiled at every corner, covering her mouth in disbelief that time had stood still in her hometown. As we made the turn up the road to Aunt Vivi's house, I heard screams come out of a large, kitchen window. A door next to the window opened as Aunt Vivi and Uncle Georgo emerged, arms stretched wide, big smiles on their faces. Tears of happiness came down their cheeks. They hadn't seen my mother in decades. I had never met them, but that didn't stop them from squeezing me tightly when I got out of the car. Uncle Georgo lifted me up in a hug and twirled me around.

"Kita tin omorfoula mas" (Look at our little beauty)!

"Ithia Mana" (Resembles her mother exactly).

"Elate, elate" (Come in, come in) …

What my aunt and uncle lacked in riches, they made up for in purity. They were the most sincere relatives I would ever come to know in Greece—loving, humble, good people. With little means, the house they lived in belonged to my uncle Georgo's parents. His mother, my aunt Maria, was Yiayia's sister. Aunt Maria was still alive in 1984, and this would be the last summer before she became bedridden.

Yiayia and her sister, Maria, were total opposites like Country Mouse and City Mouse. While Yiayia had a modern hairdo of strawberry blonde, Aunt Maria's all-white hair was pulled back in a greasy bun. Yiayia had the latest fashion circa 1980s from Sears, and Aunt Maria had a cotton housecoat with old, masculine, black slippers. Yiayia was completely Americanized in appearance, and her sister exuded the essence of rural mountain village. Looking at my aunt, I imagined this was what Yiayia would have been like if she stayed in Greece. Despite differences, however, Aunt Maria was just as fun loving as Yiayia, and the two mirrored one another enormously. They were closer than ever, and they hugged each other tightly when Yiayia got out of the Audi.

Since my mother was named after my aunt, I could tell Mom had a special place in Aunt Maria's heart. They embraced with tears, and I knew as much as they held onto each other in joyful reunion that they also were embracing in grief over my aunt's death. I fought back the tears as I watched them console one another. Soon, we were invited inside by my aunt and uncle. As is typical with Greeks, the first order of business is always to sit down and break bread with relatives or friends. We hadn't driven to our house yet, which was only around the corner, and we didn't bother to unpack bags. Our arrival in Vassara was all about reconnecting with family, enjoying the food, and showing our love. This meant coming together for a traditional meal in our relatives' home. Uncle Georgo said that Aunt Vivi had cooked all morning in anticipation of our arrival. We were led through their giant, green door to a small outdoor courtyard and then passed under a stone overhang to enter their kitchen.

Standing by the stove was a girl only a year older than I. She was my cousin Despina, Aunt Vivi and Uncle Georgo's daughter. Despina was a lot taller than I with a sweet smile and coarse, dark hair that she wore parted on the side in a chin-length bob. Despina's face was gentle and kind. She wore no makeup and had a tomboy figure. At the refrigerator door was her older brother, Petro, who immediately began teasing me like a sibling he had known all his life. Petro had dark hair and was tall, as well. His was an animated face, with a happy-go-lucky grin similar to his father's. Petro and Despina resembled one another, and I could tell they were good friends as well as brother and sister. I was shy and a bit intimidated around them at first, but at the same time, I was happy to discover kids my own age. Petro made a crack about my wearing makeup and dressing up, pointing out that, after all, this was just a village. Despina told me to ignore him. She told me to ignore most of what people would say to me about my American ways and that he and all his friends were clueless. I liked her. I could tell we would be instant friends. We were just that.

Aunt Vivi's kitchen was long and narrow. As our family filled the small space, we bumped into one another as we took our seats at their long, rectangular table. The room seemed all about that table as it stretched from the big window looking out onto the village street to the other side of the room close to the opposite wall.

Not far from the table's edge near the door was Aunt Maria's bed. Across from her bed was a small stand with a black-and-white television next to a green rotary telephone. There was also a modest cupboard that stood high, and as Despina told me later, it hid inside all the many sweets my aunt Maria baked.

Uncle Georgo set out glasses across the table and poured his homemade wine. We clinked our short, thin glasses and drank a toast to the summer. The wine tasted strong and bitter. Despina handed me a Sprite from the fridge after she saw my face crinkle after a first sip. After pleasantries were exchanged, the room grew quiet. Within minutes, everyone began to cry about my aunt. I felt so awkward. I did not want to start crying in front of these people I had just met, and now they were all crying and talking about her beautiful, short life. Despina came from behind the counter and sat next to me, putting her hand on my shoulder, giving me an understanding look. Mom tried to explain to the relatives about her sister's death in general terms, but just as it was hard to get out the facts, my aunts and uncle didn't require details. We sat. We cried. We said little. After a while, Uncle Georgo told everyone that my aunt would not want us to live in despair, and he insisted we go on with our lives in happiness. They all agreed. Wiping their eyes, the heavy sadness in the room slowly lifted as they began telling stories from their childhood. Grief-stricken expressions were replaced with smiles.

All together and all at once, my relatives decided to grieve no longer and continue forward with life. I sat speechless at their transition and looked around the table with wonderment. Despite their pain, my relatives found a way to remember my mother's sister with joy instead of tears. I was amazed by their strength. Like a wake-up call to my soul, I sat up a little straighter and changed my expression, as well. I realized that the time had come for me to move on, as well. For the first time in months, I thought about the future with a sense of optimism that hadn't existed in a very long time. Yiayia always said our family's strength and spirit was as strong as Mount Taygetos. In that moment, everything changed. A black cloud that seemed to hang over my life for the past three months started to evaporate. This was the summer of transformation. I could feel something new and exciting in the warm breeze that blew through the open window in Aunt Vivi's kitchen and was eager to discover whatever was coming my way.

As trays of feta cheese and olives passed between fresh-baked baskets of bread, a man's deep voice called out from the street. His voice grew louder as he approached the corner. Outside of Aunt Vivi's house, the shadowy figure stopped just short of the window where we all sat on the other side of the screen. He called out again, louder, for his American cousin Maria, whom he hadn't seen in years. Mom smiled and stood up, eager to see him. The voice's silhouette now stood in the frame of the kitchen window. He was an old man with a cane. Everyone at the kitchen table cheered. They knew him well. The voice belonged to my mom's first cousin, Stathi, and with his arrival, the party was about to begin.

Chapter 3
Koulouri's Magic

Upon Stathi's entrance, the mood in Despina's kitchen lifted even higher. As if someone had painted the room a different color, nothing after Stathi's presence was the same as before. His jovial energy radiated to the rest of the family. Stathi was a good time on wheels. Wherever he went, drinking, singing, and dancing soon followed. A simple lunch to celebrate our arrival in Vassara quickly became the party of the year. Cameras flashed, Greek bouzouki music blared, and before long, my aunts were dancing around the kitchen table, waving white cloth napkins in the air. Villagers passing by Despina's house heard the hoopla and were invited in for a drink. Before we knew it, Stathi was standing on a chair, holding a plate of Greek meatballs and spaghetti, acting out stories to the crowd from their childhood adventures. Anecdotes included all of the adults in the room, and they laughed themselves to tears while occasionally shouting back corrections to Stathi's version of the truth as he embellished the tales for excitement.

Despina looked at me and rolled her eyes. She had heard these stories a hundred times. Figuring I was bored, as well, she took my hand to leave the table.

"I'm taking my cousin to see the village," she announced.

No one paid attention. Stathi went on storytelling, and the partiers continued to laugh. We got a nod from my mother and Aunt Vivi and were

19

out the door. I was thrilled to escape with someone my age. As the old wooden door slammed shut, it quickly swung open again. Petro came out after us.

"You weren't going to leave me in there with them, were you?" he asked.

"Well, I gave you the signal, but you are oblivious!" Despina said, laughing.

Petro continued, "C'mon, let's go. I can't take any more of Stathi's stories. If I hear the one about the refrigerator falling off of the truck again, I'm going to bust!"

"Do you need cigarettes?" Despina asked her brother.

"Nope. Got 'em."

"Good. Give me some." She turned toward me. "You smoke, right?"

I was embarrassed to tell the truth, but I was not about to try to prove anything. "No. Sorry."

Despina didn't seem to care either way, but Petro looked at me strangely. "What's with you Americans that don't smoke?" asked Petro angrily. He seemed angry when he talked about America.

We walked quickly away from Despina's house as if her mother might come out any second and call us back inside. Heading down a steep hill, they turned right and went toward the *platia*. I picked up the pace to keep up with my cousins. My inappropriate Candies sandals clicked loudly on the cobblestone streets.

Petro continued, "It's as if everyone in the States suddenly became concerned with their health. Meanwhile, your Hollywood actor president is planning to bomb us all into oblivion."

"Leave her alone! You just met her, and already you're being a jerk. Go away so we can talk!" Despina demanded.

"Okay, okay, I'm sorry. I'll lay off you, new girl, but only because you're my cousin. I promise I'll be nice, and I also promise that you'll have a lot more fun than you were having in boring, old Magoula. Weren't you bored there?" Petro said with a smile. Before I could answer, he continued, "Consider me your personal tour guide to the village. I'll introduce you to all the right people, keep you away from all of the idiots, and bring you home safely after showing you a fabulous time. You do drink beer, don't you?"

"Yes," I lied and smiled.

As we walked downhill through the village streets, listening to only the sound of our footsteps and the echo of Petro's voice, I remarked on the quietness of the village.

"It's *mesimeri,*" Despina said. "Everyone is sleeping. They eat a big lunch like what you Americans eat for dinner, and then they all nap until evening."

"You guys, too?" I asked.

"No," she laughed. "Napping is for the very young and the very old. Kids our age usually hang out at the *platia,* play soccer at the *Yipetho,* or even go up to Koulouri if it's not too hot."

I was confused. "What the heck is a *Yipetho?* What is Koulouri? Doesn't that mean cookie in Greek?" Petro began laughing.

"All in good time, cousin, all in good time." He walked ahead.

"*Yipetho* is where we play soccer," Despina explained.

"I thought that was called the *cambo?*" I asked.

"*Cambo* is the area. *Yipetho* is the actual soccer field area," Despina described.

There was obviously a lot to learn about this place. *Yipetho, cambo,* Koulouri! Vassara had its own lingo.

When we approached the *platia,* I couldn't believe how altered the area was from just a few hours earlier. Despina was right. All of the little children were gone, and the adults, too. Only teenagers remained, hiding out from parents, as well, I guessed. Three American-looking guys sat on a bench just outside Brikakis' café and general store, covered in shade behind a tall tree. Right outside the entrance to the general store were two little tables with a group of ten or so watching village kids play *tavli,* or backgammon. Across the town square was another set of benches under a row of olive trees with some girls sitting on them, drinking Cokes out of little bottles with straws.

The whole area was quiet except for the occasional shout of victory by the backgammon crowd. Mrs. Brikaki, the proprietor, wore her white apron and stood inside the café swatting flies. Mr. Brikaki was inside, too, watching EPT1, the only television channel, on a fuzzy, black-and-white television next to the cash register.

"*Ela!*" Despina said. "C'mon. We'll get some Cokes and then show you what Koulouri is."

As we approached the *platia's* main area, everyone stared at me. They knew my cousins and must have figured that I was a relative, but they had to

21

check me out just the same. Their stares reminded me of Stathoula. Petro went by the boys playing backgammon, and Despina showed me into Brikakis'. This was the one and only café and general store in Vassara. With a large patio area filled with chairs around the outside, Brikakis' was a center for villagers to congregate. Little tables filled the area, and Mrs. Brikaki served them from what she sold inside the store.

"Mrs. Brikaki, this is my cousin from Chicago."

"Chicago!" As she opened her mouth to speak, I could see her blackened teeth. Her weathered, animated response startled me. "Oh, my!" she exclaimed. "Do they carry guns on the streets? Aren't you afraid?" Despina went on the defensive again.

"Not everything is like the movies, Mrs. Brikaki! Two Cokes, please, with straws."

"Nice to meet you," I said quietly. Her stained, white apron stretched across her stomach over a blue floral housedress. Her salt-and-pepper-colored hair was cut short and blunt. This woman seemed to have no time for herself, as the café absorbed every bit of energy out of her tired body. Mrs. Brikaki went over to the cooler to grab our Cokes from the bottom shelf. She shuffled across the linoleum floor in her torn, heavy, black slippers, walking slowly as if we might be her only customers for the entire day. Her lethargic stride seemed to tell us that there was no need to hurry. We were in Vassara. No one was going anywhere. What seemed like ten hours later, Mrs. Brikaki came back with two bottles. Despina paid her, and we walked outside to join the backgammon crowd.

The crowd cheered when one of the boys won the game. Some stood up and began walking away from the table. Despina introduced me to a few of the locals. I couldn't remember their names. They smiled. A few of them said things to me in Greek that I just pretended to understand. Despina winked at me, knowing I had no clue what they were saying, but she kept my secret.

Petro called to me from across the *platia*.

"Let's show you what you think is a cookie! *Ela,* Despina. Bring the *American*."

"Koulouri!" One of the old men sitting outside the café jumped in. "Don't you think it's too hot for Koulouri?" he asked.

"It's fine, Mr. Natakos," Despina answered. "The sun is going down in a little while. We'll be fine."

Mr. Natakos shook his head in disagreement and put his hands up in the air. "You kids are crazy! Be careful. It's a long walk up there!"

I looked at Despina for reassurance. She smiled. "It's fine," she said. "We go up there all the time during the day. We'll just take it slow."

Feeling part of a new group, I walked with Petro and Despina as we headed out of the town square, Coke bottles and straws in hand, toward the same road that Pappou had driven up to reach Despina's house when we arrived. The layout of the village was like a puzzle to me, and I was completely confused by the winding streets.

"I'm so lost around here!" I said to them. "Every street looks the same, and none of them are marked with names. How do you find your way?" They both laughed.

Petro smiled and stretched his arms wide. "This town is so small that by tonight, you will know your way around Vassara. Just remember, the *platia* is at the bottom of the village, and our houses are in the middle. Everything else is straight up. If you ever get lost, look up for the steeple of the church, Agia Triatha." He pointed. "Then find St. George's Church underneath it, and remember that your house is to the left." I was confused more than ever but nodded again in false agreement. We passed a street just outside the *platia,* and they both stopped.

"See this cross street?" Despina pointed to the left. "This road takes you straight up to my house. See? Right up that way is my big kitchen window. If you listen closely, you can still hear Stathi telling twenty-five-year-old jokes. Listen!" We paused in silence. Sure enough, we could hear Stathi's deep voice in the distance, followed by laughter. The partiers were still going strong.

Petro pointed ahead. "We'll continue on this road, and way up there, we'll take a right turn for Koulouri. Are you game?" he asked.

"You bet," I assured him, wanting to fit in with their crowd. I loved spending time with kids my own age for a change. I didn't care where they were taking me. All I knew was that this place was full of people, full of teenagers, soccer games, and partying.

After about eighty feet, we came to a fork in the road that split between a paved surface to the left and a dirt road to the right. A sign said Verroia / Tsintzina—2 Kilometers. Despina explained that the paved road continued to the next village, Verroia, and that beyond Verroia was the village of Tsintzina. To the right, however, was another section of Vassara, where Koulouri was located. We followed the dirt path and made a steep climb past many houses. The incline was so steep that our bodies bent over to make it up the hill. Now I understood Mr. Natakos's warning. My feet were killing me in my Candies sandals, and I couldn't imagine making the climb during the hottest time of day.

When the road leveled off, we seemed on top of the entire village. Walking further past the last remaining houses, the area became all rocks. I realized that we were on a flat surface at the edge of a mountain. This cliff, or Koulouri, as locals call it, overlooks the entirety of Vassara on one side, while offering a spectacular view hundreds of feet down as Parnonas cascades into a valley on the other side. This was the most amazing spectacle of nature. I felt as if I were standing on the edge of the world, looking out into the vast unknown ahead.

As I stepped forward, my feet reached what looked like a round, stone circle.

"This is why we call it *Koulouri*. It's the shape of a round cookie, see?" Despina explained. The cliff sloped down to what was a flat, stoned surface in the shape of a giant circle with a steel pole in the middle. "It's actually what's called an *aloni*, or circle. This is where they used to tie up donkeys in the olden days and walk them around the pole in the middle to separate the hay from the wheat."

"Why were they crushing wheat?" I asked ignorantly.

"To make bread," Despina explained.

I found it ironic that an old harvesting area was now a cool place for teens.

Looking up to the left stretched the grandest green mountain, standing high in the sky and as it cascaded down in front of us. The countryside full of evergreens and cypress trees reached out as far as the eye could see. Down to the right, the forest continued until the landscape of the town appeared. All of Vassara was visible from Koulouri, which was probably why the kids liked it so much. Despina pointed out Brikakis' café in the distance and the road leading out of town.

"It's great up here, isn't it?" asked Petro. "We can see it all, but no one sees us. That's why we party up here at night." He laughed. "You'll see ... wait 'til we get you drunk up here later." He laughed. My eyes grew wide.

"Ignore him," Despina said, puffing on her second cigarette.

We stayed up on Koulouri's cliff for a while, enjoying the marvelous view of the village. The vastness of mountaintops brought about a serenity that put me in a daydream state. I was unable to look away from the luscious, green treetops that stretched across the Eurotas River.

"This is amazing. It's so peaceful up here. So quiet," I exclaimed to Despina.

"I know," she said, looking around as if appreciating the view for the first time. "This is what I miss the most when I return to Athens for school in the fall." She continued, "Koulouri is even better at night when the stars come out. They light up the whole sky. We'll come back when the sky is dark."

"I can't wait," I replied in feeling of wonder.

My daze at the landscape was broken with the sound of a new and unfamiliar voice. I was surprised since I thought the three of us were the only trespassers to this hidden section of Vassara. As I turned around, I saw the stranger. He appeared out of nowhere and was talking to Petro. He wore blue jeans and an American-styled green polo. His arms were folded, and he stood with his feet apart. The boys were discussing something in Greek, talking too fast for me to decipher the conversation. I thought I heard something about soccer.

"That's Stavros Antonopoulos," Despina said as she casually pointed. "He grew up here, too."

"Oh," I said, a little startled. She went on describing her life in Athens, but I wasn't paying attention. As if a Greek statue had just come to life, I gasped at the boy who stood erect with a perfect build and a stately presence. The details of his facial structure were like a museum's statue. Stavros was tall with a light complexion not typical for Greeks. He was slender, but muscular—obviously athletic. He had such a serious look on his face. I had never seen a teenager look so intense. Beyond his stern expression, his was a beautiful face. This boy was perfect. "Who in the world was Stavros Antonopoulos, and where did he come from?" I wondered. I had met my Adonis, and he was only seventeen.

Awkwardly, I realized I had been caught staring. He smirked while still speaking to Petro and held my look for a minute. His sea green eyes pierced through my body. While the boys continued their conversation, I couldn't help glance over toward him repeatedly. Despina continued smoking her cigarette. I became nervous, thinking about how stupid I looked. Petro and Stavros walked over to us.

"This is Stavros," Petro said.

Stavros reached out his hand like a politician and shook mine. *"Herete. Kalosorisate ston Vassara"* (Greetings. Welcome to Vassara).

"Do you speak English?" I asked.

"Just a little," he lied. His English was next to perfect, but reluctant to show off his bilingual skills, Stavros spoke only Greek to me. To say it was love at first sight may be a little melodramatic. Still, at the tender age of fourteen, I was completely swept off my feet. Stavros had an air of confidence about him that I found intriguing. The sound of his voice stopped me cold. From what Despina told me later, Stavros was well respected in the village and played a major role in organizing activities for our group of teenagers. He arranged dance parties, coordinated day trips to the sea, and ran a large portion of Vassara's festival at summer's end. In many ways, Stavros was Mr. Vassara, even at his young age.

Sunset approached, and, as my cousins informed me, it was time to return home, grab a quick bite, and get ready for Vassara's nightlife. We left Koulouri and returned back down to the village. Stavros walked with us back to Despina's house. As we said good-bye outside of my cousin's giant, green door, I could still hear Uncle Stathi telling jokes on the other side of the kitchen window. The party crowd had diminished, but those remaining were still enjoying themselves.

Stavros smiled politely. "Nice to meet you," he said. "I hope to see you later tonight."

"'Bye," I said timidly.

Petro, Despina, and I went through the giant, green door and into their mother's kitchen, hoping Aunt Vivi had something for us to eat.

"Who was that?" Aunt Vivi asked as she brought out a platter of spinach pie and Greek salad.

"Just Stavros," Petro answered.

"Which Stavros?" his mother persisted. Aunt Vivi needed to know every detail of her children's lives.

"Antonopoulos?" Uncle Stathi asked as he looked directly at me. I flushed.

"Yes! Stavros Antonopoulos! What's the big deal?" Petro snapped, irritated with the questioning.

"Nice kid ... comes from a good family," Uncle Stathi pronounced to my mother as he turned, giving me a wide-eyed look. I was sure my uncle read the feelings I was trying to hide. "Typical for Uncle Stathi," I thought. The man, I was told, knew everything about everyone. I couldn't escape his quest for information no matter how I tried. Uncle Stathi smiled at me and went on telling his story to the adults in the room. Meanwhile, I knew my secret was discovered.

Finally, the wine stopped pouring, and the stories wore out, giving us a chance to see our house around the corner and unpack. We headed up the street, turned right, and saw our home. Buttercup-painted stucco walls on the exterior gave our house a cheery appeal, and the luscious grapevines that cascaded down from the upstairs balcony over the white metal railings provided a shaded oasis from the sun. I should have been more interested, walking through the house that my grandmother grew up in and where my mother spent her summers as a child. Following along in a daze and distracted by thoughts of Stavros, I was led along by Mom and Yiayia as they examined room by room, reliving their past. It took me some time before I snapped back into reality and paid attention to their explanations for each room. We entered a large eating area at least thirty feet long that held a long table built for at least twenty people to eat at one sitting. Behind the long dining table sat a barrel set under a ceiling drop shaped like a crescent moon. The barrel contained wine made by Tatzaforo. Each summer, Yiayia and Pappou filled the barrel for the season's enjoyment. This was the party place. Mom and Yiayia told me they used to keep animals tied up under the low, curved ceiling when the room had only a dirt floor.

Through a doorway was the kitchen, adorably decorated in red and white check. Just one year earlier, my deceased aunt came to Greece and redecorated the kitchen. Fighting back tears, I looked around the room, noticing my aunt's taste all over the walls and counters. She had purchased new dishes and towels that were on display. Surely she planned to revisit and appreciate her renovated kitchen, never believing cancer would win. The room was perfect, as if Mom and I had decorated it ourselves. A large, white refrigerator stood in the corner of the kitchen with a suspiciously long gash on its side that faced the wall.

Mom turned to me and started laughing. "This is the one."

"You're kidding! I thought that was just another one of Stathi's stories!" I gasped.

"No, it really happened, honey! What did you think?" Mom asked as if Stathi never exaggerated anything. I couldn't believe that this was "the" refrigerator that fell off of the truck driven by Stathi and my mother's brother, Uncle George. Supposedly, they were bringing the appliance back to the village and had the appliance strapped to the back of their flatbed when they decided to stop for a few beers in Sparta. As the story is told, they made several stops for beer along the way, and when they finally reached Vassara by nightfall, my uncles were shocked to discover that the flatbed was empty. The refrigerator had fallen off the back of the truck somewhere along their journey and had rolled down a mountainside. The next day, the two weary men retraced their steps along the mountainous roads until they discovered the dented, white metal box lying halfway down a cliff.

I opened the door to the refrigerator, which was loaded with food and beverages and turned to Mom. "I don't know what surprises me more—that the fridge actually works or that one of Stathi's tales is actually true!" I laughed.

I took out a Coke Light and cracked it open while we headed up a small, metal staircase that was awkwardly placed next to the refrigerator and led upward to a second, orange-painted metal door. We had to duck our heads down so as not to get cracked in the skull by the plaster ceiling. When I opened the door, we were somehow outside again and standing atop a set of outdoor stairs that led up to the balcony of our Vassara house. This bizarre architecture left me wondering if my ancestors who built the house were as drunk as my uncle George and Stathi when they lost the refrigerator.

The balcony, however, was a fantastic sight, covered in grapevines that shielded an overbearing sun. Not as fancy as our terrace in Magoula, the Vassara balcony was strategically placed all the same. From this point of the street, we had an excellent view of the village and could see down the road in both directions, as well as straight ahead to the courtyard of St. George's Church, the main church in Vassara. St. George's bell tower was within one hundred feet of our front door. I would quickly learn that our proximity to the bells meant rising early on church days.

Meanwhile, Mom and Yiayia had gone off into other rooms, gasping at memories that flooded their conversation. I stood on the balcony looking every which way, wondering which direction led to Stavros's house. Was this a busy street? Would he ever pass by to go to church? I was just understanding the lay of the land around Vassara and had a million questions, all of which

I knew my cousin Despina would answer later. I walked to a set of yellow double doors that led into the upper level of the home. Seeing the inside of the house brought to life so many stories I had heard as a child. There was a fireplace in the bedroom off to the left and a sitting room next door with large, brown, patterned couches that pulled out into beds. The second upstairs bedroom was filled with our old bedding from home. Each spring, Yiayia gathered our discards, packing them for the houses in Greece. Being inside our Vassara house was like walking down memory lane. I hadn't seen that old bedspread since I was seven.

Behind the second bedroom was a green bathroom, long and narrow. Why the showerhead was placed directly over the toilet, no one will ever know, but this was apparently the place to wash up, and that was all that mattered. Still, the Vassara house's bathroom made the Magoula house's shower look like the Ritz Carlton. Looking at the clock on the wall that showed 7:30 pm, I remembered that Despina said she would be back around 8:00 pm to pick me up for the night. I had just enough time to figure out what to wear on my first night out in Vassara. I had no idea what that the local kids did at night or any idea of where we would be going. All I hoped was that I would see Stavros again.

Chapter 4
First Night, First Love

AFTER TRYING ON NEARLY everything in my suitcase, I finally settled on wearing white parachute pants and a bright blue crop top. The stylish, circa 1984 ensemble wasn't complete without big hoop earrings. I was a sight, or at least I thought so. Electric blue eyeliner tied my look all together as I changed my painful Candies sandals to a pair of white leather flats. Vassara was all about walking and climbing, and I needed better shoes to survive the terrain. With a few drachmas in my pocket and a new tube of pink lip gloss, I was ready. Despina arrived and called to me from beneath the balcony. I swung open the double doors and shouted back for her to come upstairs. She wore white jeans and a red and white striped top. Everyone dressed up for summer evenings in Vassara, which made the nights feel special. Despina came into my bedroom smiling. She read my face like a book and knew instantly that I was nervous to see Stavros again. I told her I was fine, but she knew better.

My cousin wasn't a makeup kind of girl, but she was beautiful all the same in a natural way. Her huge smile and warm demeanor lit up her round, porcelainlike face. Despina seemed to glow in a state of peace and happiness, and a soft, sweet disposition was hers at all times. Unlike me, my cousin took no interest in the local boys from Vassara. Since she had grown up in the village, to her, they seemed like brothers. Despina was also indifferent to the boys from America who visited the village for the summer, as she had a hard time relating to them. Instead, as she confided in me earlier, she had her sights on a boy at school in Athens named Tasso. He studied art, and together they shared an instant connection over the esthetic aspects of life. Even though Despina and I had just met, I felt close to my second cousin. We clicked. Aside from our shared family tree, we enjoyed many common interests involving the arts. She came from a rural village, and I grew up in Chicago, but Despina and I were more alike than different. The only thing I disliked about Despina was her smoking habit. She never went anywhere without cigarettes, and she always kept them in her back pocket, poorly concealed from her parents.

"Have a great time!" Mom said with a big smile as she sat down to a cup of Greek coffee in the Vassara kitchen.

"*Prosehe*—be careful—and stick with Despina," Yiayia chimed in.

"Don't worry—I'll take good care of her." Despina always knew what to say.   Heading back into the town square, I asked, "Where's Petro?"

"Oh, he's showering. The boys had soccer practice earlier. There's a big game tomorrow at the *Yipetho*," Despina answered.

"Really? Cool!"

"That boy Stavros—he's the captain." Despina smiled at me. "Of course he's the captain," I thought. "Mr. Wonderful is good looking, intelligent, *and* the captain of the village soccer team. What else?" I asked, "Who do you play? Other villages?" I chuckled as I asked such a ridiculous question.

"Yeah, actually, we do. Tomorrow, we play Tsintzina, the village that comes right after Verroia," she answered. I felt stupid for laughing. Soccer was obviously serious business in Greece. Walking down to the square, we saw a group of kids hanging out in front of Brikakis' café. I paid more attention to their names this time. John, Lia, and Elena all came from Boston. There were some Greek kids, too—Kosma, Prokopi, Thora, and Mihali, who was Mrs. Brikaki's son. They seemed nice, but I didn't see Stavros. I scanned the *platia* for sight of him. Despina and I bought two ice cream bars from inside the café and sat outside on a bench to eat them. Slowly, the group of teenagers gathered together, and before long, our group filled the town square. There must have been thirty or forty teenagers spread about the square on benches and at tables. I was the only one from Chicago. Most of the American kids were from the East Coast.

Despina explained that a large group of villagers emigrated to Massachusetts in the 1950s. I envied the girls from Boston, who seemed to have a close-knit group. Together, they were connected both in Vassara and at home, and they obviously knew each other well after spending so many summers together in Greece. I felt like the awkward new kid.

Finally, the moment I had waited for all afternoon came. Stavros arrived, walking down from the main street into the *platia*. He wore a white Izod shirt. Stavros smiled at me as he joined our group, and I put my head down, turning red. One of the other girls looked up and smiled at him, saying something in Greek that sounded sarcastic. He nodded back to her casually. I doubted if I was the only girl who found Stavros intriguing.

Loukas, one of the kids from Vassara, stood up and made an announcement that I didn't understand. His sister Anastasia, who sat on a bench next to him, shouted back, and roaring laughter broke out among everyone. I pretended to understand, not wanting to pester Despina for constant translations. I kept quiet and went along, feeling intimidated by everyone's knowledge of the Greek language.

"Looks like we're heading over to Moustokotou's for some beers," Despina stated.

"Mou-tso-ko ... *what?*" I had to laugh at that name.

"Mou-tso-ko-tou's," my cousin pronounced slowly. "It's a little tavern up the road on the way to Koulouri. We passed it earlier today."

"I don't remember," I confessed.

"Well, it's the *only* taverna in the village. You can't miss it. It'll be fun. We'll have some beers, listen to some music, and then go for a *volta*," she explained.

"Okay, you got me again. What's a *volta?*" I asked.

"A *volta* is a walk—an outing. There's more to see in Vassara—especially at night." I had never drunk beer before, but since Greece had no drinking age, I figured this was just another step in blending in with the locals. I had wine at family parties back home and liked the taste, but I was unfamiliar with beer.

Our large group of kids slowly headed out of the *platia* toward Moustokotou's tavern, leaving the town square empty and quiet. I felt sorry for Mrs. Brikaki, who stood in the doorway of her café, watching us desert the place, leaving behind just a few old men in the courtyard. Truly the life of Vassara was its youth. Our group of teenagers populated the village, bringing excitement and liveliness for the summer months.

Down the road, near the turnoff to Despina's street, was Moustokotou's, a tavern open to the outside, named after the proprietor. The large patio stretched across the full length of the restaurant. The only indoor portion was a tiny kitchen attached to the back. Near the entrance stood a large, uncovered fire pit where Mr. Moustokotou maintained the evening's specialty over a hot fire. He was a rugged old guy, with salt-and-pepper whiskers covering his unshaven, wrinkled face. His voice was deep and loud. He called out to his wife when he saw us approaching from the street. His worn, white shirt and apron wrapped tightly across his thick belly.

A big, orange gated door opened and led down a set of concrete stairs to the open patio that held several small tables. Mr. Moustokotou continued to shout out to his wife in the kitchen as we approached, and a little old lady in a black dress rushed out to the patio with baskets of fresh baked bread. The owner left his fire pit and pushed some tables together with the help of a few guys and made an arrangement of plastic white chairs for our party. Greek music blared out of a speaker in the corner next to the kitchen, while a delicious smell of marinated pork kabobs, lamb, and other barbecued Greek specialties wafted through the air in puffs of white smoke from Mr. Moustokotou's grill.

At the other end of the restaurant, a small kitchen window gave a glimpse of Mrs. Moustokotou and her mother, an even older old lady, dressed in black from head to toe. She never spoke, but she carefully watched all of us every night through her big eyes that peered out of her black kerchief. That old lady probably knew everyone's business, watching the action from her little kitchen window. Stavros walked over to the owner and coordinated a large order for our group, counting out pitchers of beer and platters of french fries. The tavern was a happy place—a party place. Our group took over the restaurant, and the laughter was nonstop. Friends reconnected. New visitors like me were introduced to the group. We laughed. We drank. The beer went down easily with heavily salted french fries passed up and down our tables on large platters. We ate grilled pork kabobs on small sticks called *kalamakia*. The food—even the meat, surprisingly—was delicious.

As the night went on, I had a chance to get to know most of the kids in our crowd. Everyone from the village was happy to reunite for the summer. While some kids went to school in Athens or Sparta, this was their time to reminisce and party the warm weeks of August away. I met Stavros's two brothers, Lefteri and Vasili. Lefteri, the older one, was taller and good looking like Stavros, but he had a slightly receding hairline. He wanted to know all about my life in Chicago and asked me endless questions. Vasili, his little brother, was an awkward preteen, but he was happy to be out with his older brothers and their friends. No one was excluded from the group. The older kids let the younger ones join us without complaint. This inclusive attitude was the beauty of the kids from Vassara, as our crowd consisted of kids of all ages. Even Panteli, the thirty-year-old local bachelor, joined us every night. We called him "old man," because to us, he seemed ancient. As the rounds of beer continued, we laughed, Greek danced, and told jokes for hours. My only regret was that Stavros was sitting too far away on the far side of the table.

The beer poured and poured and poured. We drank Amstel Light out of little, clear glasses that looked like as if they were made for orange juice. I'm not sure how many little glasses I drank, but I quickly felt a strong buzz. Stavros continued to order for our group that totaled thirty-five kids at one long table. Despina sat next to me, and I tried not to catch Stavros's eye after he smiled at me a couple of times. He was talking with his friend Niko, who I found out was my third cousin. At one point, Stavros winked at me across the table, and I almost fell out of my chair. "Must be the beer," I thought. Later, Mr. Moustokotou came over with our bill written on a small piece of paper. We pooled our money together, left the tavern, and headed up to Koulouri.

When we turned to make our way up the hill, I knew for certain that the beer had gone to my head. I hung onto Despina as if she were my seeing-eye dog. Attempting a climb up to Koulouri at night was nearly impossible, and I was amazed at how quickly and easily all of the locals climbed the rocks with little light to show the way. The night sky in the mountains was intensely black. The further we climbed, the scarcer the streetlights became. I couldn't see a thing. We continued up one last steep hill.

"*Then vlepo tipota* " (I can't see a thing)! I kept saying out loud. The other kids laughed as they kept on ahead of me.

"That's okay," Laine from Boston said. "After a few trips up to this place, you start to memorize each step, and you don't need to see."

Lefteri came up to us on my left side. "*Entaxi* " (Are you okay)? he asked with a big smile.

"*Nomizo*" (I think so).

"*Alli fora, na pinis perisotero*" (Next time, you should drink more. That way you'll be able to walk straight), Lefteri answered sarcastically. I liked him and understood quickly why he was best of friends with my cousin Petro.

Finally, we reached the top. A full moon hung in the blackness of the night sky, offering a glow to starlit haze. Summer moonlight illuminated the mountaintop. Koulouri looked magical. Steep mountain peaks across the cliff faded into deep shades of indigo. Athough the beauty was enrapturing, I didn't dare get too close to Koulouri's edge. The cliff was an entirely different place at night. Instead of its vastness of green with endless hills to admire, Koulouri was now a mysterious, dark world. Cool air blew across the mountaintop, and in the distance, coyotes howled. With only the light of the moon and stars, I stumbled my way across the clearing, adoring this enchanted setting. Standing in the dark with little light made it nearly impossible to see faces, leaving only voices and shadows to identify friends. Out of nowhere, someone would appear, and I wasn't sure if they were standing there the whole time or not. I'd wait, listen, and then know who was talking. This was especially hard for me, since the only person I knew well enough to recognize by voice was Despina. I thought I was standing next to her, when out of the dark, I heard a new voice. I looked up and saw a gigantically tall shadow.

"Who goes there?" I slurred.

"I am Demetri," the giant said pleasantly. He held out his hand. I went to shake it, but grabbed his wrist instead. He laughed.

"Sorry," I said, laughing. "I can't see a thing!"

"Welcome to Koulouri at night, and welcome to Vassara!" he exclaimed as he held up his beer bottle to the stars. "Isn't it gorgeous up here? I'll bet you don't have anything like this back in Chicago!"

"No, definitely not. I love this place," I replied.

"So do we. That's why we don't tell anyone about it. It's just for us. We come up here to get away from the watchful eyes of the village. How was your first day in Vassara? How do you like Greece?" So many questions, but he seemed sincere. Before I could answer, he interrupted and solemnly said, "Sorry to hear about your aunt. I'm sure she was a wonderful woman." His honest comment caught me off guard. How did he know about my aunt?

"She was," I answered. "Thank you."

I decided to change the subject and told him about Magoula and how I liked this place so much more. I explained how nice it was to be around kids my own age, and he assured me that this was the place to be for the summer.

Demetri told me about another soccer game the next day against a town called Vresthena. His was a friendly voice, a warm voice, and I immediately liked Demetri. His genuine demeanor made me trust him immediately. Over by some large rocks, we heard guitar music begin. Someone was playing a traditional Greek tune.

"Who's playing?" I asked Demetri.

"That's Kosma," he said. "Our town musician. And the girl next to him is his sister, Yiota. Where's your beer?" he asked as if it was a crime not to have one.

"Oh, she's had quite enough. I'm responsible for her," Despina said as she pushed him away.

"You Americans," he said, laughing. "You don't start drinking beer until you're twenty-one! What is that?" He sighed. "Well," Demetri paused. "I hope you have a marvelous time here in our little forgotten village. I'm sure we'll talk more tomorrow when I can see what you look like and am a hell of a lot more sober!"

Some boys started singing in Greek. Loukas's shadowy figure arrived and pulled Demetri away. With arms waving to the music and legs kicking up to the stars, they Greek danced toward Kosma and his guitar. Instantly, there was another body next to me, and it wasn't Despina. The shadow was male and smelled like clean soap. He let out a warm breath.

"Despina?" I asked, intimidated.

"She went to have a cigarette. It's Stavros," he said.

"Oh, hi." I paused, surprised. "This place sure is different at night."

Stavros looked up and took another big breath of the evening's fresh mountain air. "Have you ever seen such beautiful stars?" he asked.

I looked up, too. "They're incredible."

"Come," he said. "See them from over here." He started to lead me away from the group, around a corner where there was a large pile of rocks next to a small stone structure.

"Oh, I'd better not disappear. Despina will be looking for me. Despina! Where are you?" I called out for my chaperone.

"Don't worry—you're fine," she called back into the dark.

Stavros led on. "See? She's still here. Come."

He helped me down a small drop on the opposite side of the stone structure. We stood on the other side of Koulouri, atop a flat area that overlooked the whole town. Little white lights illuminated the village from up high. Vassara looked like a fantasy land. Stavros walked me to the edge, and together we stared out over the town.

"Be careful not to fall all the way down!" he said as he pretended to push me over the cliff. I grabbed his arms for safety,

"If I fall, you're coming with me," I said as I hung onto him.

We laughed. Taking my hand, he led me away from the edge to a large rock. We sat on the stone and looked up at the stars. "This is paradise," I thought, buzzed from the beer. The next thing I knew, Stavros's lips were on mine. I couldn't believe he was kissing me. Looking back now, I realize what an unsuspecting, gullible girl I was to think he honestly brought me around the corner to show me the stars. But I liked Stavros. I really liked him. He was beautiful and strong. His tanned, smooth skin smelled fantastic, and kissing him was heaven.

We sat under the stars for a long time, staring at the moonlight and the little white lights of Vassara. Stavros didn't say much that first night, except "I want to get to know you better before you leave."

Stavros seemed friendlier when he was away from the crowd. He was sweet and even sensitive. As we left, I assumed he would walk me home. Everyone else had gone, leaving the cliff dark and empty. Even Despina had walked on ahead with Yiota, probably assuming Stavros would look after me. But Stavros said he couldn't walk me any further than the *platia* in the center of town. I didn't understand. Where I came from, a boy always walked a girl home. That obviously wasn't the case in Vassara.

"That's just not how it's done in Vassara," he said again, sounding a bit annoyed with me. He also mentioned something about everyone watching and everyone knowing. I was confused. "If he really liked me," I thought, "he'd walk me home and not care about what other people thought."

"You have stupid rules in the village," I told him. He just shook his head and held out his hand to lead me down the road.

"C'mon. It's getting late. I'll see you tomorrow, okay?" He put his arms around me and gave me one last kiss before we turned the corner where a row of houses stood.

When we rejoined the others in the town square, I was faced with Petro, who stood in front of me, both hands on his hips like an angry father.

"Where've *you* been?" he asked, smirking, knowing the answer as he looked into my guilty eyes. Stavros passed behind me to catch up with his brothers without looking at us.

Before I could utter an answer, Despina danced over. She slurred out a folk song and grabbed me away from Petro. We danced off, two happy souls, away from questioning and away from the group. As we headed home together, skipping and tripping through the dark streets, singing Greek songs I barely knew, I found myself madly in teenaged love. That's when I vowed to my cousin that I would never leave the village, ever.

When we arrived at my house, our plan was to quietly sneak back inside without a sound. However, the plan was short lived as I realized I didn't have a key. Instead, we decided to go to Despina's house for a midnight snack while we figured out a solution to our problem. Outside her great, green door, she put a finger to her lips and made a loud "Shhh." Despina showed me a secret hole in the rocks just below her large kitchen window. Inside the crevice was a large rock, which she removed, revealing her "hidden" house key. I couldn't stop laughing. The key was the size of a banana and made of thick, heavy metal. It looked like something out of *The Flintstones.*

"You've got to be kidding me," I said, laughing.

"Oh," she said. "We all lock our doors at night, you know. I'm just showing you where we hide it, in case you ever need to get in." Her stern expression led me to believe she was completely serious. We quietly went through the front door and into Despina's kitchen, careful not to stir Aunt Maria, who slept on a bed only a few feet away from their large table. After a round of cookies from Aunt Vivi's cupboard, my cousin seemed to have another plan.

"I think I have another idea to get you inside. C'mon! Let's walk you home. You'll see what I mean," she said confidently. I followed Despina out the door.

When we rounded the corner from her house to mine, Despina pointed to the balcony and suggested that I climb over the railing. Not my favorite choice, but seeing no other option, I decided to put my cheerleading skills to work, trying in hysterics to hoist my body over the railing. We couldn't stop laughing. Every time I attempted to swing my second leg over the railing, one of us burst into chuckles, making my feat pitifully unsuccessful. My cousin and I made so much noise that eventually we woke my mother. She opened the door in her nightgown, eyes half closed.

"What are you trying to do, kill yourself? Are you drunk?" she whispered. We all laughed.

"You guys are out *late*. Did you have a good time?" She didn't seem mad.

"Good night," Despina said quickly and left, unsure of any fallout to come.

"See you tomorrow," I slurred.

"Not too early!" my cousin warned.

Mom put her arm around me as I walked through the door.

"I drank beer!" I proudly announced.

"Congratulations. Don't be loud or you'll wake up Yiayia."

Thank God she wasn't mad. I suppose knowing that Vassara was a safe place had a lot to do with my mother's leniency. While the village was full of visiting families that knew each other for generations, we had little to fear. Even late at night, we were safe to walk home on our own, free from worry. Mom never gave me as much freedom as she did those summers in Vassara, and I couldn't have been happier with my newfound independence.

A bed was turned down for me in the sitting room on the upper level, only steps away from the double doors that led to the balcony. Mom slept in the bedroom to the right, fixed up with pink bedding from my sister's old room. The bedroom to the left had a small twin bed and a double bed in it, separated by an old fireplace. Our suitcases were spread all over them. So for that night, I was sleeping in the sitting room. Mom said I could make the other room into my own bedroom if I wanted. I was too tired to care. I laid on my back on the makeshift bed, staring up at the ceiling in amazement at the night's events. What happened? Stavros, Stavros, Stavros was all I could think about. So mature, so good looking, so strong. I quickly fell into a deep sleep with beer on my breath and love in my heart. Unlike Magoula, there were no roosters to wake us up in Vassara. The village was dark and quiet for now.

Chapter 5
Off to Church

W<small>HAT FELT LIKE ONLY</small> seconds later, the double doors to the balcony slammed open, allowing blaring sunlight to beam into the upstairs bedrooms. The bright, hot rays hit my sleeping face.

"*Kalimera*" (Good Morning)! exclaimed my aunt Maria, who had a better night's sleep. Yiayia's sister shuffled her rotund body across the room, making the floor creak with every step. She was loud, she was bold, and I was not ready to be part of the world.

"*Prepi na sikothite*" (You must get up), she exclaimed.

"Yeah, honey, wake up." My mom passed by the foot of my bed. "Those bells are going to ring any second, anyway. Didn't I tell you that we are going to church?"

My eyes were still shut as I murmured, "What?"

Mom was fully dressed and stood opposite the hallway mirror putting on her lipstick as she continued, "That little church that we passed on our way into Vassara—that's St. Sotira. Today is the feast day. There are church services at—" *Bang! Bang! Bang!*

I almost fell out of bed. It was the loudest noise I had ever heard in my life. Louder than a fire alarm going off inside of a firehouse, the sudden clamoring of bells made my heart race. Mom closed the double doors and attempted to shout over the muffled clanging.

"That bell tells everyone in the village that it's a feast day! There are church services in a half hour! C'mon! Get dressed!"

I shouted back, "Are you serious? It's too early!" Silence. The banging stopped. It was quiet again.

I rolled over and pulled the covers over my head. "I'm sleeping," I muffled from under the covers.

"Oh, no, you're not. We're *all* going. That's what you get for staying out late last night. You're going. Yiayia will insist. C'mon. This is one of the biggest feast days of the summer. The whole village will be there."

"The whole village?" That would mean Stavros. With a renewed sense of motivation, I decided to be compliant, wondering how I was going to make myself look decent in only thirty minutes. Head pounding, I wasn't certain if this was my first real hangover or a residual effect from the church bells.

"Why does our house have to be so close to the village's bell tower?" I moaned.

Yiayia laughed.

Mom answered back, "Because that's where your great-great grandfather decided to build. Now go get ready!"

I headed to the shower with slow, deliberate movements. This was not the way I wanted to see Stavros for the first time since last night. If I'd had my way, I would have picked out a special outfit, fixed my hair, chosen the right shade of lip gloss—the works. Instead, I grabbed what had the fewest wrinkles from the suitcase. Within twenty minutes, I pulled a fashion magazine makeover on myself. That's one lesson Vassara taught me right away—how to get beautiful as quickly as possible. Yiayia handed me a small cup of Greek coffee as Mom closed up the house. I took two small sips from the hot demitasse, and we were out the door.

Stepping out onto our balcony, I stopped dead in my tracks at the sight in front of me. Waiting in the street for us was my uncle Tatzaforo's white pickup truck, morphed into a self-created, multi-passenger vehicle, parked at the front gate. Uncle Tatz had transformed his flatbed by attaching six of Aunt Kiki's kitchen chairs tied to the sides with rope—three chairs on each side. The ropes had thick, nautical-looking knots tied around each leg to secure them into place. Apparently, as Mom informed me, we were going to travel up the mountain in this makeshift limousine from hell.

"*Ela!*" He shouted in a loud, authoritative tone. He had also gotten a good night's rest, I assumed.

"You're *crazy!*" I dramatically told my mother. At fourteen, life was all about drama.

"Oh, don't be such a suburbanite. It's fine! How else do you expect to get up there? Walk? You'd never make it in *those* shoes." She pointed at my feet. Mom and I proceeded to debate back and forth, while Tatzaforo's wife, Aunt Kiki—wearing high heels, dress, and all—climbed into the back of the flatbed. She held a white patent leather purse on her lap and wore bright pink lipstick. This was a sight. I tried to hold my ground.

"There's *no way* I'm climbing up there dressed like this!" I proclaimed.

Around the corner came Despina. I thought, "Thank God—someone that will understand me."

Shockingly, she waved me off and said, "Oh, just get in. It's fine. You're going to make us late if you don't!" Despina appeared as cranky as I was and certainly not in the mood for an argument. What happened to my loyal cousin? Was she brainwashed overnight like the rest of my relatives? Finally, I let out a big sigh and decided not to make any more trouble. I climbed in and took a seat next to Kiki. Uncle Tatz's face looked angry in the rearview mirror, so I decided not to put up a big fuss about how ridiculous we looked and how unsafe we were riding in tied-up chairs. No one seemed to care about my concerns. Mom, on the other hand, apparently had preferred seating in first class and comfortably got in the front seat of the cab, sandwiched between Tatzaforo and Uncle Stathi. I suffered climbing over the truck's side railing, complaining under my breath the whole while. Stathi got a big kick out of my grumbling, laughing at my breakdown. Surely I came across like an American princess.

Aunt Vivi climbed in next and sat beside me on one of the chairs. She reached over and took my hand, holding it securely in hers for the whole ride, as if I needed comforting. To Aunt Vivi, there were no problems in life that couldn't be cured by a warm meal or a tight embrace. Tatz started the engine, and I wanted to become invisible. How embarrassing. There I was in my minidress, all dolled up to see the boy I had kissed the night before, but sitting on a kitchen chair tied to the back of a pickup truck. "If Stavros sees me like this," I thought, "I will certainly die."

Humiliation seemed to be the least of my worries as our bumpy ride up the mountain sent all of us in the back leaning side to side, nearly falling on top of those we sat next to. Complaining about the ride would have proved pointless, for I learned early on that Tatzaforo was not a man to be messed with. The only thing that would be worse than this nightmare of a ride would be to make him angry. Despite my uncle's eighty-some-odd age, his fierceness was unparalleled. This was a unique man.

Tatzaforo, related to us by marrying Yiayia's niece, Kiki, was a weathered man, with leatherlike skin and small, beady eyes. Tatz, as we called him, had a full head of white hair and muscles that rivaled any young man's. His walk was authoritative. His looks were intense. His voice was raspy and loud, with a ruggedness to it. Although he was a man of few words, it was clear early on that when he spoke, people around him obeyed. In 1984, Tatz still had a lot of fire in him. A retired Greek forest ranger, Tatz nonetheless donned his blue uniformed shirts with navy pants and walked Vassara as if he owned the village. Everyone respected him, or rather feared him. His reputation for tough justice was legendary among the villagers. Surely, some stories had been embellished, especially if told by Stathi. But not all tales of his antics were exaggerated. He truly was a tough old man.

Although he was outwardly cool most of the time, I knew he loved my mom a lot, and he most assuredly loved my aunt. Tatz had a great deal of affection and respect for Yiayia, as well. He would do anything for my family, and I know that he felt responsible for us while we were in Greece without my father. This was both a blessing and a curse. Tatz saw to it personally that wherever we needed to go, he would escort us. If we wanted to go to the bank in Sparta to exchange money, he took us. If we asked about a festival in a neighboring village, he offered to escort us. We were under his care 24-7 in Vassara, even if this meant riding in his scary, white pickup truck. My uncle had his own speed limit—fast and faster.

Tatz married Kiki in 1955. They had two daughters, one that lived in Sparta with her family, and one that moved to Canada. His wife, Aunt Kiki, was just as tough. She was a physical, hard woman who carried the difficulties of living a rural life on her face and body. Strong as she was, Kiki tended to our every need while we were in Greece, seeking to fulfill our every culinary wish that rivaled the best of chefs in the world. Through her kind smile, Kiki's face was resilient. She had solid, weathered skin, and the lines around her eyes and mouth told a hundred stories of difficulty and survival. She was a tall woman, with broad shoulders and large hands. Her legs were strong and thick, and she wore big, clunky shoes like most of the village women. Her eyes were multicolored with a little brown and a little green. Her hair was thick and short, and her coloring was light like Yiayia's. Her lips were thin but always turned up in a grin. She was an enigma in many ways, as she had been through hell in her lifetime of war and hunger, but she still managed to exude a joyous spirit. Her sense of humor was legendary. Kiki was constantly telling jokes. Like her brother Stathi, she was always making those around her laugh. Kiki's laugh was an unmistakable cackle. Loud and piercing, the sound of my aunt's laughter became infectious. She loved having Mom and me around and would tell us repeatedly that our summer visits were the highlight of her year.

From the moment we first met in 1984, Aunt Kiki regarded me with special care. Loving me went way beyond cooking me a favorite meal or brewing up a hot cup of Greek coffee the moment I walked into her kitchen. Aunt Kiki was curious to get into my adolescent head and learn all about my world. I was her young, American grand-niece, an impressionable teen, and as I grew more enamored with her village, Kiki suggested I stay in Vassara permanently. I thought she was crazy at first, reminding her that I had yet to begin high school. But Aunt Kiki kept up her quest nonetheless. Perhaps she hoped that by my staying in Greece, I would somehow undo the exodus of so many villagers a generation ago. In this way, a resurgence of life might begin again in Vassara, filling the village with new life well beyond the end of summer.

The road up to the Church of the Savior was as breathtakingly beautiful as it was scary. The mountains around us were endless, and I noticed for the first time how beautiful the view of the village was leading out of town as well as into town. We had been there less than twenty-four hours, and I was falling in love with the village ... or was it Stavros? My fascination with this new boy and new place seemed tied up together, and I wasn't sure which was which. Tatz's pickup truck continued to bounce up and down, slamming atop rocky roads that led up to the church. In the distance, we heard chanters through a speaker as they sang the hymns of the liturgy. One voice in particular stood out deep and strong. His was the loudest.

"That's Stavros's dad chanting," Despina informed me with a smile. Aunt Kiki and Vivi both looked at me, smiling. I was silent.

Atop the tall, green hill stood the Church of the Savior, a tiny beacon with its white building and dome-shaped top. The little church's capacity was surely less than twenty, but a good two hundred Vassareans were bustling about the outside of the church. Ironically, the small churches like the Church of the Savior that are located in the surrounding hills of villages all across Greece stand vacant year round, hibernating in the hills and remaining peacefully quiet in prayer without disturbance. Villagers worshipped elsewhere, populating the larger, more modern churches like St. George, which was the church just outside our house in the village. However, on special feast days, these forgotten summits of God came alive with popularity, bringing the masses to pray on the name day of the church. As this was the day honoring the Transfiguration of our Lord, the entire village came out to worship at the forgotten church. This was a nice custom, I thought, and I enjoyed seeing everyone attend liturgy.

Our nightmare ride ended as Tatz pulled up to a clearing next to the church and parked aside several other vehicles covered in dust from the dirt road. There was a long line of cars leading to the church. I was happy to see we weren't the only victims of a village inventor. Several other trucks had kitchen chairs tied to the back, and I wondered who the first Vassarean was to come up with this brilliant idea of turning a two-seater truck into a twelve-passenger mobile unit by bringing out their kitchen furniture. Yiayia, Mom, Aunt Vivi, Aunt Kiki, Despina, and I made our way in a slow procession into the church to light candles. Somewhere along the way, we lost Tatz, Pappou, and Uncle Stathi. The men remained outside of the church, smoking cigarettes, while the women were inside worshipping. The whole thing seemed so medieval and ridiculous.

"Why aren't they coming in?" I asked my mother.

"I don't know … that's their tradition. It's not like home. The men and boys stay outside. I guess it's because the church is so small—it can't accommodate everyone," Mom offered.

As if religion was only a concern of the female gender, we approached the *iconostasio* to light our candles, passing by several old ladies dressed in black from head to foot. All of them turned in unison to stare at us as we approached. They reminded me of a club. They came in packs. They moved in unison. When one old lady sat down, they all sat down. When another did her cross, they all crossed themselves. Surely, the old ladies were harmless, although I found them a little intimidating as they stopped me several times while walking around town. They would ask in Greek, "Who do you belong to?" The correct reply was a brief explanation of my Vassara lineage. To that, the old ladies smiled, nodded their heads, and welcomed me to the village.

On our way out of church that morning, I finally saw Stavros talking to some men. He looked at me but didn't smile. In fact, he seemed indifferent. I was disappointed. Afterward, when church was over and a live auction was about to begin, the village gathered in front of the bell tower of the church. I thought for sure he would see me there and say hi, but he didn't. The same old man who was in charge of ringing the bell at St. George's Church earlier that morning was also was in charge of running the auction. He held up items like cakes and breads and sets of sheets to be sold for funds to keep the Church of the Savior running until next year. His last item auctioned off was a live chicken, and my uncle Tatz won the bid. Was that going to be lunch? I shuddered and prayed the animal didn't have to ride in back of the flatbed with me.

Stavros gave me the cold shoulder most of the morning at church. I didn't know if he was just playing it cool in front of his family or if he had taken another look at me in the daylight and changed his mind. Just as we were leaving, sitting atop my kitchen chair tied to the flatbed, Stavros passed by our truck, looked up at me while my relatives were busy discussing the auction, and winked. I was reassured, but annoyed. Why did he act like this? He treated me the same way over the next few days, distant and standoffish when he saw me around town and then warm and affectionate at night with the rest of our crowd. We routinely managed to leave the group toward the end of each night and sit beneath the summer moon in each other's arms. After a few days of this on again/off again behavior, I decided to ask him about his inconsistency. Hesitantly, I approached the topic one night while we sat in the dark on our rock at Koulouri.

"Well, what did you expect me to do when I saw you after the soccer game? Run up to you with open arms? It doesn't work that way in Vassara. People are watching. People talk," he said patronizingly. I didn't like his tone, and I was already regretting confronting him, afraid I might push him away.

"But you acted like you didn't even know me. I just thought—"

He interrupted my words with a kiss. Then he took my face in his hands.

"In this village, we must be careful at showing our emotions in public. It's not like where you come from," he explained.

"But it's okay to hold me in your arms up here on the cliff where only the kids know we are together? I don't understand. Why are you so afraid of even *talking* to me in front of other people?" He said nothing. I could tell by his squinted eyes that he was getting angry, but I had to press him further. I had to know more. "What would people say if they saw us together, and why would that be so horrible?" I asked.

"That's just not how it's done. I can't always do what I want," Stavros insisted.

"Why not? Why can't you do what you want to do?"

He looked at me sternly and then made a big sigh. He looked away from me and across the cliff to the mountain and said, "You are young. You don't understand. When you are older, you will learn that there are times in your life when you don't do what you want—you do what is expected. You don't argue with what is right. Someday, you will see what I mean."

I didn't understand. "No," I thought. "I'm just different from you. If I like someone, I'm not afraid to show my feelings. I'm not intimidated by some old lady gossiping around town. I have my own mind and my own dreams, and I don't go along with the program just to please other people. That's not immaturity—that's independence. That's also the American way of life. Something *you'll* never understand." I kept these thoughts to myself to end the argument. I didn't want to ruin things just as they started. I could tell I had hit a nerve with him. I knew our disagreement wasn't really about holding hands in the *platia* or any other type of public display of affection. Our debate was about something else in Stavros's life. I told myself at the time that either he just didn't like me as much as I thought or that he was frustrated with growing up in an isolated town, separated from the rest of the world. Why else would he tell me that he was from Sparta and not Vassara? When I told Despina, she cracked up laughing, shaking her head at his ego. He had actually tried to convince me that he was from Sparta that first night up at Koulouri, when in fact, he was a villager just like the rest of them. Why would he lie? Did he think I would be more impressed if he came from a larger city? Stavros seemed all too consumed with other people's impression of him.

Despite his irregular behavior, the subsequent weeks in Vassara unfolded like a dream. Each morning's activities were usually delayed from staying out late with the other kids. We hung out in the *platia* until 2:00 or 3:00 am when the streetlights turned off. Long afternoons were lazily spent under a tree's shade outside of Brikakis' café, drinking a Coke or playing backgammon. Later, Despina and I would visit Kiki for the daily coffee talk. Evenings were the best. After an hour or two of alone time to write letters home or make an occasional journal entry, I'd get dressed up for the night and pick up my cousin around the corner. Despina and I were consistently ready before Petro, so we would head down to the *platia* without him. Mom always made sure I had money on me, and the rest of the night was like a summer fantasy. As soon as all of the kids in Vassara—American and Greek—had gathered in the *platia*, we made our way as one enormous group down to Moustokotou's taverna, pushing tables together to make our party. We ordered beer and french fries and sometimes souflakia. The fire pit grew, and the music blared, always the sweet songs of Glykeria, a popular singer.

After a few rounds, the Greek dancing began, and it wasn't long before Stavros and his brothers, along with Panteli, Demetri, and Niko, took over the dance floor with the traditional male dances. No one danced better than the boys from Vassara. Hands down, they were the best. Kosma would grab his guitar, and we'd spend the late nights under Koulouri's stars, listening to music and singing. Slowly and secretly, a few couples broke off from the group and disappeared into Koulouri's darkness to be alone. Stavros continued to be tender and sweet on those nights, but as the summer came to a close, he started to distance himself from me, and I could tell our bond had loosened. As he grew colder, I became increasingly more attached to my new home and friends in Vassara. The village had everything I ever wanted, and as the festival arrived at the end of August, I felt as if I could have taken Kiki's offer to stay forever. But Vassara just like Stavros was quickly slipping away, no matter how hard I tried to tighten my grasp.

The night before the big festival, which was to be our last night in Vassara before returning home, Stavros wasn't himself at all. He barely kissed me while we sat looking at the moon. "You know," he began, "we're going to stay friends."

"Well, of course we're going to stay friends. I already gave you my address. You'd better write me as much as I write to you."

"That's not what I mean." He paused. "I mean we're going to end this as friends."

"End this?" I wasn't sure my Greek was translating well here.

He spoke authoritatively like he was making an announcement. "We will be friends now."

"Nothing more?" I asked.

"Not now. It doesn't make sense. You're *leaving*," he emphasized.

"So what?" I was desperate. I didn't want to lose him. "Why do things have to change because I'm leaving? Okay, obviously we're both going to go back to our worlds with school and stuff, but I still have feelings for you."

"You will start dating others now. I may, too."

"What about next summer? I'll be back, you know." He smiled as if to say, "That's what they all say."

"We'll see," he said.

"I *will*, Stavros. I *know* I will."

"Don't make promises you can't keep. You have no idea what may happen in a year. You may not be able to come."

"I *am* coming back to Vassara next summer, Stavros, and I hope you will be waiting."

That was the thing about Vassara—every visitor found themselves promising to return. The feeling was inevitable. I wanted nothing more that to return the following year and would do everything in my power to make it happen. I didn't see why we had to end the summer as friends.

"What about tomorrow night, the festival?" I asked.

"We make our good-byes tonight," Stavros said solemnly.

"No! Why?" I started to cry. "I'm not ready to say good-bye."

He wiped away one of my tears with his thumb. "Tomorrow night is very busy. There will be hundreds of people from all over coming for the festival. We will have a hard time getting away from everyone. This is one of the biggest summer festivals in the region. I will be working. We won't have time to—"

"We *have* to be together to say good-bye tomorrow sometime!"

"We'll see. Don't count on it. That's why I'm saying we should make our farewells now." I wrapped my arms around his neck and held on as tight as I could. I was probably choking the poor guy, but I didn't want to think of not seeing his face for another year. We kissed under the stars of Koulouri, which had emptied of kids by now, as they had gone to the *platia* without us. Our friends had made their way back to the town square. Despina would be waiting for me there. Slowly, we came down the hill and into the main section of the town. As we held hands, he stopped walking just as we were about to turn the corner into the *platia* where everyone would see us.

"Good-bye. Have a good winter."

"I'll miss you," I said solemnly.

"Friends," he said. "We are friends, remember? Not sad. Smile."

I couldn't. How did he expect me to turn my emotions on and off like this? How could I go from being his summer love to a friend? I was in love with him, although I never told him. Surely he would laugh at me—the innocent, young American girl who makes her first trip abroad and instantly falls for a local. I didn't care what he thought of me or how ridiculous I seemed. I was truly, madly, completely head over heels for him and this place, and nothing would convince me otherwise. I had never felt such yearning in my heart, and my age was irrelevant. My feelings were real.

Within this magical summer in Greece and, more specifically, within the last few weeks in Vassara, I had found myself. I was grounded. I no longer feared life. I loved life. I loved the trees and the sky. I loved the Mediterranean sun and its warmth. I loved the glow of the night sky as it cascaded down the mountaintops. I loved the cobblestone streets of the village and the voices of the residents calling to one another across the *platia*. I loved Brikakis' café, dirty and dusty as it was, where I was greeted each day with a smile from Mrs. Brikaki. I loved Demetri's jokes and friendliness. I loved Lefteri's dancing. I loved Niko's athletic skill that helped our village win so many soccer games. I loved how the girls from Boston were so at home in Vassara after spending consecutive summers here. I hoped to be like them someday, totally settled in this summer oasis. I loved my afternoon coffee with Kiki, and I loved seeing Mom and Yiayia so happy in their hometown. I loved watching them reconnect with everyone. I loved Stathi's gregarious personality. I loved Aunt Vivi's annoying questions about where were we going. I loved Despina's sneaking cigarettes out of the house, and I loved Petro's smart-alecky answers to every question. Oh, how I loved Koulouri, as it meant time with Stavros, and I loved nothing more than him. How would I ever get over him, and how could I ever forget this place? I rejoined the others in the *platia* and sat with watery eyes on a bench, looking around at everything I would miss. One night left. One last dance. One last kiss. It had to be the best.

Chapter 6
Festival Day

As THE SUN BROKE through a patch of gray, puffy clouds, I stepped out onto our Vassara balcony, Greek coffee cup in hand, and smiled at the quiet morning. Still too early for St. George's bells to ring, I drank my first warm sips of coffee, enjoying the quiet streets below. Only an occasional rustle from nearby kitchens rattled as village residents awoke to this long-awaited day. Thankful to have set my travel alarm clock the night before, I felt content as I soaked in the peaceful morning of August 23, 1984.

The subdued calm would not last long. This was the day of the festival, and more importantly, the feast day of the Virgin Mary. This was also summer's farewell. Nearly everyone in the village would be leaving within the next forty-eight hours, as the end to our golden days in Vassara approached. Even local kids like my cousin Despina were packed up to leave, preparing to return to school campuses in Athens and other large cities far away from Sparta. Summer had gone by so quickly.

While no one wanted to see Vassara's streets empty, none of the Vassareans were eager to be the first to leave. Saying good-bye to Vassara was all too sad. The festival of the Virgin Mary marked the end of everyone's visit. For those few who stayed behind like my aunt Vivi, Uncle Georgo, Tatz, and Aunt Kiki, this was the saddest time of year. While the town square became an explosion of activity, setting up the evening's party, my relatives' eyes grew glassy knowing the season's hours ran thin. They would be alone now in a forgotten town with a population dwindling to one hundred from one thousand in a matter of two days. With only one another to pass the long winter months, these last remaining Vassareans would wait for the following spring, when life in the village would begin again. They were like the last petals of a beautiful flower, offering only a hint of what was once a beautiful garden. I can't imagine what it was like for the old folks to live in an empty town.

Barely able to think about our own departure for the States, I knew if I dwelled on the idea, I wouldn't be able to enjoy myself at the festival. I tried to keep my mind in the present. Surely there would be time to sulk the next day and sit on Magoula's terrace, reminiscing over the last few weeks while we packed our bags for Chicago. Mom and I had one day left in the Magoula house before leaving for Athens.

I walked back through the balcony's double doors into what had become my bedroom. Clothes and shoes were scattered about just like home. I unplugged the curling iron and converter from the wall outlet and pulled out my travel cosmetics bag from the side table. Pink lip gloss matched the flowers on my spaghetti-strapped floral tank dress. Swiping the applicator across my lips, I looked at my reflection in the bedroom mirror, realizing that despite my sadness that summer was over, being in the village made me happy for the first time in months. Although I hated to go, a part of me was excited for what lay ahead in high school. I truly believed the summer magic I experienced would carry me through any uncertainties ahead. Just as my thoughts drifted back to Chicago, St. George's Church bells started to clang, announcing the time for liturgy. Smiling in memory of the first time I heard the bell's toll, I shut the door to the balcony, muffling out the sound, and went back into the bedroom to primp.

A few minutes later, the clanging subsided, and I heard my uncle call. Heading through the double doors again, I grabbed for my white shawl to make Yiayia happy and laughed out loud at the sight of Tatz's white truck in front of our house. Nothing would bother me that day. By that time, I had ridden Tatz's vehicle creation countless times and feared for my safety no longer. The roped chairs, however, were still embarrassing. Mom and the gang of relatives came out of the kitchen on the lower level and loaded themselves into the truck. We took our usual places, including Mom and Stathi in the front cab. Tatz drove us off to church, and Aunt Vivi held my hand as we bounced up and down on our chairs in the back. Her sweet smile was lovely.

This time, we weren't headed to an actual churchlike structure. Instead, we made our way past the *cambo*, past Ourania's monastery, to the Virgin Mary's church inside a mountain cave, located within the outlying hills of Vassara. Very high up inside one mountain is a small, rectangle-shaped hole cut in the rock. During the four-hundred-year Turkish occupation of Greece, which ended in 1821, local villagers hid in this grotto to escape invaders who terrorized Vassara, stealing livestock and kidnapping young girls. At night, Vassareans conducted secret schools in the mountain's hole and taught their children the Greek language, culture, and religion. All of this was done secretly in an effort to preserve their ethnic culture. Grottos like this are found all over Greece, and many of them like the one in Vassara were made into churches after the Greeks won their independence. Each year, on August 23, the village of Vassara celebrates the feast day of the Virgin Mary at this cave church called *Panayia sto Vraho*, or The Virgin Mary on the Cliff.

With this feast day comes Vassara's annual festival, or as the locals say, *panigiri*. Each village in Greece has their own local *panigiri*, or festival, where towns celebrate themselves with a huge dance in their town square, complete with food and drink. During summer months, festivals are held almost every weekend in one village or another, and party-hungry travelers migrate from town to town enjoying local fare. The festivals are the biggest and most anticipated day of the year. Vassara's *panigiri* is also one of the largest festivals in Peloponnese. After listening to accolades about our festival for weeks, I was jumping with excitement to finally see the event with my own eyes. I was told the *platia* would swell with hundreds of people, dancing and merrymaking until sunrise. A big celebration was only fitting, I thought, since it marked the end of the season. People from all over Sparta's countryside would come to give summer one last kiss before Vassara nestled in for a long winter's nap.

The road to the mountain church only took us so far, and the rest of the journey had to be made on foot. I was glad to be wearing flats, just as Despina had advised. The narrow path we climbed zigzagged upward to the cave's opening, and a flat area allowed worshipers to witness the liturgy from just outside the rock's opening. Our local priest from Vassara led the service, dressed in a golden robe. The Church of the Savior seemed as big as a cathedral compared to the Virgin Mary's grotto, as only the priest, a chanter, and a few old ladies fit inside the cave. The rest stood outside. Even the man-made clearing didn't accommodate the increased congregation. Latecomers lined up on the road that led to a row of parked cars.

Despina and I lit yellow beeswax candles and placed them in tall, golden holders that were set up on the clearing. My cousin motioned for me to follow her to a place that had more room to stand. All of the kids wore their Sunday best—Demetri and his brother Vasili, the Boston girls, Kosma and his sister, Loukas and Anastasia, and even my cousin Petro, who came before the service ended with Stavros and his brother Lefteri. They nodded to us, but Despina and I stayed still. We didn't dare join the boys, even if Despina's brother was among their group. As the end of summer approached, I had become well-versed in the village's game of protocol. This was one aspect of the village I would not miss.

"Did you see them?" Despina asked softly.

"Yeah. I'm trying to ignore him, but it's not working."

She laughed quietly.

When the service ended, a live auction began to raise funds for the church. Many Vassareans offered items to be donated for the live sale. Yiayia and Mom brought a set of bed sheets from Chicago. The old man who rang St. George's bell began the bidding. "Beautiful sheets from America! They will make any bed as soft as a cloud! Do I hear five hundred drachmas?" he shouted as the bidders held up their hands.

Mom and Yiayia were ecstatic to see their donation fetch a high bid. They stayed behind to watch the rest of the auction, while Despina and I made our way over to the boys. Now it would be acceptable to talk to them as most of the villagers moved about.

"Best wishes for your mother's name's day!" Stavros said as he approached me.

"What?" I asked.

"It's your mother's name's day, isn't it? She's a 'Maria,' right?" he asked.

It took me a second, but I made the connection. Holiday celebrating the Virgin Mary ... Mom's name is Maria ... okay, got it.

"In Greek, we say *Xronia Polla*. It means 'best wishes,'" Stavros explained.

"*Xronia Polla*," I said. He shook my hand with his typical, cold, "we're-in-public" look. I wanted to shoot him. From behind, an arm came around my shoulder. It was Demetri.

"*Xronia Polla!*" he joyfully exclaimed.

"*Xronia Polla,* Demetri," Despina and I said in unison. Throughout the crowd, there was a chorus of "*Xronia Polla*" as the villagers greeted one another with smiles and kisses on both cheeks.

A few moments later, Yiayia came happily up to us, saying, "*Yia kita ti pire i mama sou*" (Look and see what your mother bought)! She held out a large, cakelike bread round covered in powdered sugar and wrapped in cellophane with small wildflowers pressed against it.

"What *is* that?" I asked Mom as if she bought Martian food.

"It's a *kouloura*—a sweet bread. We'll cut it for lunch at our house—everyone's coming to celebrate my name's day," she stated. I was surprised we were having an impromptu gathering.

"I didn't know anyone was coming over!" I exclaimed.

"Neither did I! We just decided, so let's go. We've got a lot of prep work before the masses come."

We piled back into Tatz's truck and headed to the house in order to prepare for guests. I knew having company meant I wouldn't be able to leave. This was not good. I'd have less time in the *platia* and less time with the kids on our last day.

Mom, Yiayia, and I quickly transformed the downstairs of our Vassara house into party central. Despina and her mom helped us set the table and bring in extra chairs. Then Aunt Vivi went home to get Greek sweets she'd baked for the day's celebration. Kiki was busy in her kitchen with a lamb Tatzaforo killed especially for the day. The idea of a large meal in the middle of the day no longer made me sick to my stomach. So many dislikeable traits of Greek life faded away in the hills of Parnonas.

"*Xronia Polla!*" shouted Stathi, who came around the corner holding a large, orange jug of homemade wine. With that, the party began. Since August 23 was also my aunt Maria's name's day, Yiayia's sister was the guest of honor. The wine poured, the feta and Greek salad hit the table, and before long, Tatz and Kiki came through the open doorway holding two large platters of lamb and potatoes. They stood before us with their offerings, holding out the platters for everyone to see. We all cheered. Mom brought out the *kouloura* and *fasolia* that Yiayia had prepared. The feast was complete.

Smells of the authentic, Greek village meal filled the air, tempting my stomach and filling my soul.

Within minutes, we were a loud, eating, explosion of a family, everyone talking at the same time, laughing and telling stories. I sat back in my chair and observed, trying to soak in the scene. I wanted to freeze-frame the moment. Stathi began his monologue of tales from yesteryear. Tatz filled and refilled everyone's glasses with wine, telling us to "drink more, drink more." He loved showing off his new English phrases. Kiki and Vivi ran to the kitchen every five seconds to replenish platters. Despina and I ate at the somewhat quiet end of the table, interrupted only by Petro reaching across our plates for third helpings.

"Girls," Mom said, looking at Despina and me, "can you run down to Brikakis' and grab six more Amstel's?" She winked at me, knowing we would relish the opportunity to escape to the *platia*.

"No problem!" Despina cheerfully answered as she stood up from her chair.

"Oh, that's okay, Aunt Maria. *I'll* be happy to go for you while the girls stay and clean the dishes," Petro said obnoxiously, knowing how badly we wanted to see who was in the *platia*. He gave me a big grin and stood up from his seat, as well. "After all," he continued, "those bottles are heavy."

Despina put her hand up to negate her brother's offer. "We'll manage; we'll each carry three."

I quickly took the money from my mother's outstretched hand and raced out the door with Despina before Petro could say another word. We laughed as we turned the corner, thinking we had beaten her brother at his own game. Heading down to Brikakis', the *platia* was under an enormous transformation. The bench area was covered in a makeshift wooden platform to serve as a stage. Drums were set up, as well as a few microphones belonging to the band. Next to the platform stood four huge speakers, two on each side.

"This is going to be one heck of a party," I said as we approached.

Opposite the stage, tables with plastic coverings had begun to appear all over the *platia*. Stavros directed a large crew of boys and girls setting up chairs. I could hear his deep voice across the *platia* commanding younger volunteers, and I dared not talk to him since he was busy. Despina and I headed into Brikakis' to buy the beer. Petro surprised us from behind, catching up to us just as we entered the general store. He was as eager as we were to see what was happening in the village's center, and he began helping Lefteri move tables.

"How many will be here?" I asked Despina.

"Oh, at least five hundred people," she answered.

"I can't imagine them all fitting!"

"It's busy, and it's a blast. Let's hope those clouds stay away." We looked up at the gray sky that had grown darker since the morning. "It looks like it might rain," Despina warned.

"Not today. Not the day of the festival. It can't!" I protested.

"Don't worry, cousin. We'll celebrate either way."

Our lunch party ended a few hours later, and the last of the relatives left for siesta. The *panigiri* was a just a few hours away. The excitement of the day made it impossible for me to nap, so I took the opportunity to walk around the village by myself and take a few scenic photos. Wanting to capture Vassara during the prettiest time of day as the sky turned pink, I enjoyed the solitude. I strode through the streets wearing my new, strapless green and yellow floral dress, relishing the day's last moments of calm before the evening activity unfolded. Like a best friend, I shared my thanks with my village for a beautiful, life-changing summer and felt its love returned to me in a unique moment of bonding. How I adored my village.

After exploring some little streets I had missed throughout the summer, I stopped at a clearing to overlook the mountainous region. That's when I heard loud American music coming from a nearby house. A voice called out from an open window. I looked up and saw a young woman leaning over her balcony.

"Hey, there! What are you, lost? C'mon in! My sister and I are just about to make some frappe," she said as if we were old friends. With that, she vanished from the window and came out the front gate to welcome me.

"You're from Chicago, right?" She showed me through their front door and into her kitchen. "You're the American girl that's been hanging around with Stavros," she said, smiling. "I'm Nia. My sister and I came in from Athens last night for the festival." She paused. "I think I met you in the *platia* last night, right?"

"Uh, yeah," I said, and then I paused hesitantly. "Yeah, I remember you."

I remembered her for sure, but only because she stood out so much among the other girls. Her wild, curly, brown hair reminded me of Medusa. She had heavily black-painted eyes and red lips. Nia was thin and wore a tank top with straps that fell off her shoulders. She was tall and moved seductively when she walked.

"Who's here?" another voice called out. A shorter, blonde girl with bouncy curls but similarly painted black eyes came out from behind the bathroom door. Soula, her sister, was much shorter than Nia and a little heavier. Still, both sisters had voluptuous figures that their clothing accentuated.

"Hey, what are you doing up in our neck of the woods?" Soula asked. Before I could answer, Nia offered a chair and brought out a bowl of cold green grapes from the refrigerator. "You're American, right?" Soula asked more questions as she took her full head of curls and twisted it around a clip, making a sloppy updo.

"Yeah," I said. "Aren't you?" They both laughed. Nia took a strand of grapes from the bowl and offered them to me.

"Ah, no. We're Canadian. Our mother is from here, and our dad is from the island of Spetses. We live in Athens now and come here for the summer like everyone else. You should stay for a while. We love visitors."

"Well, okay," I agreed hesitantly. "You live in Athens permanently?"

"Yeah. It's awesome. The nightclubs are fantastic. Ever been?" Nia inquired.

"To Athens, yes. To the nightclubs, no," I confessed.

Nia continued about Stavros. "You know, Stavros and I are old friends. We go *way* back." She had a suggestive look on her face when she said his name that made me uncomfortable.

Nia went over to change cassettes in her a large boom box by the window. Soula came to the table with three tall glasses containing a frothy-looking cold coffee drink. "My sister is just being obnoxious. Ignore her." Soula sat down and put a glass in front of me. "Have you ever had a frappe before? It's like an iced coffee." I had seen the cold coffee drink in Sparta's restaurants but had never tried it. Soula assured me that I would be hooked forever. I was. The cold coffee mixed with milk and sugar had a whipped topping and ice cubes in it.

"These are fantastic! Why haven't I been drinking these all summer?" I exclaimed as I sucked half of it down.

"Easy. They're really strong. You'll be flying from the caffeine," Soula warned.

Nia looked me up and down. "Your dress is pretty," she said. "I'm sure Stavros will like it."

"I'm not sure he notices anything these days," I said, and then I regretted my comment. But before I realized, an hour had gone by, and I was still at Nia and Soula's kitchen table. Now on my second frappe, they became like bartenders, and I found myself telling them all about my summer romance. The more we talked, the more harmless they seemed, and I couldn't help but be intrigued by their frankness. The sisters treated me like a lost friend whom they had finally found, and although I was suspicious of their sincerity, I couldn't resist asking them for advice. Nia and Soula were relationship gurus in my eyes and obviously knew a lot more about dating than I did. Finally, I had to ask Nia if she ever dated Stavros.

"You're not serious!" she almost shouted, and then she laughed hysterically. "No way! He's not my type. Too controlling," she answered.

"So what's going on with you two now?" Soula asked from the kitchen.

"Nothing," I answered. "I'm not even sure he's interested anymore," I confessed.

"Oh, he's interested all right," Soula reassured me.

"Yeah, *that* we know," Nia chimed in.

"What do you mean?" I asked. "Has he said something to you?"

"Let's just say he asked me for some advice earlier today," Nia said, smiling. I found it hard to believe that Stavros would discuss anything with these two.

"Advice about what?" I asked.

"He didn't want to push you, but ..." she said and then paused. "He's been a little ... frustrated."

Out of nowhere, a huge thunderbolt cracked from above as if God was listening, and within seconds, a downpour began. We jumped from our chairs, and Soula began to close the windows.

"Oh, no!" Nia yelled. "My laundry is hanging outside. I'll be right back."

Soula came and sat beside me. She put her hand on my shoulder.

"Don't worry about it. Stavros Antonopoulos is just another guy, and they're all after the same thing. You're young, and you don't need to get messed up with some *village* boy!"

Wow. I had never heard him called that before. In all this time, I had never thought of him as a village boy. "I think I love him," I blurted out before Nia came back into the room. As the words flew out of my mouth, I regretting saying them aloud but knew they were true. Thankfully, Soula was sympathetic.

"Of course you do. You're young, he's good looking, and you're in a foreign country for the first time. Falling in love is inevitable." Soula sounded as if she understood.

"I don't know what to do. What should I do, Soula?" I asked earnestly.

"Whatever you do, *don't* do anything stupid. Look, I wasn't going to say anything, but my sister will end up telling you, anyway. Stavros has a girl back at school in Athens. She's from Vassara also but lives at school year round. She's very cold and unfriendly, and everyone here hates her. Her name is Fotini. Nobody can figure out why he's still with her. Stavros must be worried that she will show up for tonight's festival."

The next lightening bolt broke my heart in half. I never suspected there might be someone else. How could he do this to me? I sank back in my chair and tried to hide the tears. Nia came in with a pile of clothes and looked at my distraught face. She turned to Soula. "You told her, didn't you? *I* wanted to tell her."

"What's the difference who tells her? The point is she knows now. He's a jerk. They all are." Soula touched the skirt of my dress. "And you look too pretty to be upset."

Nia joined in Soula's advice. "Forget about him. Oh, and don't worry about Fotini. I hear she's not even coming this year."

I tried to talk without crying. "I just didn't suspect ... I really thought ... well, I guess it doesn't matter what I thought. It's done," I muttered.

Nia threw her arms up in the air. "Just another frustrating day in this small-minded village!"

"Nia, lay off!" Soula retorted.

"I mean it," her sister continued. "This place messes with your head. You just can't let yourself get caught up with one of the natives." I had to leave. I got up from the table and brought my glass to the sink.

"I think I'm going to go, guys. The rain is letting up, and I want to get back. I'm sure Despina is looking for me." Nia and Soula looked at each other as if they had just done something wrong.

Soula forced a smile. "We'll dance tonight, okay? I'm sorry about the bad news. I just figured you needed to know."

"Yeah. Thanks."

"Wait." Nia came toward me. "Don't let anything ruin your last night here. Go have fun and try to forget about it."

I left Nia and Soula's like a wounded dog. As I made my way back down the streets toward St. George's, I felt a lump in my stomach. The rainwater dripped from the roofs, making little puddles in the cracks of cobblestone on the streets. The air grew cool after the storm, and I took a deep breath, inhaling the smell of rain that hung in the air. Vassara's colors seemed muted. A gray sky and foggy haze covered the mountains and seemed to wash out their beauty. As if a veil was placed over the village, everything looked sullen.

My eyes dried up by the time I got all the way down from the girls' house and turned the corner by St. George's, but when Despina approached, she knew I was upset.

"There you are! Your mom said you went for a walk."

"Despina, who is Fotini?" I asked as I approached my cousin.

"Who told you about Fotini?" She put her hands on her hips.

"Why didn't you tell me Stavros has a girlfriend?" I couldn't hide my frustration.

"She's *not* his girlfriend," Despina said, laughing.

"That's not what Nia and Soula said!" I contested.

"Nia and Soula! Is *that* where you were? Oh, please. Don't believe a word they say. They have no idea what they're talking about!"

"They said he has a girl back in Athens," I protested.

"That was years ago. Fotini has been hanging on forever, and he's been trying to get rid of her. That's why I didn't tell you. There's nothing to tell!" Despina insisted.

"Whatever. I'm leaving, anyway. What's the difference?" I shook my head.

"You don't mean that. You think he betrayed you because he didn't say anything. Listen to me." She grabbed my arm. "Stavros is a decent guy. If you have a question about Fotini, ask *him*. He'll tell you himself."

"Despina, I can barely get Stavros to talk to me lately. He avoids me like the plague," I confessed.

"He's probably bummed that you're leaving," she suggested.

"I don't know," I replied sadly.

"C'mon! Let's go down to the *platia*. Your mom and my parents and Stathi are already down there, and they're saving a table. We're going to dance tonight. We're going to have fun. No worries." She put her arm around me as we headed to the party.

Chapter 7
Good Winter

GREEK FOLK MUSIC BLARED through the streets as Despina and I headed down to the *platia*. Traditional sounds of the clarinet made a festive tune, and our steps seemed to pick up the beat as we walked down the cobblestone streets to the center of town. Vassara morphed into a metropolis in only one day. Foreign cars lined up bumper-to-bumper on village roads that were built hundreds of years ago and meant to be only wide enough for donkeys to pass. Large groups of partiers strolled by. We didn't recognize anyone. There must have been between five hundred and a thousand people in the town square, jammed table to table, chairs stuck in every corner.

Traditional Greek folk songs blared through the air as crowds of people formed dance lines, encircling the space allowed to serve as a dance floor. Brikakis' café buzzed with customers. Trays of pork were brought out from the back of the store, and empty crates of beer bottles reversed the trip, going back into the café for storage. Mr. and Mrs. Brikaki wore gregarious grins, happy to see their business booming. Streams of white lights stretched over their store and onto the poles of the *platia*.

I searched the area for Stavros but didn't see him. Surely he was dictating something to someone, somewhere. Now I understood what he meant when he said good-bye the night before. I'd be lucky to find him in this chaos, let alone be able to steal away for a while or even ask him about Fotini. The crowds were too big and the festival too busy. I tried to get used to the idea that I might not have another moment alone with him before leaving for the States. Although I craved an explanation about this other girl, part of me didn't want to see him, anyway.

"*Elate, Oli* "(Come, everyone)! Stathi shouted with his arms stretched wide. He smiled at our table with great pride, boastful of his banquet of relatives from near and far. Tatz sat quietly for the time being at the head of the table. His watchful eyes cased the crowd like an intelligence agent on guard for trouble. Kiki, Mom, and Aunt Vivi drank wine in short glasses that Stathi refilled after every sip. They were like old drinking buddies from a fraternity house. Despina and I didn't stay at the table long, anxious to join in the dancing.

Loukas, Demetri, Lefteri, and Petro were working the crowd like madmen, bustling between tables, carrying trays of salad and french fries, and even taking turns behind the small cash box set up near the bar. Behind the counter outside Brikakis', I finally saw Stavros pointing fingers and directing food servers.

"You've got to put it over *there* so that we have more room to pass through!" he shouted at a group of young boys. I was glad I wasn't working for him that night. He didn't notice we were there.

Despina and I went right to the dance area and joined in on a line of *sirto* dancing that took us swiftly across the dance floor in a circular pattern. Everyone held hands as we did the forward-three step, backward one-step dance pattern, making a circle with our long line of friends. I caught on quickly. The famous Greek pop star Glykeria had her songs streaming out of the band, and by now, I knew every word from her latest album. Truth be told, I didn't understand the words I was singing, but it felt good to sing along with my fellow Vassareans. As our line turned round and around, I looked at everyone's faces, trying to memorize the features of those I would dearly miss over the winter months. Anastasia's long orange sweater swayed along with her hips as she led the line of dancers.

Eventually, as the shift of volunteer festival workers changed, most of our friends—Vasili, Thimosteni, and the rest—came out from under Stavros's rule and joined us on the dance floor. With everyone together, hand in hand, our enormous line stretched the full length of the *platia*. Each of us took turns leading the line and followed the head dancer with various moves, and everyone had a slightly different style of leading. Girls like Anastasia and

Potoula used more swaying movements with their torsos much like belly dancers, while the boys, especially Demetri and Lefteri, took gigantic steps with their long legs, making the line move a lot faster. I had to race along to keep up with them when they led the line. We went on like this for hours, forgoing any food or rest, for to leave the dance floor meant missing out on a minute more of the magic when all of the Vassara kids came together.

Even Stavros, who hadn't so much as looked at me all night, joined in as the night settled down, and only Vassara's residents remained at the festival. Visitors' cars slowly drove away, and like the end of any party where only the host and a few close friends remain, so the *panigiri* beheld just us kids. We were the last remaining partiers, and no one wanted the night to end.

Finally, out of sheer exhaustion, I left the dance line and sat for a moment in a nearby plastic chair, my feet throbbing from dancing on the hard stone ground for hours. Demetri joined me, bringing over two cold Amstel Lights.

"Thanks!" I said as we clinked our bottles together.

"It only took you seven weeks, but you finally learned to drink beer." We laughed.

"When are you leaving for Athens?" I asked him.

"Tomorrow ... like everyone else. I hate to see this place empty. It's too depressing. My mom has already started to pack me enough food to last until Christmas." We laughed, knowing how all of the mothers in town spent their days before the festival cooking, baking, and gathering packaged goods for their children to take back to their school campuses. Even Aunt Vivi had gathered multiple bags of food for Petro and Despina to bring with them to Athens. My uncle Georgo made a fresh round of feta cheese for each of his children. I wondered what they might be packing up for me to take home to Chicago, praying it wasn't a live goat.

Sitting back in the chair with my dress fanned out across my legs, I sighed as I looked out onto our crowd. Despite all of my insecurities over Stavros, I somehow managed to have a fantastic time at the party and was grateful for such an amazing summer.

"Well?" Demetri said, waiting for the impressions of my first *panigiri*.

"Amazing! Just as good as you guys said it would be," I answered.

"Told you." He grinned as he held his bottle up in victory.

"I had the best summer of my life here," I said, sighing.

Demetri smiled as if he took the credit. "I knew you would," he said proudly.

Before we could say anything else, Lefteri jumped forward and grabbed Demetri out of his chair for a *hasapiko* dance. This is a dance typically done by men alone, with onlookers who cheer on the dancer by squatting down on one knee near the dancer's feet and clapping their hands. Lefteri, Stavros, Demetri, and Vasili were some of the best *hasapiko* dancers I had ever seen. I sat with my beer and enjoyed their skill on the dance floor. Despina and some of the other girls clapped away, encouraging them to continue.

It was well after 3:00 am when the little white lights around the *platia* finally shut off, and the band began to pack up their bouzoukis and drums. Our crowd sat on the benches outside Brikakis' café, most of us buzzed or exhausted from dancing—or both. Mr. and Mrs. Brikaki left the closing of their store to their son, Mihali. He was the most intoxicated of us all. Swaying in the doorway of his parents' store, Mihali still heard Glykeria's tunes in his head as he sang them out loud, by himself, and off-key. By then, Stavros closed up shop, finally joining our group. When streetlights turned off at 4:00 am, we were left in near darkness. The kids finally decided to call it a night, saying their good-byes for the summer to one another.

"*Kalo Ximona*" (Good winter), I kept hearing them say to each other. What a befitting farewell.

Most everyone hugged and kissed each other. But Stavros, who finally acknowledged my presence, came up to me and stuck his hand out to shake mine. He said, "Have a safe trip back to Chicago. *Kalo Ximona*."

I stood with a blank look, not knowing what to say. There was an awkward, quiet moment that seemed to hang in time while all the kids looked at Stavros and I. Even they thought his send-off was cold. Some of them laughed and started imitating him, going around to the others and shaking hands, copying his politically correct tone. Pretty soon, everyone was shaking hands and making fun of Stavros and laughing. He just shook his head and walked away. That was it. That was my good-bye. I waited all night, hoping for one last moment between the two of us, but the moment never came. Sinking with defeat, I tried to keep a smile on my face while making my last good-byes. Stavros was serious, I thought, recalling our last night at Koulouri. How I wished I had kissed him one more time.

The next day, we left Vassara. After sad farewells to our relatives and a tearful hug to Despina, we promised to exchange letters, and I promised to return. The winding journey out of the Parnonas hills went by all too quickly. I tried to hide tears that streamed down my cheeks as I looked out of the window of Pappou's Audi. Twenty minutes later, we were packing suitcases in Magoula, and twenty-four hours later, we were on KLM flight 612 leaving Greece for the United States. Sitting on board the airplane, I had to wonder whether the whole experience really happened. My next week would be filled with cheerleading tryouts, buying books, and settling into freshman year of high school. The two worlds couldn't have been further apart.

Chapter 8
Finding a Friend

THERE I WAS IN the back of Spiro's cab again, a year older, but not exactly wiser. Still, fifteen seemed more mature than fourteen, and with a year of high school under my belt, I felt invincible. Surely this second summer in Greece would be fantastic. The cab hustled through the congested, polluted, and overpopulated streets of Athens, heading out of the capital city to the main highway. A layer of dusty dirt covered a gridlocked group of cars that beeped incessantly at one another, and bus fumes filled our stuffy car. As the urban chaos of Athens invaded my senses, an escape into the Parnonas region seemed ideal. For within those hills, the other half of my heart waited.

My head swelled with expectations. Dreaming of Vassara all winter long and reliving the previous experience in my mind repeatedly, I felt certain this summer would be even better than last. I closed my eyes to tune out the unpleasant ride and pressed play on my Walkman, setting into motion Sade's *Smooth Operator*, which soothed my ears as well as my heart. Her sultry music and heart-wrenching lyrics proclaimed deep love like no other.

My thoughts once again drifted to Stavros, who was no less in my head twelve months later. Memories of our teenaged summer romance flooded my everyday existence. Throughout the past winter, I thought of him constantly, wondering with every decision I made whether he would approve or disapprove. Whenever a blue and white striped airmail envelope appeared on my kitchen table, my eyes grew wide with anticipation. He kept our correspondence consistent over the winter, but I was always left wanting more. Void of any real emotion, Stavros wrote platonic, stale notes that seemed more like a homework assignment than a love letter. They sounded the same:

Thanks for writing. School is tough. I'm studying a lot. Went to Vassara, but it wasn't much fun because no one is there, and the streets are empty. You sound busy. Good luck at ... or congratulations on ... See you in the summer. Say hi to your family.

Friendly, Stavros

Without any real feelings behind his thoughts, I didn't have the nerve to ask him about Fotini. The subject was ignored. Why did it matter? By the time I knew about her, Stavros wished us to be "friends." I knew I had no right to question him. Still, as the snow melted and my plans to return to Greece took shape, I hoped for something warmer in his writing, especially after I told him that Mom and I planned to return. To my disappointment, that spark I sought never appeared. Perhaps his life in Greece was dull, I thought, although I couldn't imagine how. Maybe to Stavros, living in Sparta wasn't that exciting. In the meantime, I was occupied with cheerleading, getting elected onto student council, going to dances, and learning to drive. I was growing up, and despite all of the distractions of a normal teenaged life, the excitement to get back to Greece was immeasurable.

Our ride to Magoula was surreal. Looking out the window to see the famous palm trees that line the center of Sparta's main drag, I sat back in the cab wearing a wide grin. We made it. We were here. Memories of 1984 came flooding back, and what seemed like so long ago suddenly felt like yesterday. Everything was exactly the same. Once again, Yiayia and Pappou had opened the Magoula house a few months earlier. Mom's excitement mirrored mine as we reached the end of Sparta's main road and turned toward St. Demetrios Church, entering the suburb of Magoula.

Yiayia greeted us at the big, green gate that again swarmed with bees. I laughed as I made my usual duck and run under the buzzing orange flowers to greet my grandmother with hugs and kisses. The familiar fragrance of Yiayia's roses filled the courtyard. Home at last. Our flight was long, and I was eager to collapse in the bedrooms that waited upstairs. I ran up the exterior marble staircase and took a long, deep breath, inhaling the fresh mountain air. Greece was beautiful, especially Peloponnese, with its luscious Spartan greenery and scenic Mount Taygetos. Standing atop our terrace, I gazed across the sea of green treetops toward the group of mountains that held my beloved Vassara on the other side, wondering what would await me there this year. Would he be there? The anticipation held me tight all winter. Now I was here—*actually* here. Inspired by the moment, I ran inside for a piece of paper and jotted down a poem I titled, "Waiting up there somewhere." I couldn't believe I was back on the Magoula terrace once more. I couldn't believe tomorrow I'd be in Vassara. Summer in Greece was real again.

Opening the heavy brass door to the upstairs, I noticed a new mirror Yiayia had hung in the hallway. My reflection looked tired. Still awkward and geeky-looking, I hoped Stavros would find me attractive even though I still wore braces. My hair was much shorter, cut into an 80s-style bob. The updated summer wardrobe I packed was full of Madonna-like outfits consisting of multiple layers and big shoulder pads. I left the unpacking for the next day, too tired to begin a big project. Mom and I went to bed, listening to dogs bark in the streets and laughing to one another about the little annoying reminders that our "convenient" suburban life was thousands of miles behind us. We didn't care.

The following day, jet lag wore off quickly as I awoke to the aroma of Yiayia's *patatoula* omelet, made of potato slices fried in olive oil and scrambled together with fresh farm eggs. After horrible airline food, I was glad to eat something familiar. I devoured my lunch and checked the bathroom for scary critters, knowing there was no time to lose during this busy first day in Greece. Our agenda was different from the year before. Mom and I perfected our itinerary way in advance. We would visit Vassara right away, getting our fill in the village immediately. We planned to stay about a week and then head down to Leonithion, a local beach town, and eventually get over to Agia Marina and the island of Paros to enjoy the ocean and sun. Mom must have known that if we didn't go to the village right away, I would bust.

We headed to Vassara later that day after stopping in Sparta to exchange money at the bank and buy some necessary groceries. At the last minute, we ordered a few pizzas from Magoula *platia*'s pizzeria. I wasn't completely ready for traditional Greek food, and pizza was a welcomed transition. Deliciously familiar aromas of cheese and pepperoni filled our Audi as we headed into the hills of Parnonas.

Our twenty-minute ride to Vassara felt like twenty hours. Although we set out much later in the day than Pappou and Yiayia wanted, this was my favorite time of day, which made our homecoming even better. The sun started to set just as we arrived, presenting the mountains in a way that was even more enrapturing than usual. The sky was breathtaking, blending its blue into deep pinks and oranges. Like a newly opened present, the village unveiled itself again out of the vast, thick Parnonas hills. Vassara was still there. I made sure to be dressed for the night ahead of time. My "return to Vassara" outfit was something I took weeks to choose before we left.

"See!" Mom said, laughing. "And you said it was all just a dream!"

We honked our way up the narrow streets to the *platia,* and I was like a puppy in the backseat, anxious with excitement to see who had arrived for the summer. Brikakis' café was filled with crowds of visitors in the *platia.* Mihali was watching the store for his parents and stood in the café's doorway just like his mother once did. He looked older and more mature as he took orders from customers that looked American—probably from Boston. I rolled down the window and waved to him with a big smile.

"*Kalosorisate* " (Welcome back)! he said as he waved back.

The sounds of local Vassareans greeting Americans echoed throughout the square as the village repopulated. Locals took their evening stroll at a slow, leisurely pace. Time seemed to slow down right away as I looked around at the villagers already adjusted to a smooth summer stride. I scanned the *platia* again for Stavros, but there was no sign of him. When our car reached Aunt Vivi's giant, green door, Pappou honked loudly and drove up the road to park our car outside our house. Mom turned around from the front seat of the Audi and said to me, "I know you're anxious. Leave the bags. We'll worry about them later. Just say hi to the relatives and off you go with Despina. I'm sure the kids are gathering at the tavern soon. Do you have enough money?"

I was relieved. The last thing I wanted to do right then was unpack and worry about setting up house. "Thanks, Mom. Yep, I'm fine. Don't wait up."

"Not too late."

Yiayia jumped in, "*Then exi faie to paithi*" (But the child hasn't eaten anything)!

Mom reassured her. "That's okay, Ma. She'll eat later. She's too excited to see everyone."

After endless hugging outside Aunt Vivi's doorway, Despina and I were off. Uncle Georgo said Aunt Maria was already asleep in her bed inside the kitchen, so we didn't disturb her. Petro was at the *Yipetho* for some soccer practice, Despina explained, so we headed down to the *platia*. I figured Stavros must be at the game, as well.

Despina and I trotted down the cobblestone streets toward the town square. We had a lot of catching up to do; somehow, this was easier done in person. She looked different—better. Her hair was longer. She still didn't wear makeup, but she was definitely taller.

Down at the *platia*, I was greeted by Anastasia, Evangelia, and most of the other girls. They were very happy to see all of the Americans that returned. A few of the guys had already returned from soccer practice. They were at a table just outside Brikakis', drinking Coke and covered in dirt. Stavros was among them. When I first saw him, my stomach dropped. Demetri and his brother Thimosteni were there, too, and they got up before anyone else to greet me.

"Welcome back!" Demetri said as he gave me a big smile.

"Back for another year, huh, Chicago girl?" Thimosteni winked.

"*Kalosorisate ston Vassara*" (Welcome to Vassara), Stavros said as he nodded to me.

"Thanks," was all I could say. I knew he wasn't about to leap up and kiss me, although I wouldn't have minded. Forced to play it cool, Despina and I took a seat on one of the benches, and after a while, the boys left to shower and change before meeting us at Moustokotou's tavern.

Glykeria's music vibrated throughout the tavern, and the smell of Moustokotou's fire pit was unmistakable. Stavros sat at the other end of the table and looked angry. My cousin negated my suspicions and suggested that I drink to celebrate my return to the village, leaving boy problems for later. I did just that. After about four or five "little" glasses of beer, nothing bothered me, and I decided to play Stavros's game. I did my best to ignore him and joined in the Greek dancing with my cousin. When we got too tired to dance, we sat for a while to catch up with the rest of the girls.

Around midnight, our group decided not to go to Koulouri, much to my disappointment, and instead headed back to the *platia*. Just when I had given up on getting a chance to talk to Stavros that night, he walked over and asked if he could walk me home.

"I thought you said that wasn't acceptable in this town?" I asked.

"Just c'mon," he said, still grimacing, and he started walking up the street. I turned around to Despina, who waved me ahead. I followed him out of the square, and together we walked up the road past his house toward mine, taking the long way.

In the shadows of the dark streets, he reached out and held my hand as we made our way slowly down his street and around the corner. Baffled by his behavior, I grew nervous, not knowing what to expect. "So much for being prepared," I thought. Stavros said nothing. We walked the whole way in silence. I had no idea what to expect, so I just went along, happy to hold his hand. The streets were black, with only a few streetlights giving a small, concentrated glow every block or so. The air was cool, and the village streets were silent except for the echoing sound of our shoes hitting the cobblestone road.

When we approached my house with its streetlight shining down on the front step, Stavros leaned his back up against the building and pulled me close, wrapping his arms around me. He held me tight without saying a word. The world felt right again. His warm body enveloped mine. I waited for him to pull back and kiss me, but he didn't. After a few minutes, I broke our embrace and looked up at him with concern. I could feel he was hesitant.

"Thanks for your letters," he said with a forced smile.

"You didn't say much in yours," I answered.

He looked down at the street and paused for a minute. Then he said sadly, "We can't."

"Can't what?" I asked, looking straight into his bluish green eyes.

"Not this summer, sweetheart," he said softly, looking down again.

"What do you mean?" I searched his emotionless face, confused.

"I … it just can't happen this year." He took a piece of my hair and put it behind my ear, forcing a smile for a second, acknowledging my new hairstyle.

"Why not?"

"There's …," He paused uncomfortably.

"You have a girlfriend." I was guessing, but I knew with a sinking feeling that I was right. He looked down.

"Yes … and she'll be here at the end of the summer for the festival." He seemed almost ashamed.

"Who is she?" I asked. He didn't answer. A cold chill came over me as a gust of wind blew through the trees. "Please don't tell me it's Fotini."

"Yes," he said.

I felt my face flush with anger. Backing away from him, I looked away. "So Nia and Soula *were* telling the truth last year!" My arms fell to the sides of my body.

"No. No they weren't." He stood upright and took a step toward me, reaching for my hand. I pulled away, but he took my hand and held it in between his. "Petro told me you heard about Fotini after the festival. I didn't bring it up in my letters because I didn't want to explain. We weren't together then. But we are now, and it just wouldn't be right. It has nothing to do with you. Fotini and I had broken up last summer, but then things changed again in the fall when we went back to school. If you and I get together now before she gets here, everyone will talk, and she'll find out and—"

I pulled my hand away and put it on his chest to stop him. "Stavros, I don't care," I said before he could continue.

"What? What do you mean you don't care?"

"I mean I don't care if you're with her." I paused, not believing my own words. But the truth was, in that moment, I didn't care about anything else besides here and now. After seeing Stavros again, standing so close, I didn't care about right or wrong. I didn't care who knew or didn't know. I just wanted him. "Look," I continued. "I didn't expect you to stay true to me all winter long, especially after you said we were *friends*. But I'm *here*, I'm actually *here*, and it's *summer,* and I want to be with you. So what if you're with her back at school? I want you while I'm here—now."

Stavros looked down. "We can't. People will find out," he warned.

"No, they won't. We'll be really quiet about it. I won't tell a soul. I won't even tell Despina." I reached for his face. "I've waited all year to see you again, and I can't spend the next seven weeks without you." He said nothing. He just shook his head.

"Stavros, please." I was desperate. "I love you." I couldn't believe I told him.

He took my face in his hands and gently kissed my lips. "I'm sorry," he whispered.

Tears streamed down my cheeks, and though I tried to hold back, I couldn't help but cry. He held my head to his body as if I were a young child.

"Please, Stavros, please," I begged.

He pulled my face up from his chest and looked at me. "You're going to be okay. You're going to have a good summer, okay?"

I closed my eyes in disbelief, as what endeared me to Stavros also crushed my heart. Whether I liked it or not, he was all about right or wrong. In Stavros's world, there was no in-between. Even though he was breaking my heart, he tried to let me down gently and not ruin my summer. I wasn't angry with him. I just felt sad. Deep down, I understood that this was his world I entered each June, not mine. I had the luxury of dating people back home without him knowing, but Stavros couldn't do the same. He was too decent to lie and knew I would find out about his girlfriend. After all, there was no hiding the truth in a village like Vassara. I wanted him back so badly. I felt like someone was cutting off my air. Summer wasn't summer without him.

"Tell me we'll stay friends, okay?" he asked.

"Boy, you're big on that whole 'friends' thing," I said as I tried to dry my eyes.

He smiled and held me for while longer. He said he didn't want me to hate him. How could I? In my eyes, Stavros was still perfect, which made me want him back even more.

I didn't sleep most of that night. Rewinding the evening's events over and over in my head, I wondered what I could have done differently, knowing in the end, nothing could have changed the outcome. He had another girl. I'd have to get used to the idea. At least now I had some explanation for his hot and cold behavior. While Stavros and Fotini weren't together last summer, obviously they weren't completely over, either. I was sure he had both of us on his mind last August. I figured that's why he ignored me in public. If there was one thing to feel good about, it was that I finally understood him a little bit more.

The next morning, and for most of the next week until we left for the ocean, I hung out with Despina and some of the other kids from Boston. I tried to look happy when Stavros was around even though I was dying inside. Like learning how to breathe or walk again, I found that I had to learn how to be in Vassara without being "his." Everything in the village reminded me of

Stavros. I knew I needed to make new memories, but my heart ached. In the meantime, Fotini was nowhere in sight. "Thank God," I thought, dreading the day she returned to Vassara.

I was glad to leave the village for the islands as scheduled, and I welcomed time at the sea. I didn't say anything to Mom about Stavros or Fotini. She was cool enough not to ask for details, but she could tell I was upset about something. I didn't feel like explaining the whole mess and instead tried to concentrate on enjoying the beach. We traveled the local Mediterranean islands and got a feel for the local fare of Greece outside the village. There was an entire country to enjoy outside Vassara. The hot sun was therapeutic, and after many days spent on the water, I not only developed a nice tan but began to feel better inside, as well.

Mom and I got back to Vassara just before St. Sotiras's feast day. I knew being near Stavros would be difficult, but I had to face him. My cousin did her best to lift my spirits. We hung out all over the village, day and night, and even took the bus into Sparta by ourselves to shop a few times. Eventually, summer worked its magic, and I was able to enjoy life in the village once more. Nights at Koulouri were difficult. While we drank and sang and danced, I couldn't help but wander in my mind back to the time when Stavros and I would escape the party crowd and go off behind the rocks to look at the stars and love each other.

One night, while we all stood in the dark up on Koulouri's cliff, holding our bottles of Amstel Light and singing to Kosma's guitar, Demetri's dark shadow approached. I recognized the shadows now and could identify most of the kids by the sound of their voices in the dark.

"You okay?" he asked.

"Yeah, why?"

"Well, from what I and some of the others see, you don't seem okay."

"I'm okay, Demetri." I smiled.

"No. No, you're not. You're not the same happy girl I met last summer." Demetri knew me too well.

"It's just so hard seeing him and not being with him," I confessed.

Demetri stood up straight, stretching his chest to the stars. "In my opinion, you're wasting your time feeling sorry for yourself and wishing things were different. It's obvious to me that you're still chasing after him in that head of yours, wishing you could get him back. Why don't you let it go and let yourself have some fun instead? There's more to the village than Stavros Antonopoulos, you know."

I looked down, grateful it was too dark out for Demetri to see my face redden. He was right. I paused for a second and then confessed, "I know."

"Good, because there's still a lot of fun to have around here, and there's other people worth getting to know better," he protested.

"Demetri, can I ask you something?" I looked at him.

"Sure."

I was hesitant, but I had to know. "Why are most of Stavros's friends keeping their distance from me? Niko, Loukas, and Thanasi—all those guys used to talk to me, and now they act like I don't exist. What's going on?"

"They act that way because they all think all you care about is Stavros. I know better. I know you love this place for what it is even without him," he comforted.

I smiled. "You are my friend, aren't you?" I asked him.

"I'm your *kolite*." He stood upright in pride.

"What's a *kolite*?"

"It's a ... a sort of buddy ... a partner in crime, so to speak. Of course I'm your friend," he reassured me. "And next summer will be all yours. I promise." He put his arm on my shoulder.

"All mine?"

He paused and looked down, smiling. "You'll go home this year, spend the winter getting over Stavros and growing wiser, and next year when you return, this place will be all yours. I promise."

"You're the best, Demetri. You're my *kolite*."

That was the beginning of my friendship with Demetri. Along with my cousin Despina, he had the courage to tell me what I didn't want to hear. I was fortunate Demetri felt concerned about me, although I never expected to hear what he confided about the other guys. The last thing I wanted was to be thought of as the girl who got dumped and never recovered. My good times in the village were too precious to lose, and I needed to maintain my friendships with the other kids. I loved being a part of their group. Demetri's words to me that night were a wake-up call. I decided to have a good time even if it killed me. Demetri walked with me back to the group and handed me a freshly opened beer bottle.

"*Kolite*," he said as he held up his bottle and clinked mine.

After that night, I did my best to enjoy the rest of our summer, even the festival on the last day. Although the summer didn't play out like I had planned, by the time we were ready to return to Chicago, I was grateful for the trip.

Chapter 9
On Fire

I TOOK ONE LAST look in the mirror attached to the Magoula bedroom's wardrobe before heading out the door. A quick swipe of candy pink lip gloss and I was ready. Pappou, Yiayia, and Mom waited in the car with the motor running just outside the orange-flowered gates. I turned sideways to check the rear view of my body, pleased with my tanned legs and new miniskirt. Facing forward again, I made a big, teethed smile at the reflection, showing myself straight, pearly whites for the hundredth time. What a difference with braces off! At last I could smile without a mouthful of silver. My teal tank and electric blue eyeliner matched perfectly. Summer of 1986 was off to a great start.

As I trotted down the Magoula terrace steps to add my bag into Pappou's trunk, I smiled to myself, remembering the last two weeks and how much I enjoyed time on the islands. Our ten-day jaunt to the Greek port towns of Poros, St. Marina, and Edipso brought out a golden glow from within, and I felt a new sense of confidence emerge, as well. Mom's suggestion to delay our arrival to Sparta and start off our Greek vacation with beach time proved ideal. We always talked about visiting local islands, and knowing Stavros wasn't waiting for me, I felt no rush to return to the village. I was happy just to be in Greece for one more summer. We were able to unwind, walk the sands of the Aegean, and decompress from our lives in the States before heading south to Peloponnese. While on the beautiful beaches, my mind went back to a year earlier when the same sun therapy helped mend my broken heart.

I was a stronger now and ready for the four weeks that remained for us to spend in Vassara.

I found it ironic that only a month earlier, I was taking finals, finishing up my sophomore year of high school, and looking at colleges. As caught up as I was with my agenda back home, nothing could stop my thoughts from returning to Greece come springtime. Determined to return, I worked at my father's office on breaks and after school, finally making enough money to pay for an airline ticket. Mom was eager to visit Greece, as well, as our trips were becoming more of a routine.

By 1986, I grew to appreciate the slow, European lifestyle, and I even enjoyed quiet afternoon siestas, especially on the Greek islands. While local merchants closed their tourist shops midday, Mom and I spent peaceful time connecting with our love for art. She painted watercolors. I wrote poetry. We soaked in the hot sun and enjoyed daily iced coffees at oceanside cafés. I ingested all of Greece's picturesque beauty, from the way the sunlight glistened across turquoise water to the charm of whitewashed churches dotting the coastline and the daily arrival of weathered fishermen bringing ashore catches of octopus. My inner spirit blossomed as the Grecian golden days freed me from a routine life at home and allowed me to connect with a different part of my soul I didn't know existed.

Even Magoula felt more like home when we arrived. I rediscovered summer clothes and a blow dryer left behind. What a great welcome to find things exactly where I left them. This time, I had no romantic expectations for my trip. Demetri was right, after all. I spent the winter maturing as he'd predicted, and I put my thoughts about Stavros into perspective. I knew I'd always hold a bit of love angst for him, but I couldn't allow old memories to rule my life. That fling had flung, and now the time had come for pure vacation fun.

When the day arrived to return to Vassara, my excitement could not be contained. Even without Stavros, I knew an amazing experience waited. We headed off in the Audi once more and soon arrived at Vassara's outskirts near the village school. After another embarrassing round of Pappou's horn announcing our arrival into the *platia*, we headed for Aunt Vivi's house. The same crazy, happy greeting exploded from Uncle Georgo, Aunt Vivi, Kiki, and Tatz outside Despina's big, green door. My cousin was even taller than the year before and completely towered over me as if I had forgotten to grow. We laughed at the difference.

Looking around, I noticed that Aunt Maria was missing, and I learned that she had become unable to walk with ease. Confined to her small, twin bed beside Aunt Vivi's sitting room, we went inside to greet her. Aunt Maria was quiet and had a distant look in her eyes that made me sad. I wasn't sure if she remembered me. I held her hand, kissed her cheek, and smiled into her aging face. While the fleeting years were turning Despina and me into young women, Aunt Maria was slowing down, and I knew life would not hold still for any of us.

The same was true for Petro, who left just before our arrival in order to serve in the Greek army. His enlistment papers called for him to report for duty in Athens, and by law, he could not refuse. Petro's two-year service kept him away for most of the summer, including Vassara's festival. Lefteri was gone, too. He was finished with the army but was working a new job in Athens. I thought it sad that the two best friends were both gone for the season. Summer would be different without them. Petro and Lefteri were the first of our group to move on with their lives, and they offered a scary glimpse of the inevitable.

Despina and I were impatient to get out of the house. We remained at the table with our parents only as long as necessary, eating our meal quickly and answering questions about school. The first chance we had to leave, however, we made a dash for the door. Freedom! Without a word, each of us had the same plan, as our agenda remained consistent. First, we would stop to buy Cokes from Brikakis' café and then walk to Koulouri to dish the latest news. Even though Despina and I exchanged letters over the winter months, some juicy details had to be explained in person. Koulouri was the place for assured privacy. Despina updated me on her romance with Tasso, an architect student she was seeing in Athens, and I filled her in on the stories of my previous year. Despina knew how much I loved being up at Koulouri and how much I missed the view. Somehow, the cliff gave me a sense of calm unmatched anywhere else in the world.

After buying cigarettes from Mrs. Brikaki and avoiding a multitude of questions—"When did you get back? Who came with you this year? How old are you now? How long are you staying?"—we walked up to Koulouri, pausing for a minute to greet a group of friends that were coming down from the cliff. Niko, Thanasi, Anastasia, and Loukas were there, as well, and spoke outside a corner house. We stopped to say hello.

"Back for another year, hey, Chicago girl?" Thanasi asked.

"Yep," I answered.

"Welcome back!" Niko shook my hand with a smile.

"Good to be back." I smiled in return. "Where's Demetri?" I asked Despina.

"Still in Athens. He should be back here in about a week," she answered.

Stavros came out of the house they were standing near and looked at me with as much surprise as I looked at him. I wasn't prepared to see him until evening. Stavros put his hands on his hips and gave a winning grin, as if to say *"Well, look at you!"* Like a knee-jerk reaction, I couldn't help but smile broadly back at him. He winked at me. I smiled more grandly.

"Oraia" (Beautiful), he said.

His hair was cut shorter than before, emphasizing his strong facial structure. Why did he have to be so attractive? I shook his hand, nervously laughing.

Later that evening, our large group of kids gathered again at Moutsokotou's. With the school year over, we reunited in our far-away home across the globe to drink beer, dance, and celebrate summer. Tables were pushed together quickly. Despina and I counted sixty kids in our crowd. We took up more than half of the tavern. With Demetri missing from the village, his brother Grigori sat across from Despina and I, trying to listen to our whispers. He was always hungry for scoop. Amstel Lights passed up and down the tables, and our small glasses filled with beer. We toasted to another great summer. Sharing updates of our lives, we discussed our latest accomplishments, plans for the following year, and news of who was going into the army and who was just about to get out. We reconnected. Stavros said he expected his own enlistment papers to arrive over the winter. I couldn't imagine his absence. Our crowd seemed incomplete without Petro and Lefteri, let alone Stavros. Even if we weren't together, Vassara would never be the same without him.

Our happy, drunken crowd left the tavern hours later, near midnight. Most of us made our way up to Koulouri in the black of night. Some of the younger kids returned home. Some of our older friends like Panteli returned home, as well, since he had to work the next day in Sparta. Panteli was in his midthirties at the time. His dark, bushy hair had started to recede and show his age. Panteli was a barrel of laughs. We teased him relentlessly, calling him our token "old man." In our youthful eyes, he seemed ancient.

Kosma, always devoted to his guitar, broke out classic Greek tunes on top of the cliff as our group filled Koulouri with song, beer, and cigarettes. I talked with the girls but noticed that Stavros broke away from his group and stood alone by the edge of the rock. I smiled, remembering our old signal, wondering if he was up to his old tricks again. I let him stand by himself for a while, enjoying the thought that he might be waiting for me. But like a magnet, I gave in and walked over toward him.

"Took you long enough. What were you trying to do? Make me wait forever?" he asked.

"You deserve to wait," I answered with attitude.

"Why? Because of last summer?" He looked at me sympathetically.

"Yep," I said coldly.

"Ah, last summer. I was an idiot. Fotini and I are long over."

I froze. He stared at me with his intense eyes, and I helplessly tried to appear cool, when in reality, I was entranced.

"Did you have a good winter?" he asked politely.

"Yeah, it went by fast, but I'm glad to be back. Thanks for the Christmas card."

"I'm glad you're here this summer. You look fantastic." He sounded sincere.

"It's just the braces. They're finally off," I explained.

"No. It's not just that. It's *you*. You're really growing into a beautiful young woman."

I turned my head away, hiding the smile that beamed across my face. His flattery was enticing, but I knew I was playing with fire. Still, no matter how hard I tried to forget him, there was no fighting my feelings. Something always brought me back to Stavros.

I followed him as he slowly walked down the rocks, away from everyone else. Before disappearing around the corner, I looked back at Despina, who shook her head at me, grinning as she puffed out the smoke from her cigarette. So much for growing a year wiser.

"I'll catch up with you," I called back to her.

She smiled as if to say, "You stupid American, here you go again. Go ahead—I tried to warn you." I knew I looked like an idiot.

Out of sight from the others, Stavros pulled me close. I'd forgotten how wonderful his embrace felt. Without a word or explanation, we were crazy for each other all over again. He kissed me passionately, and I was in heaven once more. What a perfect moment—the summer, the stars, the village, the midnight mountain air, and Stavros. Life didn't get any better than this. All that was missing was for him to tell me how much he cared about me, how sorry he was for hurting me last summer, and that he loved me forever. But this was not my Cinderella moment. Instead, he got up, took off his shirt, and threw it on the rock next to us.

"What are you doing? It's cold up here!" I asked him, puzzled.

"Did I tell you how beautiful you look?" he asked me, ignoring my comments.

"Yes, you did. What are you—?"

Like a large rock thrown at my head, his intentions hit me out of nowhere. Instantly, my perfect moment vanished. Stavros stopped when he saw my shocked expression. Frustrated, he plopped himself back down next to me and let out a long sigh. I searched his eyes, but instead of sincerity, I only saw irritation.

"Don't you want to talk to me?" I entreated him. There was so much to say, I thought, so many feelings to express. If he wanted me back, surely he knew I needed some explanation of where things stood between us.

"But we've only got a short time together. We'll talk later. C'mon ..." He kissed my neck. My eyes grew watery as I turned away, hurt and disappointed.

He sat back and smirked. "You're still a *virgin*, aren't you?" he asked sarcastically.

I swung my head back toward him and snapped, "It's not about that."

"Yes, it is. I should have figured. You ... *Americans*." He sighed again and grabbed for his shirt. "Too bad." He looked up at the moon. "We could have had a lot more fun if you weren't."

Stung by his hurtful words, I stood up in anger, too shocked to speak. I brushed myself off and headed back around the corner to be with the other kids. Stavros didn't try to stop me. When I reached the flattened area of the cliff, I saw that our crowd had already left. Forced to climb down Koulouri alone in the dark, I was even more upset. My mind raced as I hurried along the rocks, blown away by Stavros's behavior and anxious to reach the first lit cobblestone road. There was so much left unsaid between us. I didn't understand him. "What was he thinking? I'm only sixteen. Is he crazy?" My steps quickened, fearing what might jump out from behind a rock.

Stomping down from the cliff, I made my way hurriedly through the dark, desolate streets toward the *platia*, where I knew the kids gathered. Thankfully, I remembered each turn and bump, and I needed little light to find my way. I berated myself with each step of my clapping sandals for being so stupid, for thinking he finally cared. I couldn't believe Stavros's intentions were merely physical.

I reached the town square with a flushed face and fast breath. Despina took one look at me and instantly knew. She came over and led me away from the others, putting her arm around my shoulder as if to tell me a secret. We walked to the opposite end of the town square, where she told to me to take a deep breath and to calm down and that we'd talk about it later. Despina was great about not making a scene—better than I.

Stavros rejoined our group only moments later and walked past me with his head down. When he rejoined his friends, they started teasing him for taking such a "short walk up to Koulouri." Obviously, we weren't expected back so soon. I ignored all of them. Finally, Despina suggested that we call it a night, and we walked home together. As I told her the details, she shook her head, equally as surprised by Stavros's behavior. She offered little advice except to say that I was right to leave. After all, he still hadn't expressed his real feelings after all this time.

By the next day, most of the kids heard about what happened. I knew Stavros wasn't one to spread rumors, but suffice it to say that people in a small town have a way of putting pieces together. I wished my friend Demetri was around. He would have had something to say to make me feel better about the whole mess. Meanwhile, in the days that followed, Stavros grew colder and more distant. I wasn't surprised. Surely I had damaged his pride, challenging his reputation of always getting what he wanted. About a week went by, and while I did my best to avoid him, a confrontation between the two of us finally occurred while we visited another town.

Our group had traveled to the village of Vresthena, a forty-five-minute drive from Vassara. We made the excursion for their village festival, loading into cars and vans to party the night away in the neighboring village. At first, Mom was reluctant to let me go, but Tatzaforo convinced her that I would be safe with all of the older kids, especially since we were going as a large group. Stavros organized the caravan and suggested that Despina and I ride with Loukas to the festival in his maroon Mazda van. Loukas became our designated driver that year since Lefteri wasn't around.

Vresthena's festival was huge just like Vassara's party. The villagers even hired the same band. Our group took up a large section of their *platia* and sat at several long tables. Everyone drank beer in short, little glasses except Stavros. He held a plastic cup filled halfway with orange Gatorade and explained that he was training for a marathon. "Whatever," I thought.

I got up from our table to order my cousin a refill of wine, and Stavros followed, asking if I would step outside with him for a moment. I complied, thinking he might want to apologize for being such a jerk. I brought Despina's carafe of wine to our table and told her I'd be back in a minute. Stavros followed me away from the tables and into the street.

He took my hand as we waited for oncoming cars to pass by, full of partiers still arriving for Vresthena's big party. Walking down a dark street, he kept my hand in his. While I wanted to pull away, I didn't, feeling sorry that things had soured between us so quickly. A cool breeze blew over us as we continued down the road, and the temperature seemed to drop. Stavros stopped for a moment to give me his jacket. I wrapped his white parka around my shoulders and smelled his familiar scent. We stood by a little house at the end of the stone road overlooking Vresthena, the moon high in the evening sky. He took both of my hands into his.

"I—" He started to speak, but something in me snapped. I couldn't hold back.

"What was that about the other night?" I interrupted.

"I just thought ..." He paused. "Look, most girls by now—"

"Most girls?" I stopped him. "I don't even know how you *feel* about me!"   Stavros came closer, wrapped his arms around my waist, and drew me in. "You know I care about you. I missed you very much over the winter, and I will miss you even more when you leave this year. Let's just have a fun summer. Maybe you'll change your mind."

Change my mind? Was he kidding? I let go of our embrace and took a step back. What happened to him? This wasn't the Stavros I'd known for the last three years. I looked up at him, and his whole face seemed different. He waited for me to say something, but I couldn't. All I kept thinking was that he didn't look the same. I felt like I was standing next to a stranger. I was so hurt, so angry, and I felt so stupid. Stavros wasn't interested in a relationship. That was clear. I had put him on a pedestal higher than he deserved. He wasn't perfect. He was insincere.

Feeling as though someone had just punched me in the stomach, I walked away from Stavros and rejoined our group still partying at Vresthena's festival. Stavros was too prideful to come after me. I sat back down at the table, and Despina put a fresh beer in front of me. She toasted to the rest of the summer. I toasted to the end of being stupid. She laughed, and we both knew it was finally over. Even at sixteen, I realized my heart needed more love than he could give.

The following afternoon, Despina had to practically force me to go to the *Yipetho* with her to watch Vassara play Verroia in a highly charged soccer game between bitter rivals. I secretly routed for Verroia the whole time, hoping Stavros would have to swallow the bitter taste of defeat. We beat them 4–3, and instead, Stavros gloated with his pals after scoring the winning goal. I couldn't help but hold onto my anger after spending the night sleeplessly turning the events of the past week over in my mind, wondering what I'd missed. In the end, I had no sign that Stavros truly cared for me.

Despina stayed after the game ended to celebrate with her fellow villagers, but I decided to walk home alone. Heading up the dirt road that led from the soccer field, I turned left and walked toward the old school. Up ahead and across the path approached a little old lady dressed in black. She was short in stature with a sweet face. As we neared each other, I recognized her as Ourania, the nun who had built the monastery. I hadn't seen her since the day we first arrived to the village in 1984, and yet she remembered me right away.

"*Kalispera koukla mou*" (Good evening, my doll). She held out her arms as she crossed the road to greet me.

"Ourania! You remember me?" I asked her as she embraced me, wrapping her long-sleeved arms around me. How did she survive wearing all black on such a hot day?

"Of course I do—although look how you've grown! Far from the little girl of fourteen I met two years ago." She looked me up and down with a smile.

We exchanged heartfelt greetings, and I agreed to send her best to Mom and Yiayia as she instructed.

Before we parted, she gazed her sparkling, beaming eyes into mine and said, "May you walk with *Panayia* (Virgin Mary), my angel, and may she always be with you, every day, with every choice you make. May her strength be with you always and keep you close to God."

She kissed me on both cheeks and headed off down the road past the soccer field and the *Yipetho*. I stood there for a minute and watched Ourania, wondering if my inner thoughts seemed so obvious. I wondered, "How does she always read me?" With a smile on my face, I headed back into town, walking a little taller, armed with a new affirmation of my principles and with less self-doubt. Someone would be the right one for me, and whoever he was would be worth waiting for. The important thing was that I knew who I was and felt strong enough not to compromise my principles for anyone, including Stavros.

Eventually, Despina and I stopped talking about him, and I returned to enjoying summer. During the evenings, we managed to sit at tables far from Stavros at the tavern and kept away from him up at the cliff. Although I was heartbroken at the loss of my first love, I knew time had changed Stavros— and not for the better. As the days of my vacation continued, I did my best to soak up the village before saying good-bye. Kiki took Mom and me into the mountains to harvest tea. Aunt Vivi and Despina showed me how to make Greek french fries, and Tatz even attempted to teach me to drive stick shift in his scary, white pickup. Demetri finally arrived, and with him, the best days of the summer were saved for last. We Greek danced every night until dawn, telling jokes until we were bent over in laughter. He was like a male version of Despina—carefree, easygoing, with no hidden agendas or hang-ups.

One day, after pitifully trying to play basketball with Demetri and his brother and being told to stick to cheerleading, I passed through the *platia* on the way home, hungry for lunch and thirsty for a cold drink. Tatzaforo called me over to his table at Brikakis', offering me an Amita juice. I was exhausted from my efforts and happy to rest in the shade for a moment. My uncle had a man sitting with him. He was tall, with dark hair and dark features. He was extremely good looking like a model. I greeted him politely as I sucked down the juice, but I was anxious to get home, knowing Mom was making our last box of Kraft Macaroni & Cheese. After eating lunch, I went over to Despina's to hang out. We sat in her bedroom like we did on many lazy afternoons, listening to my American cassettes and talking. She showed me some of her latest paintings and sketches. We talked about her degree in technical drawing and her dreams to become an architect.

A few hours later, I returned home to change for the evening. Coming up the street from Despina's, I heard loud voices from my kitchen and assumed we had company. Tatz sat at our dining room table with the same man. His name was Ari Kostopoulos, and he was passing through Vassara on his way to Tsintzina, where his father owned the local restaurant. Pappou joined the men, and they sat smoking and talking, with a soccer game showing on our black-and-white TV. Meanwhile, Aunt Kiki stood at the stove, preparing Greek coffee for the men. As soon as I passed the dining room, my aunt winked at me with a suspicious smile. After Mom looked at me and rolled her eyes, I realized my aunt's agenda.

Mom handed me a bowl of fresh grapes to bring our guests and said, "Ari is Kyriakos's son. You know, Kyriakos from Tsintzina? Kiki and Kyriakos grew up together." Her unauthentic tone gave the truth away.

I returned after putting the fruit on the table and whispered to her, "How old is he? They're nuts!"

Mom laughed and shook her head. "Oh, he's at least ten years older than you if he's in his late twenties. In fact, he's already finished his army duty!"

The words "arranged marriage" were written all over my aunt and uncle's faces. As soon as I connected the dots, I literally laughed out loud at my backward relatives. "They're hilarious," I thought. "He's too old for me!" Besides, I was done with romance for the summer.

I politely excused myself from our guests and went upstairs to change clothes. I remember picking out this little white Greek island tank dress to wear that I bought on island of Poros a few weeks earlier. I thought I looked great for one of my last nights on the town in Vassara. I did my hair and was ready to go when I heard screaming.

Opening the door to the upstairs balcony, I came outside and saw the commotion coming from the street. Without noticing smoke or smelling fire, I saw Yiayia's face paralyzed by fear. They must have been trying to get my attention from the street for some time, but because I had my music playing loudly, I didn't hear a thing. A large crowd of people gathered in the street, all of them in a fury. Mom and Yiayia yelled at me to get out of the house. Our lower level kitchen was on fire. Smoke rose toward me from the lower level. I wouldn't be safe upstairs for long.

The entrance to our kitchen that connected with the bottom of the balcony's stairs was full of smoke and flames, so the only feasible way out wasn't an option. With ancient construction and design, the layouts of these village homes didn't make any sense. The only way to get from the upstairs to the lower level was to go outside to the balcony and down the connecting staircase that was on fire. My only choice was to jump off the balcony. All I could think of was breaking my ankle or leg and not being able to cheer the following fall. Such are the worries of a high school cheerleader!

The crowd that gathered below shouted different things to me while I stood looking at the railing. Directions of what to do and where to go were coming at me in Greek and English, and I couldn't understand anyone. Everyone had their own idea of how to get me off the balcony. Someone yelled something about a ladder. I heard an old lady say she'd go get her donkey to break my fall. No one made sense. I tried to concentrate on what my mother was saying, as she remained the only calm person.

"You're going to have to jump down, honey. It's the only way," she said, knowing I was scared.

That's when my cousin Yianni Malikotsi walked down the street. He must have heard the fuss and came to see what was happening. My older cousin was visiting his elderly parents who still lived up the street from us. Yianni Malikotsi was Yiayia's nephew and about forty years old at the time. He was a big guy with the build of a professional football player; he had broad shoulders and thick legs. His most noticeable feature, however, was his thick, curly, black hair that was always out of place. He immediately motioned for me to jump from the balcony into his arms. Mom nodded. This seemed like the best option, and I knew he was the only one big enough to catch me. I nodded but first ran back inside house to get something. Everyone in the street gasped when they saw me go back into the house. Returning to the balcony, I clutched in my hand a bag carrying our passports, tickets home, money, my collection of costume jewelry, and makeup case. Essentials only. Mom shook her head in disbelief. Like Dorothy's ruby slippers ensuring her way back to Kansas, I could never leave behind our passports and tickets home.

"Here," I said to Mom. "Catch!" I threw them to her as I prepared to jump.

My large, burly cousin caught me in what proved to be a completely humiliating experience since everyone watched me fall into his arms. A crowd of local women encircled us with hugs and kisses as I stood in the street, my heart pounding. Meanwhile, the crowd continued to yell out different commands regarding the fire that still burned inside the lower level kitchen. Mom and I stood back and watched the horrible scene, wondering what would become of our house.

A young boy ran up our street and into the bell tower at St. George's Church. He grabbed the thick, long rope that hung from the tower and began to pull down with all his strength. The rope rang the loud, clanging bell that had previously been my alarm clock for church. Now the bell rang in a fast rhythm to signal an emergency. Within seconds, more villagers came running, splashing buckets of water behind them. They worked in a frenzy to put out the flames. That's when I noticed Ari still inside my burning kitchen by the stove. He came out moments later, covered in sweat and carrying a gas tank. He ran past us, shouting and bringing the tank far away from the house. I had no idea what he was doing but later learned that the fire had something to do with the oven, and Ari brought the gas tank outside so that there wouldn't be an explosion.

As I watched the fire continue to burn, my eyes welled with tears. How could this happen? Mom tried to calm Yiayia. A group of old ladies dressed in black smothered her, telling her God knows what. We tried to steer her away from them.

Out of the commotion, a skinny, old lady appeared, shouting as she came around the corner, running in her black dress and head scarf. She was leading the priest from St. George's Church toward our house. He was a rotund, old priest and had the physical characteristics of Santa Claus. His concerned look deepened as he trotted along beside the old lady, his big, round belly bouncing underneath shiny blue vestments. As they approached, I realized they were headed toward me.

The old lady screamed, "Here she is, Father! Help her!"

"What?" I thought. "What are they talking about? Who needs help? Me? I'm already off the balcony, you stupid, panic-stricken, old lady. What is the priest doing here?"

He held out his arms as the old lady pointed at me, saying, "She's hysterical. We don't know how to calm her down, Father. *Please help her!*"

Before I had a chance to speak, the sweaty, plump priest pulled me into his round belly and shoved my head into his thick chest. I couldn't breathe. He kept saying, "Don't cry. It's all right, my child. God will protect you. The Mother of God is with you."

I wasn't crying. I was suffocating! And why in the world did this old lady fetch the village priest? I wasn't hysterical. I wasn't making a sound! The kind old priest finally released my head as I gasped for breath. When I looked up, Mom and Yiayia were watching me, both of them laughing. I just smiled and said, *"Euharisto"* (Thank you), to the priest, grateful to breathe again.

The flames slowly diminished, and the villagers were able to put out the fire. Fortunately, the flames never spread to the living room, and the fire didn't do nearly as much damage as it could have. The quick response from the villagers saved our home. Ari stood by the balcony door, holding his left hand. His face winced as he inspected the burns that came from carrying our gas tank. Blood trickled down from the scratches on his arms. Tatz told me to get Ari some *othondocrema*. I had no idea what that word meant. Mom had gone inside to inspect the damage and wasn't around to translate. I thought maybe he wanted a Band-Aid, so that's what I brought. Ari made a big smile which led to a huge laugh. Then he asked me for toothpaste in English. Apparently, Crest heals burns.

I went back upstairs and brought him the tube. We sat in the living room together while I helped bandage his cuts. As I sat with our hero, he continued to tease me about the Band-Aid, and I couldn't help but notice his charm. Black soot covered his smiling face. "What a shame he's so old," I thought. "Twenty-eight is way out of my range." Tatzaforo brought over a bottle of banana brandy—I'll never forget it—and two of them had a drink. Ari held his glass with his bandaged hand. I sat with them for a while and then got up to help Mom and Yiayia clean. Aunt Vivi and Despina came, as well. Our house swelled with villagers that volunteered to help us put the kitchen back together.

With all of the excitement, my relatives' plans for an arranged marriage were put on hold. When he smiled, his eyes twinkled. In fact, his whole face lit up when he grinned with his beautiful lips and perfect teeth. Ari had soft, shiny, jet-black hair. Even with dirt and dust from the fire on his skin and ashes covering his clothes, he was beautiful. High cheekbones cut the lines of his face and gave him a Hollywood look. Ari was tall and slender, with strong hands. As we sat, I quickly learned Ari's charm went way beyond his looks. In addition to his heroic escapades that afternoon, he was funny, sweet, and endearing. I liked him from the moment I met him that fiery afternoon. When he left a few hours later, Ari asked if he could see me again before we returned to the States. I said sure. Then I laughed, realizing that Tatz and Kiki's matchmaking plans were off to a good start.

Chapter 10
"I Think He Means Business"

THE FOLLOWING AFTERNOON, ARI called to ask if we were all right from the fire. We spoke for nearly an hour. He was easy to talk to, and we shared another good laugh about my balcony-jumping escapades and his toothpaste-covered burns. Ari's calls continued nearly every day that week. Soon, our late afternoon phone dates were something I anticipated with pleasure. Despina hung close by in case I needed help translating a phrase—and of course to analyze each conversation as soon as I hung up the phone. Ari's openness allowed us to converse on a wide array of subjects, from what it was like being a high school teenager in the suburbs of Chicago to how he reached the decision to leave his parents' business and pursue corporate opportunities in Athens. Our friendship took off immediately, and since the clock was running out on my time in Greece, we were eager to share as much about ourselves with one another as quickly as possible, even if only by phone. Unfortunately, his job at Eurobank in Athens kept him too busy to come down to Sparta as he'd planned. Instead, he promised to see me off at the Athens airport the morning of my departure.

Since this was pre-9/11, Greece's capital city airport was like most others, offering a variety of airport cafés for people visiting with nonflying friends or relatives. In addition, Ari said he had some sort of security clearance from his job (I never understood the connection between the bank and the airport) that allowed him to bypass checkpoints and wait at our gate with us until we boarded. I was thrilled. Kiki was even more ecstatic when Yiayia spilled the beans, detailing the connection Ari and I had developed.

Although my impressions of Ari were positive from the start, I couldn't help feeling intimidated by his age. I wondered what this twenty-eight-year-old man wanted with me. I wanted to approach the subject but thought it best to wait until I saw him in Athens to ask. In the meantime, the more I grew to know him, the better I liked him. His sense of humor was a welcomed change after spending so much time with Stavros's serious demeanor. Ari reminded me more of my friend Demetri in his happy-go-lucky take on life.

"So what did you do last night?" Ari asked me this question every afternoon as if Vassara were a bustling metropolis of activity.

"Oh, you know the routine … hanging out in the *platia*, beers and french fries down at Moustokotou's, and a walk up to Koulouri to watch the moon rise," I answered.

"Walks up to Koulouri, huh? Just so long as you're behaving up there on that cliff. I know what goes on late at night!"

"You do, huh? Tell me!"

He laughed.

I didn't think Ari really knew, but I wasn't about to offer unnecessary details since Stavros and I were through. I smiled at Despina as I held the green receiver. "We're just hanging out, enjoying the summer."

"Good, 'cause I haven't had a chance to take you on a first date. I wish I didn't have to be here in Athens, but the bank is busier than ever now that it's tourist season," he explained.

"Those annoying tourists!" I responded. We laughed again. "Next summer," I demanded, "I want the first date of a lifetime!"

"You got it!" Ari exclaimed. "I'll take you to the ocean."

"Deal," I answered enthusiastically.

"Just promise you're coming back next year," he said.

"I promise," I replied. There was a pause, and then I heard a coworker say something to Ari in the background. He had to go.

"Okay, so next week, it's KLM flight 610 to Amsterdam, leaving at 7:00 am," he confirmed.

"Yep, see you there," I agreed.

"*Y'iasou koukla*" ('Bye, doll).

We had three days left in Greece and only one more day left for Vassara.

Where had the summer gone? That year, we were unable to stay for the festival because I had to get back early for junior varsity cheerleading practice. As disappointed as I was, I had no choice if I wanted to cheer my junior year of high school. This was difficult to explain to everyone, even Despina. When our relatives asked why we were missing the festival, I tried to explain my commitments back home, but failed. In the end, I just told everyone that I had to get back early for school. Mom and I scheduled ourselves to return to Chicago the night before cheerleading camp. That meant I had the plane ride home to get my head out of the clouds—literally—before diving headfirst back into my American life. The transition always felt awkward, but since this was our third trip, I was better at adapting quickly every year.

I purposely avoided Stavros and didn't say good-bye. My disenchanted feelings toward him festered in the back of my mind, and I felt there was little left to say.

Our last day in Vassara was depressing. Mom and I spent most of our time with Uncle Stathi, Aunt Vivi, and Despina at Aunt Maria's bedside. We didn't know if we'd ever see her again, and so our good-byes were filled with tears. She had aged so much in the last two summers. Pale and confined to her bed, she was nowhere near the energetic sister to Yiayia that we'd met two years earlier. Memories of her running out to greet us seemed like a lifetime ago.

Despina and I took our annual "say-good-bye-to-Koulouri-walk," sadly climbing up to the cliff one last time. I took a deep breath at the edge, trying to soak in as much of the mountain scenery and clean air smell as I could. My final look at the hills would have to last all winter. This was the moment I would remember all of the cold, wintry nights back home.

Despina came up behind me and put her hand on my shoulder. "You had a crazy summer this year," she said, smiling.

"Yeah."

"Think you're finally over him?" she asked.

"Stavros? Oh, yeah, it's done. I finally know where he stands."

"On to better things, right?" she asked.

"I hope so."

Despina paused and then gave me a big hug and said, "*Kalo ximona, xathefoula mou*" (Have a good winter, my beloved cousin).

"*Tou xronou*" (Until next year), I added.

We walked down Koulouri's rocks slowly back into town with our arms around one another. I saw her wipe a tear away from her cheek. Passing Brikakis' so that I could say good-bye to everyone, I tried not to tear up, as well. Even Mrs. Brikaki had gotten wind of what was being said of my early departure and wanted to know what "cheerleading" was.

I approached Grigori and Demetri, who were sitting at one of the café tables and playing backgammon. I put my hand on Demetri's back. "I'm going to miss you guys this winter!"

Without turning around, Demetri sarcastically answered, "I can't believe my *koliti* won't be at the festival." He had been giving me a hard time for days, accusing me of abandoning our crowd. I knew he was just pretending to be upset. We started laughing.

"I hear you're leaving early for 'cheerleading'? You'd better stay for the *panigiri* next time and forget about this thing, whatever that is!" Grigori added.

I laughed and thought about explaining the sport back home where girls dance around edges of football fields wearing short skirts and calling out cheers to the players, but some concepts don't translate well.

"I promise, Demetri. I'll stay the whole month of August next time."

"You'd better." He got up and gave me a big hug, towering over me. "*Kalo Ximona*" (Good winter), he said.

"Thanks. You, too. 'Bye, you guys." I held up my hand to the rest of the group. The boys got up from their chairs to wish me well. This started a chain reaction of heartfelt good-byes, even from Mrs. Brikaki. Tears rolled down her wrinkled cheeks as she placed her hands on my face. The scene was much warmer than last year's "shaking-of-the-hands" drama that unfolded with Stavros. The Boston girls made me promise to stay longer next year, as well, and I was happy to feel that my relationships with the kids in the village had solidified.

Mom and I returned to Magoula with Yiayia and Pappou. After washing massive amounts of laundry and figuring out what to leave behind, we spent the next few hours closing suitcases and getting ready for Athens. Spiro would take us to the airport in his cab. Yiayia and Pappou had plans to stay another two months in Greece and return home in October. How I envied them. Still, I knew the time had come to get real and become American again.

With an airport date with Ari on my radar, I took extra time fixing my hair and made sure to wear a nice outfit for the plane ride. Usually, I flew home in comfortable shorts and a T-shirt. That was not the case that year, or any year thereafter. Again, the trip to Athens would take at least six hours. Spiro picked us up around 10:00 pm. We drove through the night and made our usual stop at Corinth for something to eat at a twenty-four-hour roadside café. Our last taste of Greek food was to be relished, so we ordered our favorites even though we were half asleep. I slowly nibbled at my last cheese pie, feta and tomato salad, and grilled pork kabob seasoned with oregano and olive oil.

When we started out again from Corinth for the last leg of the ride, I refreshed my face in the backseat with lip gloss and powder. The idea of putting on makeup in the middle of the night during our long ride to the airport seemed ludicrous, but I saw no alternative. Spiro's cab pulled up to the airport around 5:00 am. Although the sun hadn't risen yet, an orange haze stretched across the sky with a translucent glow and seemed to mimic my emotions. My heart ached as we got closer to our departure. Although I was eager to return to air-conditioning, American food, and my friends back home, the painful reality loomed in the back of my mind that I never knew with complete certainty if we would return. As excited as I was to see Ari, I knew within a matter of hours, all of this magic would be memory.

Our plane was scheduled to leave at 7:30 am. We said good-bye to our neighbor and checked our bags at the KLM counter. I turned to say something to Mom and saw Ari, standing tall and lean, wearing a slightly unbuttoned, beige business shirt and tan dress pants. He twirled his keys in one hand and held a single red rose in the other. His smile lit up the terminal.

"*Kalimera*" (Good morning), he greeted us.

"Hi, Ari." Mom kissed him on both cheeks.

"I can't believe you're up this early," I said to him. He smiled and handed me the flower. "*Efharisto*" (Thank you). I kissed him on the cheek, just once.

"Looks like you have about an hour before boarding. Can I buy you girls a morning coffee?" Ari asked.

"Make sure it's strong," Mom complained. "I feel like I'm sleepwalking." Poor Mom had spent the entire ride to Athens talking to Spiro, probably in an effort to keep him awake.

We sat at an airport restaurant and drank the world's worst coffee. Mom and Ari talked most of the time, discussing his job and his family back in

Tsintzina. Then Mom, being ever so cool, made up an excuse about needing to get a magazine and left Ari and I alone. As soon as she walked away, he reached over and pulled my chair over to connect with his. He put his arm around me.

"Did you have a nice summer? Despite the fire, of course."

I sighed. "Yeah, it was good. Lots of changes. Lots of surprises. Something unexpected always waits in Greece."

"Something good, I hope." He looked into my eyes.

"Yeah," I replied. "Thanks for meeting me this morning. I'm glad to see you again before I leave."

"I am, too," he said, and with that, he leaned over and kissed me very gently on the lips, beaming his radiant smile into my eyes.

"I wish we had more time together," I whispered.

He leaned his forehead onto mine. "Next year."

"You know ..." I said as if I had just remembered to tell him something. I sat up with a smile and tried to lighten the mood. "You're an old man!"

"I know." He sat back, laughing and pointing to his legs. "I might have a walker next summer." I squeezed his hand. We laughed.

Mom came back, and the three of us headed to the gate. Ari put our carry-on baggage over his shoulder as we proceeded through the terminal. All too quickly, we were told to board, and we said our final farewell to Ari. I thanked him for my rose.

As he walked away, I called back, "Have a good day at work, old man."

He turned jovially and replied, "You do well in school this year, little girl."

"What's that all about?" Mom asked.

"Nothing." I laughed. "Isn't he cute?"

"He's gorgeous," Mom said. "And I think he means business."

Sparta's Valley

Magoula's 'bee' gate

Magoula house

First view of Vassara in Parnonas hills

Village of Vassara

Church: Virgin Mary the Liberator at outskirts of village

Gate outside church: Virgin Mary the Liberator

Vassara house

View from Vassara house balcony

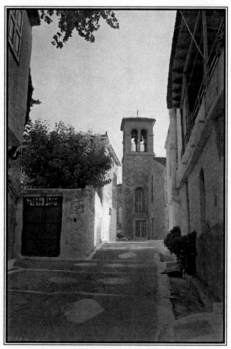

View of St. George's church from Vassara house balcony

The great green door

Village street

Village street

Vassara town square

Village tavern

Village soccer field

Church: Virgin Mary in the Rock

Townspeople worship at church: Virgin Mary in the Rock

Townspeople worship outside church: Transfiguration of our Lord

View of Vassara from the road to Koulouri

View from the edge of Koulouri

Road headed out of Vassara

Chapter 11
The Chicago Girls

ARI WAS GOOD ABOUT writing. We communicated regularly over the winter via letters and cards and even a few phone calls. He always asked if I was dating "some rich American guy." He liked to tease me endlessly that one day I would dump him for a successful Chicago business man and leave him brokenhearted in Greece. My correspondence with everyone else in Vassara continued, as well, and before long, spring arrived. As we planned our trip, I hoped to get to know this older and wiser guy from Tsintzina.

Mom and I got off the plane on a hot, July day in 1987 and found Ari waiting at passport check-in. He stood tanned and lean, smoking a cigarette to pass the time. My insides flipped over when his eyes met mine, and a wide grin quickly spread across his dashing face. After polite greetings with my mother, we passed through customs and headed to baggage claim. Our neighbor and taxi driver, Spiro, waited there, standing next to the conveyer belt. Ready to drive us down to Peloponnese, Spiro rubbed his forehead out of frustration when he saw that we didn't travel lightly. Our suitcases came off the revolving black belt, and he shook his head in disbelief.

"Already there are five large bags between the two of you! How many clothes can you wear in six weeks?" He yelled out, loud enough for everyone in the terminal to agree that we were typical American tourists. Obviously, Spiro didn't appreciate my busy social schedule with the likes of Ari. Nor was he aware that I shopped all winter long for a summer wardrobe that met every need. I was prepared for anything, including hot days at the beach and freezing, wind-blown nights up at Koulouri.

Truth be told, however, half of the items stuffed in our bulging bags were gifts Mom bought for our relatives. Mom always said she'd never forget the generosity shown to her family during World War II, when everyone in Greece was hungry and had so little. Yiayia's sister, her Aunt Pota, lived in Montana with a wealthy husband and regularly shipped boxes back to her sister during the 1940s. The large packages wrapped in twine that were sent from Montana to Magoula contained everything from coats and shoes to even sugar and toys. Receiving a box from Aunt Pota was like Christmas Day, Mom said, and she wanted to pay it forward with gratitude. Throughout the winter months, Mom and I kept our eyes peeled for sales at department stores and gathered presents for our village relatives. Nearly every time we shopped, I heard her shout over a clothing rack, "This shirt would be *perfect* for Tatzaforo!"

By the time we left Chicago, Mom and I had at least two suitcases packed with gifts. I thought about bringing something from America for Ari, especially since the Chicago Bulls were becoming national champions, and people like Michael Jordan were now international stars. But I didn't know if Ari liked basketball, and I thought the whole gift idea might have been too much, too soon. Ari, however, had a surprise for me. He asked Mom if it was okay to take me to his car for a moment to get something he "forgot." I didn't catch their conversation because I was busy having a momentary state of paranoia that my main suitcase, packed with carefully selected outfits for the trip, was lost. My bag finally arrived—the last suitcase taken off the plane. When the fuss ended, I was thrilled to have a moment alone with the man I had waited to see all winter.

We held hands through the terminal and passed through crowds until we reached the airport parking lot. He put his hand in the middle of my back, directing me through busy groups of people. Ari said he liked my longer hair that reached almost to my waist. We stopped at his red Fiat, where he leaned against the car and took my face in his hands.

"I'm so glad you're here," he said happily.

"Good to be back." I smiled.

Then he kissed me. A real kiss. Spectacular. I felt it in my toes. When we finally pulled apart, he rested his hands on my hips. "Welcome to Greece." He smiled.

"With a welcome like that, I'm never leaving!" I told him.

"I've got something for you," he said as he opened the backseat and took out not one, but two cellophane-wrapped bouquets of roses.

"The red ones are for you. The yellow ones are for your mother." He grinned.

"Wow," I said. "A dozen for my mother, too. You're *smooth*!"

Back inside the terminal, Ari handed Mom her bouquet. She shot a look at me, on to the idea that he was doing his best to lay groundwork for a summer of motherly approval. I grew nervous thinking once again about our age discrepancy and that perhaps he did "mean business" when it came to me, but I shook the insecurities out of my head for the time being. After attending junior prom only two weeks earlier, marital courting wasn't on my radar.

Twenty minutes with Ari in a crowded airport was not the romantic reunion I'd waited for, but that was all the time we had. Ari needed to return to work, and we were headed back down to Peloponnese to meet up with Yiayia in Magoula. Noticing my disappointment, Ari pulled me away from the cab to say good-bye.

"Like I said in my letter, I've got some business in Athens for the next two weeks, but after that, I'm off for a while and will be back in Tsintzina for summer break."

"Tsintzina? You mean Vassara?" I asked.

"No." He laughed. "I mean Tsintzina! I don't have a home in Vassara—at least not yet."

"Don't forget about the beach next week—Thursday," I reminded him.

"*Then xehnao*" (I won't forget), he said.

Ari kissed me on the forehead, and I got into the backseat of the taxi. Watching him walk across the airport parking lot through the back window of Spiro's cab, I wondered what went through his mind. Was he thinking I was as cute as last year? Did he think I was immature? As he moved further into the distance, I noticed his mature demeanor. Dressed in a stiff, white business shirt and black dress pants, his stride was that of an adult businessman, not any teenaged boy I knew from high school. What in the world was he doing with me? I just couldn't understand how Ari could take me seriously. We were at such different points in our lives. I was finishing high school, and he was in the midst of his career. Perhaps age didn't matter in Greece, but back in Chicago, my friends considered it headline news if a senior went out with a sophomore. With Ari more than a decade older than I, I loved the attention, but I just didn't get it.

We drove out of Athens toward Sparta while Mom and Spiro began their annual back and forth to catch up on the latest village news. I sat in the backseat with my Walkman in a sort of daze of jet lag and infatuation. Madonna's *True Blue* cassette drowned out the city noise, and eventually, I fell asleep for most of the ride down to the valley of Taygetos. Hours later, I woke just as we drove past the fork in the road leading to Vassara. "Nestled in there," I thought, "my village stirs in her sleep, moments away from waking up for a summer of fun." We continued toward Magoula, and when Spiro's cab pulled down Yiayia and Pappou's dirt road, we saw my grandmother waiting just outside the large, green, bee-infested gate.

Later that afternoon, after putting away my suitcases and inhaling my first *tiropita* that Yiayia bought especially for me from the *fourno* (bakery) up the street, I pulled up a white plastic chair on the balcony and sat in one of my favorite places to soak in the mountain air. Mom and Yiayia sat below in the courtyard drinking coffee, their voices muffled by the dark green grapevines that grew over the terrace railings. Up above, cool air blew across the peaceful oasis where I relaxed, taken in by the incredible view of Mount Taygetos wrapped in a pink watercolor-painted sky. Sunset approached, and ribbons of gold, pink, and purple colored a perfect backdrop to Sparta's distinctive landscape. Looking across at the group of mountains that contained the villages of Vassara, Vresthena, and Tsintzina, I pondered away dreamy thoughts of the summer of 1987.

No longer was I the naïve, fourteen-year-old, fooled by the likes of Stavros Antonopoulos. Still, I knew I wasn't a woman, either, and I certainly wasn't ready for Aunt Kiki to march me down the aisle to marry her best friend's son, no matter how charming he was. Stuck in between girlhood and womanhood, I understood that I had the advantage of maturity on my side, as well as the ability to remain a carefree girl, discovering herself in this ever-surprising world. Whatever came my way, I wanted to enjoy my summer of seventeen. I took a deep breath and let out an audible exhale as I looked across at my Taygetos Mountain that stood strong and steady. Like the mountain before me, I, too, wanted to stand solid.

Twenty-four hours later, after shopping for groceries in Sparta's markets, exchanging dollars into drachmas, and sleeping off the last remains of jet lag, we rode into Vassara, packed into the Audi like the four musketeers. We pulled up to our house, and I heard Madonna's "Open Your Heart to Me" blaring from the house kitty-corner to ours. The place had been vacant for years, ever since we first traveled to Vassara, and I had no idea who could be living there now.

"*Perimeni i xathelfoula sou*" (Your cousin is waiting for you)! Yiayia smiled and pointed at the music-pumping house.

"Despina?"

"No, Rania!"

"Rania who?" I asked.

"*Rania—tis Despina's ei kori*" (Rania—Despina's daughter), Yiayia answered.

"You mean Poulos, Ma?" Mom asked.

"*Nai, paithi mou*" (Yes, my child).

"Oh, yeah," Mom said, remembering. "They're from Chicago—from Berwyn. You met her at a wedding a few years ago." Mom spoke as though I was supposed to know this person, when in fact, I had no idea who Mom was talking about. Still, I was glad to learn of a potential friend for the summer, especially since Despina was delayed in Athens an additional week.

I don't recall the exact moment I met Rania, but I remember every moment since then of our sisterlike bond. Rania and I are actually third cousins, as our *yiayias* were first cousins and our great-grandmothers were sisters. What I know for sure is that we were immediate friends. We felt and thought the same way about nearly everything and almost instantaneously became inseparable. I felt as if I had met another version of myself.

Along with our past histories, Rania and I shared all that we brought to Greece and quickly made a name for ourselves around Vassara by wearing identical halter tops in different colors from the Limited Express in Chicago. Rania brought an array of them with her, including a white one, an electric green one, a fuchsia pink one (my favorite), and a yellow one. We wore them constantly, exchanging colors after washes so that we could be dressed alike. We were the coolest, or at least we thought so. We shared clothes, tapes, jewelry, and, most of all, laughs. Like me, Rania didn't go anywhere without her hairspray and makeup, and I'm sure if her house was on fire, she would have also grabbed her cosmetics and costume jewelry, too, along with her passport.

Although Rania was only a freshman, I was surprised by her maturity. She claimed to be more adultlike because she grew up in the city, quick to point out that I came from the sheltered suburbs. Any difference between us evaporated while we were in Greece. I never felt an inability to relate to Rania. In a word, she was my rock star. Rania was cool. Rania was self-assured. Rania was funny. Rania called a spade a spade, just as I did. Physically, however, we were total opposites. She was tall for her age, quite slender, and had very un-Greek-like, light brown hair and a light complexion. We also shared the same summer goal: to obtain a perfect Ban de Solei tan we could show off back home.

While Despina finished up her college preparatory testing in Athens, Rania and I immediately began a daily sun bathing routine while the rest of the village took siesta. Blasting Madonna and Richard Marx tunes from her giant stereo, we lay atop her balcony every day and tanned ourselves into oblivion. She had the Hawaiian Tropic; I had the beach towels. One or both of our mothers provided the cold, fresh fruit and lemonade. We were set. Those were golden, sun-filled afternoons. My days in Vassara would never be the same again, as we quickly became known as "the Chicago Girls."

During our relaxed afternoons, I filled her in on all that had happened since my first arrival in Vassara in 1984. Rania had only been in the village one week before my arrival that year but had already made an impression on the kids and drew her own conclusions regarding personalities. She thought I was out of my mind for liking Stavros Antonopoulos. She hated him.

"He's so bossy. He's so arrogant, so stuck up! You must have been delusional!" Rania always called me "delusional" if she disagreed with something I thought or did. There was never a time when I had to wonder what Rania thought. There it was, like it or not.

As far as Ari was concerned, Rania had yet to meet him in 1987 since he wasn't from Vassara, but she thought the idea of dating a guy in his early thirties was ridiculous. When Despina returned from Athens, we incorporated my Greek cousin into our antics and became a triad of teenaged girl power. Rania and Despina got along perfectly. Both of them smoked like chimneys. I was the dork that didn't. Together, we shared an honest component to our friendships that made the three-way relationship easy and effortless.

Still, some things are just plain "American" like sunbathing and cheerleading. Once in a great while, Despina opted out of our chosen activities during long, hot afternoons and retreated to the shade to sketch. We forgave her. Although no one could replace my ever-loyal cousin Despina, I was elated to finally have an American to pal around with, as well. There was no holding back our friendship that took off like a rocket. At night, the three of us reunited, drinking and dancing, walking to Koulouri, and sitting together at Moustokotou's. At the end of every evening, we returned to our nearby homes together, late into the night, arm in arm in arm.

Rania's witty personality won everyone in our crowd over, and together we were the life of the party, constantly cracking jokes and making each other laugh, most of the time at ourselves. Demetri loved Rania, too, and he made himself part of our exclusive club immediately. We were never afraid to act goofy and dismissed what everyone else thought. Romantically, Rania had her eyes on Vasili, Stavros's younger brother, and eventually he joined in our frolics, as well. I thought their attraction was hysterically ironic, especially since Rania hated Stavros. But Vasili was a lot more easygoing than his older brother, and he instead mimicked the personality of his eldest brother, Lefteri.

One afternoon, while Despina left Vassara to visit an aunt on the island of Crete, Rania and I sat drinking Coke Lights on a park bench in the *platia*. Panteli, who absolutely loved hanging out with "the Chicago Girls," mentioned going into Sparta to check out a new disco club for the evening. The idea sounded great but far from anything that would actually happen, as Rania and I were used to being underage for these types of activities in the States. Panteli said he'd drive, and the two of us could ride shotgun in his powder blue pickup. Lefteri and Thanasi were driving their cars, and together with some of the kids from Boston, the whole crowd could go to this hotspot called Mango. Rania and I were shocked when our mothers approved the idea. The thought of going clubbing with our friends was far more than we anticipated. Since Greece didn't have a drinking age, we were good to go for a night that would otherwise be completely illegal back home.

"Do they know I'm only fifteen?" Rania said to me. "I love this country!"

We agreed on a time for everyone to meet in the *platia* and depart in our caravan of vehicles. Rania and I headed up to our houses to change. A night out at the bars and discos of Sparta … this was too good to be true. We changed into our best party outfits—miniskirts with off-the-shoulder tops, big, colored hoop earrings, and sling-back flats. I grabbed money, along with my favorite cassettes of Madonna and The Police. Rania and I hoped to convince Panteli to play our American tunes during the ride into town.

After listening to our mothers' speeches regarding safety, we were off to meet our driver and the others in the town center. When we reached the *platia*, we couldn't help but laugh as everyone in our crowd appeared glitzed up for the night. Even the guys wore shirts we hadn't seen before. An array of never-before-used cologne hung in the hot, summer night air. Demetri sported a red T-shirt that said, "If life is a bowl of cherries, then why am I always in the pits?" Our gathering reminded me of prom night, when friends you see every day look a thousand times better and you wonder why they don't enhance their appearance all the time. Unlike so many other group outings, Stavros didn't take charge of this trip. Instead, Lefteri was the leader, telling all of the drivers where to park and where we would meet in downtown Sparta. The ride wasn't long, but since the sun had already set, I was a little apprehensive about the roads. Panteli could tell.

"*Ti fovase*" (What are you afraid of)? he patronizingly asked.

"Nothing," I said. "It's just that I'm not used to traveling these mountain roads at night."

"Oh, shut up. We'll be fine. Panteli is a good driver. Right, Panteli?" Rania barked back. "Besides," she added. "I know stick."

"Okay, the idea of *you* driving back really scares me, so Panteli, stay sober."

"*Pantote*" (Always).

We laughed, knowing this was a complete lie.

A half hour later, we reached Sparta. Coming out of the black hills of Parnonas, the city's bright lights made the glow of Sparta's nightlife eminent. Panteli parked along the side streets of Sparta's *platia*, which was as large as a football field, and we made our way across to a little nightclub with a pink neon palm tree sign that read Mango. The bar was outside like all of the clubs in Greece's hot climate. We passed through an indoor archway that led to a courtyard with long tables, a dance floor, and a crowded bar. Like Koulouri, I found it hard to pick out our friends from the village in the darkness, which was lit only by the club's neon lights and the stars above. Soon we found the table with Lefteri at the head, and we were all together. Seated at one end were the Boston girls that arrived with Thanasi, who had finally made his romance with Effie public. She was from Watertown, Massachusetts, and he was from Vassara. He was much older—probably as old as Ari. They were quiet about their relationship but always together.

Rania, Panteli, and I headed to a few empty seats in the middle of the table, comfortably far enough away from Stavros, who seemed lost in his own world that night. He wasn't talking much to anyone and didn't get up to dance. Lefteri, however, had a renewed enthusiasm. I had never seen him so alive with personality. Demetri and Grigori arrived with Loukas and Anastasia. Within seconds, Demetri was giving us a hard time about dressing alike, and he managed to fit his chair in between Rania and I, honing in on anything we tried to say to each other.

Since almost everyone in Greece learned English as a second language, Rania came up with the idea of using Pig Latin as a sort of code to comment on everything from "Hey, I just caught Stavros looking at your legs," to "Are you keeping track of how much Panteli is drinking?" Unfortunately, through our drinks and the loud music, Pig Latin became an undecipherable secret language. At one point in the night, Rania and I tried to teach Pig Latin to Demetri, but we failed miserably. We had a lot of laughs in the process, listening to his broken English get even more butchered by twisting the syllables around to appease us.

"You girls are crazy!" Demetri held up his drink. "Another round for you both."

"I think she's had enough," Stavros said from the table, looking at me.

"Oh, shut up, Stavros. She's not driving," Rania snapped.

"Asta ta koritsia" (Leave the girls alone), Lefteri said to his brother, carefree from his brandy.

"No, really, I'm fine," I answered and showed my half-full glass to Demetri. "I still haven't finished this one yet." I knew Stavros was right and that he was just looking out for me, but that didn't stop Rania from hating him on my behalf.

"Well, *I'm* ready for another," Rania announced.

"Ela, Chicago Girl. Let's go to the bar!" Panteli and Rania went inside to order more drinks.

Demetri leaned over and said quietly to me, "When you're ready for another, let me know."

I looked up at Demetri, who looked surprisingly handsome that night. "Thanks, I'm okay for now," I replied with a smile.

Although the thought had surely crossed both of our minds at one point or another, Demetri and I kept our relationship purely platonic. He was the most real guy I'd ever met in Greece. What I loved most about him was his fantastic sense of humor, always making those around him laugh. He was never afraid to be silly or to make someone smile. He wasn't consumed with the idea of impressing others. Demetri never lied to say he was from another town. His purpose was simply to have fun, and I adored him for that.

Standing over six feet tall, Demetri was handsome, as well, with sandy brown hair and green eyes. He was a fantastic athlete just like Stavros and most of the other boys from the village. Built like a professional basketball player, Demetri always joked with me about my petite size. He welcomed me into any crowd with his friendliness, whether we were watching soccer practice or simply sitting outside Brikakis' café. Demetri always made me feel I belonged. As a result, our friendship enabled me to have a life in Vassara beyond Stavros and establish my own presence among the kids. Demetri was a loyal *kolite*. In all my time visiting Greece, I only saw him sad once, and I never saw him angry.

As the drinks poured and dancing continued, Rania and I partied with Demetri, Panteli, and Lefteri, laughing until our sides hurt and our eyes watered. Lefteri was a much more relaxed when he wasn't in the village. Although always outgoing, his personality exploded the minute he escaped Vassara's borders. I suppose that was true for most of the Greek kids in our crowd, as they felt free from watchful eyes and the rumor mill.

When we left the Mango, Rania and I piled into Panteli's pickup. We three remaining partiers brought up the rear of village caravan but carelessly lost the group after stopping for gas. Oblivious to Panteli's level of sobriety, Rania and I bought some pop and chips at the gas station and climbed into his pickup without a single concern that, eventually, we would safely return to the village. When we realized we were alone on the mountain roads, the precariousness of our situation dawned on me, and I regretted not being part of our usual single, long line of vehicles as we traveled back to Vassara. Normally, our cars stayed together. Panteli assured me that even in his "not-so-perfect" condition, his truck knew the way home all by itself.

"Like a donkey," he slurred.

"We'd better keep him awake," Rania whispered to me.

"How drunk is he?" I asked.

"Oh, he wouldn't drive if he was *that* bad, but I think I'd better help him navigate. I'll sit in the middle," Rania instructed, and I agreed. I listened to her as if her Chicago street smarts outweighed my maturity.

"Okay, just don't let us die. I still have to go on that date with Ari tomorrow," I reminded her.

"You mean *today*. It's 3:00 am. Prince Charming is picking you up in four hours," Rania pointed out.

"I'm going to be a zombie."

"Maybe you should stay awake," suggested Panteli.

"Please just get us home in one piece." Then I saw a familiar break. "Look, that's the turn off, right?" I asked.

Turning off by the famous fork with its Vassara, Verroia, Tsintzina sign, I flashed back to the usual ride to Vassara in the back of Pappou's Audi. His driving didn't seem so bad now compared to Panteli's swerving.

"Cut it out, Panteli!" Rania nudged our driver to make him wake up and pay more attention to the road.

"He's falling asleep. Turn the radio on loud to keep him awake," I suggested.

The truck continued on, entering the now scary landscape with mountain drops many feet high, and of course, no railings.

"*Then thoulevi*" (It's broken), Panteli said, pointing to the radio.

"I'll do the shifting, then, Panteli, 'cause *you're* going to get us killed!" Rania snapped.

Rania took over the stick shift while Panteli did the clutch and pressed the gas and brake. I started humming a Randy Travis tune to take my mind off my fear.

"Good idea," Rania instructed me. "You sing!"

"What?"

"You sing!" Rania said. "Hey, if it keeps him awake, who cares what you sound like? And it's not like he'll remember what your voice sounds like tomorrow with the hangover he's going to have."

So I started. First it was "I Told You So" and then "I'm Gonna Love You Forever." In fact, I think I went through all of the songs on that album. I had to sing songs Rania wasn't familiar with, and that meant anything Country.

My cousin knew little outside pop radio's top forty. After what seemed like forever, we saw the small, white lights of Vassara flickering in the darkness ahead.

"You know, you're not that bad," Rania finally confessed. "You've got a decent voice!"

"Shut up. You're drunk," I told her as I crossed myself, thankful to be alive.

By the grace of God, we made it back to the village in one piece. Panteli stopped the pickup with a screech in the *platia* and waved to us as he stumbled down an incline to his family's home around the corner. Lefteri and Stavros were waiting on benches in the *platia* to make sure we got back to the village safely. I was so glad to be back. Lefteri assured me that Panteli was more sober than I had thought, and that if he wasn't, he never would have let us go home with him.

The brothers walked with us halfway up from the town square until we reached the turnoff for their house. Our walk with them was silent and awkward. Stavros still avoided conversation with me. Rania and I turned right, and arm in arm, back to our houses, humming Randy Travis. She'll never admit it, but I think she grew to like a few country tunes that night.

"You're really going to the beach with this old guy Ari guy tomorrow?" she asked.

"Yeah. That's what he said. He's supposed to pick me up bright and early."

"Don't be disappointed if he doesn't show. You barely know the guy."

I hadn't thought of that. "I'm too tired to think right now. I'm going to bed. If he doesn't come, I'll be by when I wake up for lunch."

"If he does come, be careful, and have a blast. I'm totally jealous, and I hate you. Don't forget to take pictures. I want to see what this Greek god looks like!"

We said good night, and I quietly entered the upstairs, hoping not to wake up Mom. She was out like a light. I tiptoed to my room, half believing that Rania might be right and that we'd be eating lunch together tomorrow, as Ari would not come as promised.

Still, even in my tipsy condition, optimism won out, and I decided to pack a beach bag in case Price Charming did arrive. I made sure to gather everything, even a change of clothes for later in the day if he asked me to dinner or to go somewhere special. I waited for this date with him for an entire year, and I wasn't about to let a little alcohol keep me from being as ready as Malibu Barbie. I even went into the bathroom and showered, making sure to shave my legs. At one point, I toyed with the idea of staying up the few more hours until he came, but I was too tired to make it. I had everything laid out on my dresser for the next day before my head hit the pillow and my eyes closed.

Chapter 12
A Day with Ari

"*XIPNA*" (WAKE UP)!

The shout came from the street outside. I recognized Ari's voice as soon as he called out, and I jumped from my bed. Daylight arrived so quickly. My head still pounded the beat of the Mango's disco music the night before, and a ringing vibrated in my left ear. The inside of my mouth tasted like a wad of cotton balls, and I would need much more than a cup of Greek coffee to return to a state of normalcy.

"Are you serious?" I called back to him through the open window, referring to the time, which hadn't quite reached 6:00 am. Swinging open the balcony door, I walked outside onto the terrace in my nightshirt. His eyes grew wide with a surprised smile, his guilty smirk stretching across his lips, revealing mischievous thoughts underneath his otherwise innocent grin.

"*Ela. Perimeno*" (Come. I'm waiting), Ari called back as he stood in the street beneath my balcony, both hands on his hips. His white cotton shirt was unbuttoned just enough to show hints of a tanned chest, and it was tucked into a pair of white chino pants. Standing there in the street with sleeves rolled up, Ari looked like a sexy ice cream man.

"Why are you surprised to see me? I told you *early*," he said. "Let's go! Grab your swimsuit."

"Where are you taking me?" I leaned over on the balcony railing.

"Everywhere!" He stretched his arms wide as if he intended to show me the entire country in one afternoon. "But first, Gythion."

I headed back inside the house, shouting back, "I'll be ready in ten minutes."

"*Grigora*" (Quickly)! he called out after me.

Like a tornado, I blasted through the upstairs, laughing to myself that this was really happening. "I just got home with Rania three hours ago!" I said out loud to no one as I searched for eyeliner and mascara. I threw my jean shorts and pink tank top on over my one-piece, black and gold bathing suit and was nearly ready to go. A quick application of makeup followed by a desperate round of hairspray made me presentable, despite only a few hours of sleep, a raging headache, and queasy stomach. That was the beauty of being seventeen—when a beauty makeover could be pulled off in no time. Youth was on my side that frantic morning, although I vowed never to drink whiskey shots with Rania again.

Gythion was the nearest beach town to Sparta and about a thirty-minute ride from the city. However, since we were leaving from Vassara, the trip would take us an additional half hour. I guessed that was the reason Ari was in such a hurry, determined to reach the ocean before the sun reached full heat. Rushing back inside, I tried to get dressed while my mind raced. "He came! He actually came! Thank God I packed my bag last night," I thought as I scampered around the upstairs, gathering my things and dying for caffeine and Nuprin. He said he would pick me up *first thing* in the morning for our day at the beach, but I didn't realize how early. Pounding pain on the left side of my head reminded me of my night on the town with the gang as morning light streamed into the upstairs through the white lace curtains Yiayia brought from America. Surely all of my village friends were still sound asleep.

Knowing I needed more time, I stumbled back outside to ask Ari if he could wait for me at Kiki's while I got ready. She would offer him something to eat or drink, and that would buy me at least another fifteen or twenty minutes. I assumed Mom and Yiayia were already at Kiki's drinking their morning coffee since the house was empty.

There was no time to worry about what might be said between Ari and my relatives at Tatzaforo's house. I was sure Mom could keep the conversation light and steer away Kiki's comments regarding courting and marriage. Still somewhat in disbelief that Mom was allowing me to go on this all-day excursion, it seemed enough that Tatz and Kiki were tight with Ari's family. As his parents were my aunt and uncle's childhood friends, they trusted Ari implicitly. Mom had no reason not to give me a green light for my excursion with the dark, handsome hero. Like she pointed out a day earlier, if Ari's parents knew Tatz that well, Ari had to be a perfect gentleman, or risk death from the old retired forest ranger.

When I came out of the upstairs, ready at last, Ari had returned from Kiki's, and he stood leaning against his new, white Alfa Romeo with the driver's side door open. Greek top-forty hits blasted into the quiet street from inside his car. Talk about waking up the neighborhood! I laughed out loud as I came down the stairs. There was nothing discreet about Ari, who clearly didn't choose to live under the radar. Villagers passing by the car stared, knowing immediately that the man in white was not from Vassara. That's when I realized that word would quickly spread throughout our gossipy town that I departed with a stranger for the day. I could just imagine the "*Who was he?*" and "*Where was he taking her?*" Rania would be bombarded with questions.

When I came out of the house, Ari set my beach bag in the backseat of his car, while Kiki, Tatz, Yiayia, and Pappou came out of my aunt and uncle's courtyard to see us off. We got into his car and drove off like a newlywed couple, waving, beeping the car's horn, and smiling to the family through the windshield as they told us to "have a fabulous time," and "enjoy our day together." I knew my mother was the only person out of that group that saw us as merely a guy and a girl going to the beach for the day. The rest of them believed an old-world courting tradition had begun.

Ari's Alfa Romeo bounced along the narrow, cobblestone streets made for donkeys. He turned right to pass through the *platia* and head out of Vassara. Just as we reached the center of the town square, he paused to downshift and leaned over the stick shift to kiss me softly on the lips. His timing couldn't have been better. When he put his hand to my cheek and whispered "*Kalimera*" (Good Morning) into my ear, I noticed Grigori, Demetri's brother, who always loved a good new story, walking across the *platia*. He caught every detail, so I was certain he saw the kiss and recognized me as *the girl* in *the car* with *the guy*. Word would travel fast. While the last thing I wanted to do was start a scandal, I couldn't help but enjoy the thought that some of this might get back to Stavros.

Ari's car proceeded out of the village and onto the mountain roads. I leaned my head against the headrest, feeling the Nuprin start to kick in and clear my head. I closed my eyes and smiled, happy in anticipation of the journey that awaited me on this glorious morning. I was so excited to spend an entire day with this new and wonderful man from Tsintzina.

"Everything okay?" Ari asked me when I shut my eyes.

"Everything is *perfect*," I answered with closed eyes, a big smile, and a relaxed tone.

He took my hand and kissed it and then rested it back on my leg. Ari asked if I wanted to pop some music in, and I chose my favorite male artist, Parios, from a stack of cassette tapes in his center console. The classic, deep, romantic voice of Greece's equivalent to Frank Sinatra awakened my senses with songs like "Kokino Garifalo" (Red Carnation) and "Pote then se Xehno" (I Will Never Forget You).

"Good choice," Ari replied as he reached the main road and pressed the accelerator.

I opened my eyes to watch the morning's pastel haze hover above the mountaintops as we drove out on the winding roads. What had been a fearful ride into Vassara the night before behind Panteli's not-so-sober wheel was now peaceful and calm as we exited the village. The serene scenery echoed my emotions as I felt my fate evolving in my hands for the first time. Like a glow of morning sunshine, I welcomed the opportunity to be in control of my day, my destiny. Our ride out of Vassara was an awakening as I looked out onto the hills kissed with bright daylight. This was my time. Unexpected and wonderful opportunities were out there waiting for me. A new sense of happiness and independence pulsed through my body. This would be another golden day.

The beginning of our road trip was filled with equally beautiful song and scenery while we headed through the hills and approached the main road taking us to Sparta and then onto Gythion. Ari said little, but I could tell he was appreciating the moment, looking out at the picturesque countryside through the windshield. He must have missed the wide-open landscape while living in Athens's congested urban chaos. Ari broke the silence with cheerfulness.

"So, are you up for an adventurous day?" He tapped my thigh.

"I think so. I just have to wake up a little bit more first. You've had your coffee. I need to catch up."

"Someone was out late last night, huh?" He laughed.

"Does it show?" I asked, embarrassed.

"A little. I've got a quick errand to run first in Sparta. It won't take long."

We stopped just after getting onto the main road, past the gas station at a white building with its front door open. Ari said he had to check on a bread order for his father's restaurant. The building didn't look anything like a bakery from the street; its old, rundown exterior appeared more like a forgotten warehouse. But the smell of fresh bread wafting through the air was unmistakable. Fresh loaves and pastries taken out of the ovens carried a sweet smell that made me hungry. "How different from the States," I thought, "where bakeries proudly display their creations in large windows." At this place, the production of baked goods was like a secret, only to be given away by undeniable aromas.

As Ari got out of the car and crossed the street out of sight, I sat for a minute, looking around the car to get a better sense of my mystery man. I became curious and decided to inspect the interior of his car for some insight into his personality. I found cigarettes, of course, as every European man smokes. I also found matches and some spare change in drachmas. Nothing strange. Then my hand felt a silky item stuck in between my seat and the center partition. I looked down and saw a crunched-up ball of black, shiny fabric. When I pulled it up, my jaw dropped open. This tiny, dark piece of material was a men's bottom garment—very slinky, very small. "Seriously?" I thought to myself. "Is this his bathing suit? Maybe it's underwear. Why would he keep loose underwear in his car?"

I looked up. Ari reappeared in the bakery doorway and was still conversing with an old man wearing a white apron stretched across his rotund belly. While their conversation continued, I inspected the piece more, only to discover a small label that read Speedo. Thus my fear was confirmed. This was indeed a bathing suit, or lack thereof. My stomach dropped. Would he be *wearing* this today? My heart beat fast as I suddenly felt I was in way over my head. I had no clue about boys, let alone men. Ari was over ten years older than I and obviously one mature man by the looks of this bathing suit. Who was I kidding?

Not knowing what else to do, I quickly shoved the Speedo back in the crevice between the seats and decided to stop spying in the Alfa Romeo.

I leaned my head back on the seat and closed my eyes, feeling the warm morning sunlight beam through the window and hit my face. Taking a deep breath in an effort to relax, I focused my mind on the gorgeous ocean we would see. Minutes later, I felt a cold sensation touching my leg.

"*Proino*" (Breakfast)! Ari said, holding two ice cream sandwiches. Not exactly an Egg McMuffin, but I accepted.

We continued down the main road, which took us through Sparta and onto a highway that runs about sixty kilometers to Gythion. The straight, open highway made for a peaceful trip with mountains on one side and flat, open greenery on the other. At that time, there wasn't a lot of commerce between Sparta and Gythion, and the topography was calming.

While we drove down the smooth road, appreciating the beautiful scenery, Ari and I began to talk more openly, sharing little pieces of information about ourselves, getting to know one another. Ari had nothing to hide. As Ari explained, he came from the poor mountain village of Tsintzina. His father owned the village taverna, and as soon as Ari was able, he left the village and moved to Athens after his two-year obligation to the army was over. He got a position with Eurobank. That's it. No excuses, no cover stories. He was as nice as he was gorgeous. Together with Tatzaforo's stamp of approval on him, I decided I had nothing to worry about.

As our conversation continued, Ari's sensitive side came out. He was nothing like Stavros. His down-to-earth personality reminded me more of Demetri, as we were at ease talking about every subject under the sun. When he asked me if I ever dated anyone from Greece, I felt no shame in explaining that I had fallen for someone who let me down. I didn't use Stavros's name. It didn't matter. He gave me his warning about Greek men, looking for the typical *Americanaki*—clueless American—to take advantage of. When I returned the question, all Ari said was that he was single and that out of all the girls in Athens thus far, he hadn't met "the one." The more we shared, the more comfortable I became. We enjoyed a beautiful, long morning ride to the ocean.

Ari pulled into the city of Gythion and headed down a main strip of cafés along the water. We parked across from the ocean, only a few steps away from one of the nicer cafés with white fabric tablecloths that differentiated the restaurant from others with bare metal, dented tables. Ari sat us at a corner table next to the water. He pulled out my chair and asked me how I took my coffee. As he went inside to order, my eyes followed him. He approached the owner and stood next to a lit-up pastry case under a pink awning. When the owner placed our order, Ari smiled at me as he returned to our table.

Sitting in the glorious summer sun, I tilted my head back to absorb the rays that hadn't yet reached their unbearable heat. Ari grabbed for his cigarettes again, even before the coffee came to the table. After lighting up, he looked at me as if to say, "Well, now what?" and suddenly seemed like he was about to demand a lot of answers to a lot of questions. I froze, not knowing what to say. He just kept looking at me and smiling, blowing smoke from his cigarette up into the air. Here we were, alone at a gorgeous Mediterranean beach with no chaperones and no time limitations. We could do anything and everything we wanted, but we just sat in silence, slowly drinking our coffees at the beachside café. No questions were asked. Ari sat peacefully and continued to soak everything in, including me. I followed his lead. Looking out over the water, quiet and tranquil, we gazed into each other's eyes, smiling. He was certainly a man comfortable in his own skin, not feeling the need to say something clever all the time. Ari just wanted to "be." I liked that quality in him very much.

After finishing our coffees, Ari suggested we get to the beach before the day's heat got more intense. Walking back to the car, he held my hand and then put his arm around my shoulder. Ari unlocked the car, and I opened the back door on my side to grab my bag. Imagine my surprise when I shut the back door and looked up only to find Ari taking his pants off in between his driver's side door and the door to the backseat! He was half naked, changing into that nothing piece of black fabric Speedo I found in the front seat. There he was, birthday suit and all, in the middle of the café parking lot in broad daylight, putting on the skimpiest bathing suit I had ever seen. I looked away quickly, trying not to appear embarrassed, and pretended to soak in the sea air. He shut the driver's door and emerged from between the two cars like a statue of the gods—tall, dark, tanned, chiseled muscles all over an unclothed body.

Walking down to the beach, I noticed Speedos were *the* thing to swim in among European men. Men of all shapes and sizes wore them. Some, with fat bellies hanging over vanishing waistlines, paraded across the sand like Hercules and Poseidon. I found it hysterical that every body type wore this style of swimwear, even older men with wrinkled skin and gray hair.

Hands down, my date was the most handsome of all Speedo-wearing men on shore.

We got down to the beach and picked out our spot on the warm, soft sand. I immediately set up camp. After all, sunbathing was my forte, and I proceeded to lay out my towel, taking out necessary items like Hawaiian Tropic, magazines, cassette player, lip balm, sunglasses, and gum. Ari watched my detailed setup, laughing at my routinelike procedure.

"You Americans!" he said as he shook his head with his hands on his hips. I ignored his teasing as I had learned to do with my cousin Petro.

"Where's your towel?" I asked, noticing that he had nothing with him except his cigarettes. "Did you forget one?" I asked. I didn't wait for an answer. "That's okay. We can share mine. It's big."

"Don't need one," he answered.

I shot him a shocked look. "Okay, be serious. How are you going to dry off after swimming?"

"The sun dries you off," he combated instantly, looking up and closing his eyes to the sun.

"Well, what are you going to *lie* on?" I continued. Clearly Ari and I shared nothing in common when it came to sunbathing.

"I like to lie on the sand. It feels good," he retorted with confidence.

"Okay, you're definitely weird!" I concluded.

Ari chuckled as he plopped down on the sand next to my towel and pulled out another cigarette. His toned muscles quickly became covered with a layer of sand. I decided to stop counting cigarettes, classifying him as a chain-smoker. He turned and lay on his stomach while he smoked another cigarette and watched me put on oil.

"Why don't you let me help you with that?" he asked with a smirk.

Not long after, the beating sun was stronger than either of us could bear, and we decided to go into the water and cool off. I wondered when I'd get the nerve to tell him I couldn't swim. Before I could say a word, Ari embarrassingly admitted to me that he couldn't go in too deep because he never learned to swim. We laughed when I admitted the same and went into the ocean about waist deep. The cool water seemed to evaporate the heat right off our skin. I tried to get all of the sticky sand off of Ari's arms and chest. We kissed and kissed and kissed. The sun was hot, the water was cool, and Ari was like a dream. We splashed, we embraced, and we dunked each other

131

like kids. Every so often, he'd just stop and look at me with his deep, dark eyes and smile. We stayed in the water for a long time. But when a crowd of swimmers arrived, we decided to dry off on the sand.

I sat down on my towel, running my fingers through my long hair and trying to style the mess back into place. Ari collapsed on the sand and closed his eyes. I watched him lie there, calm, relaxed, and happy. Ari wasn't afraid to show his feelings, and I liked that. Ari didn't care what others thought, and I liked that even more. "This is a man I could really fall for," I thought. Then suddenly, Stavros came to mind. The smile vanished from my face, and I unexpectedly became angry, recalling how insecure Stavros made me feel. How could I have been so stupid? Watching the ocean crash against the shore as memories—so many memories of the past three years—flashed back, I thought about the many mistakes I made behaving like a typical, gullible *Americanaki*. "No wonder Stavros took advantage of me," I thought. "I played right into his hands." Turning my thoughts to Ari, I looked at him, not realizing that his eyes were now open, and he was watching me.

"You look like you've got a lot on your mind." He paused and then asked, "Who is he?"

"Why are you asking me that?" I asked.

"Who broke your heart? A Greek? Or was he someone from home?" he persisted. I cursed myself for having no poker face. "It's not important," I answered, hoping he would let it go.

"Tell me," Ari said.

"It doesn't matter." I paused. "I'm just mad at myself for hanging on for so long. Having fun here today with you has made me realize that maybe I've forgotten what it was like to be treated well." I smiled at him and wiped my eye that had teared up. Ari sat up and stroked my wet hair that fell on my shoulder.

"You deserve only the best from *any* man. You know that, right?" Ari came closer. "Can I tell you something?" he asked.

"What?" I asked, forcing a smile.

He took a second, looked down, and then looked up at me again and said, "You have to protect your heart at all times." He pointed to my heart. "I'm serious," he said. "Maybe I'm not saying it right, but what I mean is that I don't ever want to you to fully give yourself to any man, not ever," he warned.

Now I was even more confused. What was he talking about? I shook my head, not understanding what he was saying.

"What I'm telling you is important. I'm trying to protect you," he said as put his hand on my cheek. "Not ever, not even to me. I'm not talking about your body. I'm talking about your spirit. You must always keep a part of your heart to yourself and not share it with anyone," Ari continued. "You protect your soul, understand?" he asked.

"Okay," I answered softly, feeling my eyes tear up again.

Ari leaned over and held my face in his hands, not letting me look away. "Promise me you will *never* give *all* of yourself to anyone," he said. He was so sincere.

I closed my eyes and answered, "I promise," thinking I understood what he meant—that I had to protect my heart. But he was saying much more. I'll never forget Ari's words on the hot sand of Gythion's beach that day. His insightful message was beyond the grasp of any seventeen-year-old, and many years passed before I was able to absorb all that he meant that day.

After the beach, we sat at another beachside restaurant, enjoying the delicacies of *pikilia*, a platter of fried, freshly caught seafood doused with lemon. Ari convinced me to try octopus for the first time. The calamari rings were enormous and went great with a cold Amstel Light. We laughed the whole time, telling each other funny stories about our childhood and various anecdotes of our lives. We left the café and headed back on the main road out of Gythion to return to Sparta. It was late afternoon, and most of the stores and businesses had closed already for siesta.

As beautiful and pleasant as the ride to Gythion was earlier that day, the ride home was even more enjoyable. Not only had the warm summer sun relaxed us both, but the intimacy we shared brought us together in a way like a true couple. He held my hand on the steering wheel with his as he drove, playing more Parios songs on the car stereo, and I spent most of the ride leaning on his shoulder. Every few miles or so, Ari took my hand and started kissing it. He made stupid jokes and put on a ridiculous, hot pink-colored terry cloth headband that must have been leftover from some *Flashdance* costume. He looked so ridiculous. I couldn't stand how he looked, so he kept putting it on just to bother me. I ripped the girly headband off his head a hundred times while he drove, but he was persistent.

Just as we passed the famous row of palm trees down Sparta's main drag,

Ari asked if we could stop for a minute in town. He wanted me to meet his favorite aunt, Potoula, who was more like an older sister to him, he said. They were raised like siblings, and together with her husband, she lived in a three flat with her two small children.

"She's going to love you," he said with enthusiasm.

Not wanting the day to end, I was eager to meet a person close to Ari. Little did I know that she was about to change my mind—and my life.

Chapter 13
Potoula's Warning

THE WHITE, THREE-STORY CONDOMINIUM Ari pulled up to was only one of many modern buildings on a block of newly styled homes set apart from Sparta's typically older apartments. We parked adjacent to an indoor parking garage and made our way up a long flight of marble steps with black wrought iron railings that led to a large terrace. I was impressed with the home from the moment we arrived and surprised that I never came across the avant-garde section of town before. "This," I thought, "is an area I could live in one day, with its urban appeal and Mediterranean charm. What a perfect location to enjoy summers in Greece. Who knows?" My thoughts continued, "Maybe someday."

Out of the front door came a robust, four-year-old boy who barreled over to Ari. I gathered that the preschooler adored his uncle, who spun him in the air, turning him upside down and kissing him all over. A middle-aged woman, younger than I'd expected, stood in the doorway wearing a flowing, blue tank dress with little white flowers. Her long, straight, black hair was pulled off her high cheekboned face in a silk headband. She wore little makeup. Potoula was an attractive woman, but her appearance seemed hardened by time, offering only a glimpse of lost beauty. Beneath her wrinkles, Potoula's deep, doelike eyes mirrored her cousin's, and I instantly saw a family resemblance.

"This is my *aunt* Potoula." Ari emphasized the word "aunt" as they both laughed at the idea for probably the hundredth time.

"I'm more like his sister. Did he tell you?" She embraced Ari and greeted me with double-cheeked European kisses.

Walking through the foyer, Ari's aunt immediately wanted to offer us refreshments. "Can I get you something to drink? How about some cold fruit?" she asked, showing us to an elegant sitting room decorated in contemporary colors of black and white, with hardwood floors and a white loveseat.

"*Paithi mou, exo me aufta ta paixnithia*" (My son, take those toys outside)! She turned to me and in almost perfect English said, "I love him to death, but he is exhausting!" She took a deep breath. "So," she continued. "You are Ari's girl from Chicago. I've heard a lot about you," Potoula began.

Ari smiled and sat down next to me, holding my hand on top of his leg as the interview began. I sat up straight, unused to the idea of making an impression on anyone's family. After a few rounds of initial questioning on things like age, my hometown, and family ties in Greece, Potoula excused herself into the kitchen and returned with a tray, carrying frappes and platters of cut-up melon with small forks.

"I just love your red top!" she said as she set the tray down on a glass cocktail table in front of us, pointing to my sleeveless, knit halter I changed into in case Ari took me to dinner.

"Thanks," I said. "I bought it for the trip just before we left."

"Ah, American stores. That was the best part of being in New York." She smiled.

"When did you visit the States?" I asked, surprised that Ari hadn't told me.

"Back in '82. My husband and I went to New York for our honeymoon," she explained.

"Oh!" I said, surprised. I had never thought of America as a vacation destination before. "Did you like it?" I asked Potoula.

"I loved it, but the city was way too congested for me. I think Athens is horrible, as well—so many people and so much noise! I don't know how you do it every day, Ari." She turned to her nephew.

"It's not that bad, really," Ari answered. "You're just all domesticated now. Not like you used to be." He turned to me. "Potoula was a real party girl before she met Stathi."

"Oh, stop it!" Potoula lifted up a plate from the coffee table and handed it to Ari. "Here. Eat some melon!" She handed him a fork.

Potoula quickly changed the subject and started another line of interrogatories regarding my studies back home, goals for my future, and career opportunities. Just as I was running out of answers, the phone rang. When Potoula got up to answer it, Ari said, "*Ela,*" and held up a piece of melon on his fork for me to taste. I opened my mouth as he fed me, enjoying the chilled sweetness of the cantaloupe, impressed by Ari's affection once more. Potoula carried on her phone call in the kitchen, speaking Greek one hundred miles an hour.

"She likes you," he said as he pierced another cube of melon for me. "I can tell." I smiled as he continued, "My whole family is going to fall in love with you."

He leaned forward and kissed me.

"That was Stathi," Potoula said as she came back into the room. "He's not going to make it home like he planned. Stuck at work again!" Potoula stood with her hands on her hips. I could tell she was disappointed. She looked at me with an irritated expression. "My husband works for the government. Great pay, but ridiculous hours. This country drives me nuts sometimes!" She threw her arms up in the air and retreated back into the kitchen.

"Don't worry about it!" Ari yelled out after her. "I'll be in Tsintzina for the next two weeks, until the end of summer. I'll see him before then." Ari got up and walked toward the kitchen in an effort to appease his aunt.

"I'm sorry," she said, looking at me through the doorway by the stove. "Stathi sends his regards to you, as well, and apologizes for not being here to meet you. I'm sure he'd want me to tell you that this old guy you're with isn't really all that bad. Try to ignore his wrinkles." The age difference had obviously been discussed between them. She sat back down and tried to look pleasant. I gathered that this wasn't the first time her husband broke plans.

Potoula asked if I'd like a tour of the condo. I was eager to see the place. All of the rooms appeared as fashionable as any American home. Everything in the place, from the furniture to the curtains, showed good taste and quality. Obviously, with a government job, there was money to spend on niceties. They even had a VCR and TV in the den. I had to laugh to myself, thinking of the way Mom and Yiayia adorned our Magoula house in 1970s leftovers from Chicago. Surely the olive green rotary phone we had wasn't stylish.

Ari and Potoula carried along most of the conversation while we walked up and down the halls and into each room, admiring the children's bedrooms and her husband's study. I listened as the two of them caught up on each other's lives. Ari told her about corporate politics at the bank, and she proudly detailed the latest accomplishments of her children. When we made our way onto the terrace, we were seated at a bistro set underneath a white umbrella that shielded the late afternoon sun. Looking out over her balcony, we took in a picturesque view of Sparta's valley, framed in a gorgeous mountainscape. Ari and Potoula quickly resumed picking on one another affectionately, offering me different versions of embarrassing childhood stories. They seemed to adore their formative years in Tsintzina, and both of them got a kick out of telling me one ridiculous story after another.

I leaned back in my chair, soaking in the surroundings as well as the two of them. The more I learned about Potoula, the more I liked her. Her friendly, forthcoming personality mirrored Ari's, and she was easy to know. Potoula explained that she was an elementary school teacher and left the village at a young age to study in the northern city of Patra, where she earned her degree and began teaching at a local school. Not long after, she met Stathi, and they moved to Sparta, where he began his government job. Potoula was thrilled to settle near her family's village. She continued teaching, she said, but later resigned after they had their first child. Potoula seemed an excellent, attentive mother, but she also missed working, and I knew she was serious as she explained her plan to return to work as soon as her youngest started school. Potoula smiled as she spoke, and I got the feeling she liked me, as well.

"It's just different here," she explained. "Not as many good opportunities as in the States. We simply don't have enough jobs."

I couldn't say much on the subject. I hadn't started to look for a real job yet because I hadn't started college. Part of me felt like I was playing adult in Ari and Potoula's presence, but at the same time, I enjoyed seeing what people their age lived like in Greece. Most of my experience with Greeks was with the villagers I knew in Vassara who raised goats and made olive oil for a living. I knew very few educated, middle-class people. In addition, Potoula and Ari were my only examples of the generation between my parents' age and the teenaged party crowd of Vassara. These two were living normal lives in Greece, not just celebrating the summer away. I admired Potoula for her family values and goals. She was living a life that didn't seem too far from what I wanted for myself—an education, a husband, children, and plans for a career. She seemed to have it all.

Nikko came into the room and bombarded Ari once more, this time with a soccer ball in hand.

"*Ela, Theo Ari*" (Come, Uncle Ari), Nikko said. Showing off his English, he continued, "You promising me!" The boy smiled.

"Not bad!" I praised him.

"Excuse me for a while." Ari got up. "I'm going to go outside and torture my obnoxious nephew while you girls talk." Ari kissed me on the forehead as he got up.

"Take your time," Potoula said. "Get him as tired as possible before bedtime!"

"I'm not going to bed!" Nikko shouted out at his mother while Ari put Nikko on his shoulders, barely clearing his head with the doorway as they exited the condo. Potoula and I looked at each other and laughed.

As soon as Ari was out of earshot, however, she turned to me with complete sincerity in her voice. "So, you and my nephew ... you seem to be getting close." She smiled.

"Yes." I couldn't fight back the grin that stretched across my reddening face.

"You're headed into college soon, right?" Another line of questioning approached.

"I'm planning to study literature and art." I improved my posture for the second time.

"That's wonderful." She paused for a while and then got up from her chair to sit next to me on the couch, placing her hand on my knee. "Can I say something to you?" she asked softly.

"Of course."

"I like you a lot. You're a very nice girl, and you seem to have a good head on your shoulders," she began.

"Thank you," I said.

"It's just ... well ... honey, don't," she said with a serious look.

"Don't what?" I turned to her, confused.

"Don't do it." She shook her head. "You're smart, and I don't want to see you throw your life away."

"What are you talking about?" I was puzzled.

"I'm talking about convincing yourself that you'd be happy marrying a Greek and leaving your American life behind." She had an expression of relief on her face as if she had finally said what had been on her mind for some time. Meanwhile, I felt like the atomic bomb had just landed on my lap.

"Oh, I'm not looking to get married. I'm way too young for that," I refuted as quickly as possible, assuming she knew Kiki and Tatz.

"I know you're young *now*, but if things keep going, it won't be long before …" she stopped, and then she continued as she spoke with passion. "This is *your* time. All of life's opportunities are awaiting you at this age. *Don't* let yourself get wrapped up in an older man from a foreign country. I know you're a sharp girl, but it's written all over your face that you're really falling for my nephew. If the thought hasn't come to mind yet, it will, and *that's* what I'm talking about." She had a motherly tone to her voice that was both concerned and nurturing at the same time. Before I could answer, she added, "Look, I'm not trying to pull you two apart. Honestly, he's never brought anyone around to meet me before, let alone the *rest* of the family. I just don't want to see a nice girl like you throw her life away. This isn't about Ari. This is about Greece. Things work differently in this country. Trust me, you wouldn't be happy here," she said and then began to clear the plates.

"How are things so different?" I looked up at her, still feeling as if I didn't totally understand her.

"Because although my nephew is a good and honorable man, he is a *man*, and in *this* country, that means something different from what it means in yours. You've been coming here for years, and I'm sure you think you're comfortable with the lifestyle. But this isn't real—this is *summer*. Life isn't as much fun here after everyone leaves in September."

"Oh, I know that," I assured her.

"Do you?" She looked right into my eyes. "Do you have any idea what it's like to spend a winter here? Do you know that *normal* in Greece is for a man to marry a woman, get her pregnant, and then go out every night to the tavernas 'til dawn? *That's* normal around here. We women … we are left behind."

"Is that what happened to you?" I asked.

"It's what happens to *all* of the young girls here, and don't think my beloved nephew is any different."

"I … I don't know what to say," I stuttered. I had never thought things through to that extent, imagining myself in Greece permanently. Part of me felt she was way off base, and I was almost offended that she stereotyped me as a typical American tourist, unable to see things for how they really are. On the other hand, I knew there was some credence to her comments and that her advice would stay with me for a long time.

"*Go home.* Finish your education," she concluded. "Get the job of your dreams and follow your heart. Don't leave your dreams behind for *any* man. You will regret it." She exited the room, carrying a tray of dirty dishes back to the kitchen.

I sat on the couch, speechless and overwhelmed. Then Potoula popped her head out by the stove and called out more optimistically, "If he wants you so badly, tell him to come to the States! Let him adjust to *your* world." Then she retreated back to the sink and ran the water.

I got up and followed her, walking into the kitchen and leaning against the dishwasher. Something inside me wanted to defend myself. "I appreciate your words," I said. "But you have to know that I'm well aware of my stage in life. I'm not trying to get engaged anytime soon, despite what my relatives may have in mind."

She laughed as she looked up and loaded the plates into the bottom rack. "You'll be amazed at how fast things go once the families get involved." She stopped for a while with an endearing look and said, "I didn't mean to offend you, and forgive me if I have. I've just seen it happen so many times to so many girls."

"Thank you," I said.

She put her hand on my face and smiled into my eyes just like Ari had done. Potoula couldn't have been more sincere, and that's what affected me most.

Ari and Nikko busted through the door with a rush, panting from an obvious race to the front door. Nikko let out a cheer of victory and sprinted to the kitchen for juice while Ari plopped down on the couch, exhausted.

"That kid wore me out!" he gasped. "How was your visit?"

"Enlightening," I replied, faking a smile to hide my worried eyes.

"You have a wonderful girl here, Ari. Treat her well." Potoula winked at me.

"Oh, I will." He took my hand as she retreated into the kitchen and scolded her son for spilling juice on the floor.

"We'd better get going. It's almost sunset. Your mother is going to think I've kidnapped you!" We laughed and stood up, making our polite farewells and thanks to Potoula. Nikko gave Ari's leg a big hug and then took my other hand. "I like her. Let's *keep* her!" he exclaimed to his uncle, who laughed.

Potoula nodded at me as if to say, "See!"

I was quiet as we got into the car, but I was even quieter on the ride through the suburban neighborhood. Everything his aunt said to me made sense—too much sense—and I didn't expect to get my head pulled out of the clouds so quickly.

"You okay?" Ari asked. Then I felt guilty, as if Ari knew what his relative had said.

"Oh, yeah. Sorry. Just tired, I guess. Going on little sleep, you know," I lied.

Ari laughed. "Oh, yeah, I forgot about that. See? You're a party girl, too, just like Potoula was." I felt a kick in the stomach, imagining a life sentence as a deserted, American wife stuck in a foreign land to raise children by myself while my Greek husband partied the nights away with his friends.

"Let's stop in town and call Vassara and let them know we're still alive. Then we can grab dinner in the city before returning to the village," Ari suggested.

We pulled over to use a pay phone. Mom was glad to hear from me and said it was okay to extend the date even longer. Her relaxed tone over the phone put me at ease. I got back in the car, and we continued along into town. Ari pulled the Alpha Romeo into a parking space along Sparta's main drag, and we walked through the large town square to an outside corner restaurant. Our dinner was quiet at first just like our coffee earlier that morning. Ari sat peacefully in his chair, taking in the sights and sounds of Sparta's emerging nightlife. An increasing number of people arrived in small groups, walking arm in arm, dressed in their best for a night out. Little children rode past on bikes, keeping the city *platia* alive with activity. Like Ari, I enjoyed people watching, too, and I found myself lost in thought as I admired the European custom of taking a stroll at the end of the day. "Was life really that different in the winter?" I wondered. "Where do all these people go?"

Our waiter brought over a platter of pork kabobs and french fries made in olive oil, sprinkled with oregano and salt. Ari and I shared them along with a platter of sliced tomatoes and feta cheese. We toasted our cold Amstel Lights to each other, to a beautiful day, and to finally being alone. With his arm around me, we ate slowly, savoring every bite, every word, every kiss. The time we spent in each other's company flew by, and I knew then, despite Potoula's warnings, that I was falling in love.

We drove back to the village with the setting sun, tanned, sand in our shoes, and happy. By the time we reached Vassara, the sky above blackened, and a spray of stars speckled the evening sky. I told Ari about Koulouri and how beautiful the view was and that I couldn't wait to show him the cliff someday. Without a reply, he slowed the car down and pulled over on the side of the mountain road. He threw the car in park, leaned over, and kissed me one last time before we entered the village. Ari promised to see me before the weekend. I was glad to know we would be together again soon. He needed to leave for Athens in two weeks, and I was scheduled to leave Greece at the end of the month. Time was running out.

Passing through the *platia*, I looked out of the window and saw a crowd of kids by Brikakis' café. Rania was there. She caught sight of Ari's Alfa Romeo as we turned the corner heading up to our house. I'd have a lot to tell her later. Luckily, all of my relatives were gathered at Kiki's, as we discovered when Ari and I pulled up to an empty house. We quietly parked the car, careful not to make noise and announce our arrival. I took Ari around the corner from the front door so that we could sit for a while on a little white stoop, delaying our final farewell. Ari held me tight into his chest. We embraced in silence, making our long good-bye there on the stoop. Crickets chirped in the summer night, and in the distance, bells from flocks of sheep softly rang their evening song. Occasionally, a loud burst of laughter exploded from inside Kiki's kitchen nearby, most likely caused by Stathi.

Ari finally left, heading home to Tsintzina. I went inside to take a shower before bed. I would not join Rania and the kids that night. I had all the excitement I could handle for one day.

Chapter 14
Lights Out

THE PHONE RANG EARLY the next morning, and I stumbled out of bed to answer it. Mom and Yiayia were already at Kiki's and drinking coffee. I was certain that my aunt was grilling Mom for details of my date.

"Hello," I mumbled. "I mean, *Embros.*"

"It's me, dork. Sorry to wake you up. I couldn't wait any longer. How was your date with MachoMan?"

"Rania?" My voice was faint.

"Wake up, sleepyhead. It's already after 10:00 am, and I want details!" my cousin demanded. The thought of talking to Rania over the phone never occurred to me.

"Where are you?" I asked, still a little out of it.

"Look out your balcony doors!" I opened the door as the bright rays of sunshine streamed into our darkened upstairs. Across the street and on top of her terrace stood Rania, already dressed in white shorts and a T-shirt. She was holding her oh-so-modern cordless white phone and laughing.

"Isn't this awesome? We can talk all we want!" She seemed hyper that day compared to my lethargic state.

"Rania, we can talk all we want in person, too," I reminded.

"I know, but this is cool. It's like walkie talkies, but better!"

"You *are* getting bored in this town, aren't you?" I laughed. What I initially ridiculed shortly became a beloved tradition between the two of us.

Before long, we were addicted to the phone in Greece just like home. The only difference was that Rania lived across the street from my house, a mere eight steps away. She would stand on her balcony with her cordless while I stood on my balcony with the green rotary phone cord coming out of the upstairs balcony doors. There began our "balcony talks" that occurred almost daily. We stood atop our terraces, looking at one another and enjoying our secret conversations. This was just another way to dish the dirt in a town where so many seemed to eavesdrop.

"So, start talking!" She was hungry for details and dying to describe how everyone reacted when Ari and I left the village, but she interrupted before I began with her own juicy details. "Grigori is the one who saw you," she informed me. "I can't believe you guys kissed in the car in the *platia*. He told everyone. You know how the village loves gossip!" My cousin was completely animated as she elaborated the spreading of Vassara's headline news. Worrying what the villagers said was last on my agenda.

"Listen, I'm wiped today—still feeling burned out from the Mango two nights ago, let alone an entire day at the beach yesterday. The last thing I want to do is go to the *platia* and get strange looks from everyone. What do you say we lay low at your house today and catch some rays? I'll give you all the details. I just need to wake up first," I promised.

"Fine by me," Rania answered agreeably. "To be honest, I'm getting a little sick of our village routine. At least you can to escape to your house in Magoula and visit Sparta whenever you want. I'm stuck here in the hills, and four straight weeks in Vassara is starting to get to me."

She came over by me, and we ate a breakfast of french fries and scrambled eggs—our usual—with a pint of Amita orange drink, the closest thing in Greece to American orange juice. Amita tasted more like Tang than juice, but like most things in Greece, after a while, we adjusted to it. Rania and I sunbathed on her terrace for most of the afternoon. The sun was hot, but the warm rays felt soothing on my tired skin. Despina came over and confirmed that most of the kids in town were talking about my escapades with a stranger. Only a few of them knew he was Ari Kostopoulos from Tsintzina.

The three of us occupied ourselves on Rania's terrace for a good portion of the day. We played cards and drank Coke Light in the shade when we became overwhelmed by the heat. Chilling out with good music and good friends was therapeutic. By the time the sun started to cool off, I had told

145

them all about my day in the sun with Ari. Despina cautioned me to take things slowly, warning that he might be more serious than I imagined, but Rania and I agreed that there was no way Ari wanted to settle down with a seventeen-year-old. The clock reached well past 6:00 pm before we decided to venture out beyond Rania's balcony. We cleaned up and made our way into the *platia* for the night, braving whatever comments might emerge from the rumor mill.

Wearing a pair of shorts and an old tank, Rania and I remained in a sort of "anti-Vassara" mood that night, fed up with small-town gossip, and talked instead about home and all of the things we missed in Chicago. I hesitantly approached the town square with the girls and sat on a bench beneath a large tree, out of the spotlight as much as possible. We kept to ourselves until Demetri found us. He sat down next to me, not saying a word about Ari, and acted friendly, as usual. His brother Grigori, however, had a big "I know a secret" look on his face and immediately came over to stand in front of our bench with his feet spread apart, his hands on his hips. Grigori's evil grin morphed into a snicker as he asked, "So, how was *your* day yesterday?" I ignored him.

"Leave her alone, Grigori. Her life is none of your business," Rania snapped.

"I saw some kissing going on in the *platia*. Boy, you Americans are gutsy—*kissing* in the *platia* for everyone to see!"

"Don't be a jerk, Grigori," I warned.

Demetri tried to change the subject. "What do you guys say we head over to Koulouri early tonight? We can blow off the crowd at Moustokotou's and bring our own party up to the cliff." Rania and I smiled.

"Why can't you be as cool as your brother, Grigori?" Rania asked him.

Demetri, ever the loyal friend, offered us a perfect solution to our evening's dilemma. He must have read that "the Chicago girls" were growing weary of the village's watchful eyes as we remained out of sight for most of the day. As Demetri lived in Athens year round, he understood our angst and probably felt a longing to get back to his big city and anonymity, as well. He always knew how to make an uncomfortable situation better. His brother Grigori, however, lived in the village year round and obviously didn't relate.

"Oh, I don't know," Grigori protested. "I don't think everyone will want to do that, Demetri," he complained.

"That's precisely the point, Brother. Who cares? Let them stay at the tavern." He turned to us. "You girls game?" We nodded, loving the idea of being on our own. As we got up to buy our beer from inside the store, a loud popping noise crackled from the telephone wires above us, followed by the buzzing of electrical shocks. In an instant, the streetlights went out, along with the lights and television inside Brikakis' café.

"What was *that*?" Rania shouted. We looked around. Townspeople had shocked expressions on their faces. Some villagers got up to look at the power lines.

"Do you smell fire?" An old lady in black asked.

"There goes the ice cream!" Mrs. Brikaki moaned from the doorway of her store.

Although the sun wouldn't set for a few more hours, the locals understood the looming inconvenience. A group of old men sitting inside Brikakis' café who lost their televised soccer game against Bulgaria became angry, yelling at Mrs. Brikaki as if she pulled a switch. Panteli, who worked for the electrical company of Greece, came out from inside the café and walked over to our group.

"That, my friends, is a power outage!" he said with disappointed certainty.

"What happened?" I asked.

Lefteri walked over to the Boston kids and made some announcement in Greek. He had a suspicious look on his face.

"Don't be afraid," Demetri said. "This usually happens at least once a summer. The outage comes from high temperatures day after day. Power lines can't handle the heat, and we go without electricity for while."

"I never remember this happening before!" I answered.

"I think you were in Magoula that last time we had an outage," Demetri offered.

"How long before the power goes back on?" Rania inquired.

"What do you think? A ComEd truck is on its way?" I turned to Rania. "I'm guessing it will be a while."

"Great. As if we weren't bored *before* the lights went out," Rania complained. "What are we supposed to do? Walk to Koulouri by candlelight?" I could tell my cousin was completely irritated.

Lefteri finished speaking to the group across the way and walked over.

"So, it looks like there won't be any music in Vassara tonight!" he said, looking right at me. I assumed he had heard about my departure with Ari the day before, as well as his brother, Stavros, as the tall tale must have reached their house. God only knows what was exaggerated.

"Well this is just *great!*" Rania complained. "What are we going to do in the dark?"

Lefteri smiled. "That's what I came over to talk to you girls about. Well," he paused. "We could always move the party to somewhere that has light. Like, say, Tsintzina?" He grinned.

"What?" I asked.

"Why not?" Lefteri offered. "I hear there are many *interesting* things and many *interesting* people in Tsintzina. Why don't we visit them tonight? It's better than staying here in the dark!" He gave me a big smile. Now I knew why Lefteri had the weird face. Grigori got up and started pacing in circles, dramatically throwing his arms up in the air. "Now they want to go to Tsintzina!" he said like a frustrated, overprotective parent.

"We could do that!" said Demetri enthusiastically, standing up in defiance of his brother. "Why not? We'll caravan!" I looked at Lefteri, unsure of his motives. He could have chosen anywhere, even Sparta. Why Ari's village? I determined that Lefteri was pulling my leg and told him I wouldn't fall for his joke.

"I'm serious," he insisted. "I'll drive you, Rania, and Demetri. I'm sure your mothers will approve if you come with me. The others can drive with the Boston crowd." I shook my head, still unsure he was for real.

"You don't mean it," I refused. But Lefteri pulled me aside, saying softly, "Well, I'll be honest. Just as you have, let's say, a 'connection' in Tsintzina, so do I. Her name is Katerina. But not many of the kids know about her, so let's keep it quiet. Okay?"

"You *are* serious!" I said in disbelief, opening my eyes wide. The sudden thought of seeing Ari ran like a lightning bolt of excitement through my entire body.

"Yes, I am! But we have to leave shortly because it'll get dark soon, and I'm not sure where the streetlights will kick in again on the roads. We need to go in the next twenty minutes. Go get the okay from your mothers and grab jackets. It's cold up there." Rania and I looked at each other in ecstatic disbelief.

"We're *so* out of here!" she exclaimed.

"I have to change. I can't go like this." I panicked, looking at my clothes.

Lefteri started laughing. "I mean it. Twenty minutes, you guys. Be back in the *platia*."

I turned to Demetri and put my hand on his knee, saying quietly, "Thanks."

"For what?" he asked.

"For suggesting we blow everyone off and hang out at Koulouri. That was a great idea." I paused. "You're always making things easier for me."

"No problem!" he exclaimed. I got up from the bench to head home with Rania and turned to Demetri.

"See you in twenty. Gotta go get beautiful."

"*Eisai*" (You are), he said quietly as I walked away. I stopped and turned, giving him a smile. He smiled back with a reddened face.

Rania pulled me onward. "I finally get to meet your old man!" Rania laughed.

"Shut up!" I pushed her.

As quickly as we could, Rania and I changed into our party best and headed out the door. Mom and Aunt Despina gave us the green light as long as we promised to ride with Lefteri. The adults were gathered in our kitchen with a deck of cards and had already lit some candles. We couldn't believe our otherwise dreaded day and night showed signs for potential. Rania threw on her denim shorts and an off-the-shoulder sweater. I pulled out my red minidress with the ruffled skirt, short and bold. I loved that dress. Putting my big, black hoop earrings on, we hustled ourselves down the street to pick up Despina. Standing outside her great, green door, Rania laughed at how quickly I made my hair go from frumpy to fabulous.

"Did you call him?" she asked me as we waited.

"I can't. The lines are down, remember?" I asked. "I guess I'll have to surprise him. Just hope he's there. What if he decided to go to Sparta or something?"

"He won't. You said his parents' restaurant keeps him busy. He's probably helping out tonight." Despina came out in a pair of white jeans and a striped top. She looked adorable.

"*Etimi*" (Ready)? Despina asked.

"Etimi"(Ready)! Rania and I answered.

The three of us skipped through the darkening streets, Rania and I with our mini flashlights, ever the prepared travelers. Making our way to the *platia*, we were arm in arm in arm. The three of us loved walking in a linked line of solidarity.

"Cigarettes?" Despina asked Rania.

"Check!" she replied.

"Yeah, God forbid you guys go anywhere without your smokes!" I threw in.

"What do you care? We'll be smoking and drinking all night while you're off with *lover boy*," Rania snapped.

"You mean 'lover*man*.' The guy is *how* old?" Despina teased me. We all laughed.

Down on the benches outside Brikakis' café sat the Boston girls with less than excited expressions.

"They don't seem too excited about the plan," I observed to my cousins as we approached their group.

"Are you sure they're coming with us?" Rania was equally surprised at their plain appearance.

"Yeah, they're coming. See? They grabbed sweatshirts," I answered.

"How come we're so much more excited about stuff than anyone else?" Rania asked. I had no answer.

Meanwhile, my cousins and I were jumping out of our skin with enthusiasm. In no time, we were on our way to Tsintzina in the back of Lefteri's maroon van. Demetri and Kosma rode with us, and Grigori decided not to go. I was glad. I didn't feel like spending the night listening to him tease me. Stavros's Mazda truck followed behind Lefteri with Niko and his sister Lia riding passenger.

Our caravan continued in the dark with only headlights to lead the way around curvy, blackened mountain roads. We drove past the village of Verroia and onward toward Tsintzina, which was another half hour away. A few miles after Verroia, streetlights glowed again, and we were glad to know there would be electricity at our destination. When we reached Tsintzina, Lefteri parked in the *platia* and got out of the van, gathering our group together. "Listen up," he said. "The van is parked here for the night until we leave, so this is where we'll meet to return to Vássara. Let's say midnight."

"You got that, Cinderella?" Rania nudged me.

"I'm not kidding." Lefteri turned toward us. "I'm responsible for you guys tonight, so wherever you go in this town, be back by midnight at the van so we can leave as a group. I don't want to wander around looking for anyone."

"We got it," I said. He pointed up the street. "I'm going to go see if my friend is home, and I'll meet you guys down at Kyriakos's tavern. Get a large table and order a round of beers."

As he started to leave, Stavros called out after him, "*That's* where we're hanging out? Kyriakos's?"

"Where else? It's not like this town has a million choices!" Lefteri turned away as he answered his brother and walked onward, holding his hand up in the air and waving him off. "Get a big table, guys. There are many coming," he called back to us as he headed up a road leading to village homes. I looked at Rania. She smirked back at me. We walked ahead with Demetri and Kosma, not waiting for Stavros and his passengers.

Like most village restaurants, Kyriakos's tavern was outside, and it was in a sunken level from the main road. Open to the sky, Tsintzina's main tavern resembled Moustokotou's in many ways. At street level, a large red gate led down a flight of stairs to where the restaurant spread out over a flat concrete slab. I was first to reach the gate, with Rania, Demetri, and the others following. I stopped before entering and looked back behind me, noticing a long stream of Vassara kids. Our caravan to Tsintzina was bigger than I realized.

Stavros walked up to me at the gate and said, "Go on, lead the way. This is *your* night, apparently."

I opened the gate and proceeded down the staircase. The ruffles on the skirt of my red minidress bounced off of my knees on each step, and I had a nervous butterfly in my stomach in anticipation of seeing Ari. Kyriakos let out a big shout when he saw me. I hadn't been to his tavern since my first trip to Vassara, when Ari was still in the army. I hoped the old man would remember me and wondered what he thought of me spending time with his son. My answer came quickly. Kyriakos came over and picked me up in the air, hugging me like a long lost child. Rania's mouth dropped open as she watched the big scene.

"What are you doing here?" he called out. "Does he know you're coming? I'm so glad to see you! How you've grown into a beautiful woman! Ari's mother and I were hoping to get a glimpse of you before you return to the States. Ah, the girl of his dreams! How many did you bring with you?" There was no pause in between his comments and questions, and my face turned as red as my dress. "Saranto!" he called out to his older son, Ari's brother. "The *bride* is here. She's brought her friends. Set them a long table! A large, long table!" Kyriakos took my face into his hands and held my cheeks. "Wait 'til he sees you! He'll be so happy you've come!"

"Is Ari here?" I shyly asked as my cheeks were being mashed together. Knowing our family ties, I appreciated the old man's friendliness, but when he called me a "bride," I just about died. Obviously, Aunt Kiki and Tatz had Kyriakos as part of their matchmaking plans. I innocently dismissed his father's behavior. Surely, Kyriakos was just being playful.

"Of course he's here! Look how busy we are! This is why he took vacation from work—to help us out." Just then, Ari came out from the back of the tavern carrying a large crate of beer. He wore a red, short-sleeved polo and jeans with a white apron around his waist. His face lit up when he saw me. Ari held his arms open wide as he approached.

"*Koukla mou*—my doll!—what are you doing here?" We embraced in the middle of the restaurant. All eyes were on us, which only added more fuel to the gossip fire already burning after my day at the beach with him. I felt like we were on center stage, and the tavern's many tables of customers were our audience. Ari greeted me in European fashion of a double kiss on each cheek. Before he pulled away, I planted a third kiss on his lips. He smiled as he pressed his mouth firmly to mine. He looked up at the long line of kids still coming through the tavern door. "What did you do? Bring the whole village with you?" He laughed.

"Vassara lost power," Despina added.

Ari laughed. "Vassara's loss is our gain." He turned to my crowd. "Have a seat, everyone!" he announced. "Drinks are coming!"

The kids grabbed seats at a long table arrangement in the middle of the restaurant. I took Ari's hand and followed him into the kitchen, where I greeted his mother and grandmother. They were full figured and full of smiles. Luckily, the tavern was busy, so the women had no time to interrogate me. I went into the back room with Ari as he pulled out another case of Amstels to chill in the cooler. He filed all of the bottles in place, closed the cooler door, and pulled me tightly toward him. I looked around, making sure we were alone in the dark corner of the storage area.

Ari didn't seem to care. He kissed me and then whispered, "I can't believe you surprised me like this. I haven't been able to stop thinking about you all day. What a time we had at the beach yesterday, huh?"

"Our date was perfect." I looked up into his eyes and put my hand on his chest. "I love being with you." He kissed me again as his mother walked through the door with his father. I froze. Kyriakos's smile didn't leave his face while he and his wife walked over to us together. Ari's dad put his arm on his son's shoulder.

"*Nifi mou*" (My bride), he said. "We're going to dress you in gold from your head to your feet." I smiled, not knowing what in the world he was talking about. Ari looked on as his mother embraced me. Then we returned to Vassara's table for what was turning out to be the most surreal evening of the summer.

Rania held up her hand from the far end of our group, signaling that she and Despina were saving an empty chair for me. I nodded. Demetri and Kosma were next to them with Lefteri, who had arrived with a girl I assumed to be Katerina. She was a cute, typical Greek girl with short hair and little makeup. After Lefteri introduced us, I noticed Stavros sitting at the head of the table, opposite where Rania and Despina had settled. He called Ari over, and my eyes widened.

They shook hands. Ari asked him how many more they were expecting. Stavros answered. They went on with their exchange of information about chairs and beers and food orders, but I stopped hearing the details. Their conversation became drowned out by the exploding thoughts in my head as I watched them together. I couldn't help staring at their two figures, standing opposite one another for comparison just as they had appeared in my mind so many times before.

Rania and Despina's eyes were on me, reading my mind and feeling my disbelief. I tried not to look tense as I examined Ari and Stavros's facial expressions, searching for a reaction, as they each knew about the other. Stavros was my past, and Ari was my present, but Ari knew I still carried the pain of Stavros's rejection. As they spoke, Stavros seemed cold and businesslike. He sternly spoke in short sentences with a bossy attitude, giving our group's order. Ari seemed at ease, taking in Stavros's demeanor with humor and responded in a casual tone, nodding his head amiably. I so badly wanted to know what each of them was thinking.

Our group sat and drank and ate. Greek salad with feta cheese and platters of french fries preceded roasted lamb off the spit, followed by oven potatoes baked in olive oil and lemon. The delectable smell of Kyriakos's open fire pit filled the cool evening air, while traditional bouzouki music blared through the large speakers set in the corners of his restaurant. "This is quite a party for a blackout," I thought. I was up and down from my seat at the table often, being brought into the kitchen more than once to meet Ari's friends and relatives. I tried to spend as much time with him as possible as he worked the tables. He kept whispering, "Just a bit longer—I have a surprise." I didn't know what was coming, but the time was already past 10:00 pm and, feeling anxious, I didn't want to leave Tsintzina.

"Okay, *pame*—let's go!" he said, and he got me up from the table once more.

"Take your coat," he said. "You're not coming back." He nodded to Despina. "She'll see you back at the van," he called out as we made our way away from the group.

Rania and Despina winked, informed of Ari's plan. Stavros shot me an angry look as I got up from the table. I followed Ari into the kitchen, where he explained, "Saranto is covering for me until midnight. Now I'm all yours. Let's go."

"Awesome." I was game.

"Let me take you for a walk around my village tonight. You may not believe me, but the view with the moon is even more beautiful than your Koulouri in Vassara. I'm just going to grab my cigarettes before we go. C'mon up, I'll just be a minute."

Through the kitchen, we climbed a staircase that led to an upstairs apartment atop the tavern. A large balcony ran the perimeter of the house, and below, we heard muffled sounds of the music and partying. Kyriakos's restaurant was jammed, and I was surprised Ari got away.

"So this is home, huh?" I asked as we walked through the hallway.

"Yep. This is where I grew up. Saranto and I shared a bedroom in here." He opened up a door that held only two small twin beds and an old dresser. The place was nothing like his Aunt Potoula's lavish condominium.

I stood speechless as I looked around at the meager surroundings, trying hard to hide my astonishment at the cracked walls and measly beds covered in tattered blankets that appeared coarse and hard. Now I understood why Ari was eager to escape the village and live in Athens. I thought about how drastically different our childhoods were—his spent in this old, decrepit room, and mine in a bedroom with plush pink carpeting, a big bed, and all of the comforts enjoyed by any teen living in American suburbia. I wondered what kind of luxuries he had if this tavern was his parents' only source of income.

Ari came up from behind and wrapped his arms around my waist. I was so glad to be alone with him again, still on a euphoric high from our day at the ocean. I didn't care where we were. All that mattered was that we were together again. Finding ourselves in the seclusion of his old room, Ari and I were comfortable expressing our feelings toward one another. We kissed and kissed and kissed. We never took our walk. I never saw Tsintzina's view of the moon. The next few hours melted away in an instant, the clock raced along as Ari held me in his arms. That's when Ari told me he loved me, and I told him I loved him, too. Not for richer, but for poorer. Ari was a beautiful man. He was gentle. He was gorgeous. He was funny, and he was kind. He was in love with me, and I couldn't believe it. He came from nothing, and yet, I knew I was the luckiest girl in the world to have his heart. At the time, I loved Ari, too. If only I were a little older. If only our relationship stayed that simple. If only.

Inevitably, Ari looked at his watch, saying, "We'd better get you back. It's almost midnight."

"Already?" I couldn't believe the time had passed so quickly.

"Yeah. C'mon, I promised Lefteri," he said, sitting up.

I got up and grabbed my jacket. We heard footsteps from the balcony staircase.

"Ari, you up there?" It was Saranto, looking for his brother.

"Be down in a second," he called back.

"*Ela.* Dad's looking for you." Ari's eyes widened at me, pretending that we were in big trouble. Then he smiled, and I realized he was pulling my leg. We laughed.

"Don't worry. It's fine," he said. "My dad loves you more than he loves me at this point. You go ahead out the balcony, and I'll be out there in a second.

I'll walk you to Lefteri's van." I kissed him one more time before leaving the room. "Thanks for surprising me," he said.

As I opened the door, the lights from the tavern below shocked my senses back into reality. The narrow outdoor staircase off of the balcony led back down to the restaurant. I slowly began my descent down the stairs, back into the busy crowd of tables below, tightly holding onto the metal railing as my eyes adjusted to bright lights. About halfway down the stairs, I looked out across the restaurant at our table. Everyone was happy, toasting glasses and singing folk songs. The beer poured, and the laughter was loud. My crowd was having a good time in Tsintzina. All were smiling, except Stavros. He caught my eye as I stood for a moment on the stairs and held a mean glare that pierced through me. In that one short moment, a million words were said between us, and none of them were kind.

I'm sure he made a lot of assumptions about me that night, not understanding that Ari showed gentlemanlike respect at all times. Our love affair was more about our hearts than our bodies, and being alone in Ari's room didn't mean he crossed any line. I thought for a moment about explaining this to Stavros since he looked so angry, but I wasn't sure he would understand or even believe me.

Our ride back to Vassara was quiet. Everyone was exhausted from Kyriakos's party. Even Rania was too tired to talk, but she said she would give me her full opinion of Ari tomorrow. For now, she said, he was "ridiculously gorgeous." I rode with my head on Despina's shoulder, staring at the full, bright moon out of Lefteri's rear window while my two cousins softly sang their drunken folk songs of love and despair. Some of the guys fell asleep. We reached Vassara just after 1:30 am. When the caravan pulled into the *platia*, we noticed the streetlights were on once again. Power was restored.

I turned to Stavros's brother. "Thanks, Lefteri."

"Did you have a good time?" he asked.

"Best night of the summer." I smiled.

"Good. You deserve it. See you tomorrow. Sleep well."

Chapter 15
My Utopia

THE REMAINING WEEKS IN Vassara followed along like a dream. I treasured each day, knowing the time spent in my village would fill my memory. Escapades with Rania and Despina continued. We would reminisce about our ride home from the Mango in Panteli's truck, the power outage trip to Tsintzina, and dancing at Moustokotou's tavern for the next three decades. The freedom we received in Greece was rare, making our time in the village all the more endearing.

Lazy afternoons sunbathing atop Rania's balcony, walking to the *Yipetho* to watch soccer games, and hysterical, ruthless water fights in the *platia*—some of which involved more than twenty kids at a time—sweetened summer's end. Our group's cheerful, dancing nights at Moustokotou's tavern, followed by drunken song at Koulouri's cliff, were the perfect finale to our blissful August days. As we spent more time with Panteli, Lefteri, Demetri, and the others, I felt my ties to the village deepen. Despite an occasional frustration with small-town gossip, Rania and I kept our mood light and fun. We knew the clock was quickly ticking away toward fall. As for Stavros, he kept his distance after the visit to Tsintzina. I was sure our friendship had ended.

Ari returned to Eurobank in Athens not long after my surprise visit to Tsintzina, but he stopped by Vassara briefly to see me. Aunt Potoula's prophetic words whispered in the back of my mind as I was bombarded with comments and questions from relatives. Aunt Kiki and Tatz were at an all-time high in matchmaking. I was somewhat relieved that he returned to the big city.

When he was gone, pressure seemed to lift. Although I loved spending time with Ari, I was sure that if he stayed for the festival, our village's annual celebration would turn into a pseudo-engagement party, which would have been disastrous. He promised to see me off at the Athens airport at my departure. Since his time off from work ended, I gathered that our alone time was over, as well. We made the most of our daily phone calls during the last week of my trip, talking endlessly about a to-do list for the following year, but that was all.

When festival day arrived, Rania, Despina, and I attended church up in the mountain's grotto with our mothers and grandmothers in the morning and spent the afternoon helping set up tables and chairs in the town square for the evening's party. That night, as strings of little white lights glowed in streams across the *platia*, draped between trees, poles, and buildings, the mood in the air hung thick with merriment. This particular festival seemed especially joyous. Even Soula and Nia came back to Vassara for the party. Soula said she couldn't believe how much I had changed since that rainy day I sat in their kitchen, drinking frappe coffee and whimpering over Stavros. Nia called me mature. We Greek danced, even belly danced together, and laughed to no end when Soula said she caught Stavros staring at me. I gave little attention to his unpredictable behavior.

Demetri joined me for a brief time-out from the dance floor. He said with pride,

"Well, I was right! What did I tell you? This would be the best summer yet!" He toasted my beer bottle to his while we sat on white plastic chairs near the dancing. My heart beat fast as I tried to catch a minute's rest after hours of Greek dancing.

"I'm sad it's over," I panted. He smiled. "It went by so fast," I added as I shook my head.

But within seconds, our bodies were up again, cutting our conversation off as we were pulled back to the dance floor by Lefteri to lead another line of hand-holding *sirto* dancing around the cobblestone square. I had finally learned a few Greek dance moves to lead the line. Demetri placed himself next to me, second in a long line of kids with a white cloth napkin between us as he spun me around and around. As was customary in Greece, the dancer next to the lead position holds a napkin to assist the leader to spin. Demetri and I showed off our talent, but truth be told, I hung on for dear life as he picked up the speed with his extra long legs, sending me flying around in circles, barely able to keep up with his skillful abilities.

Further down our chain and next to Rania was Stavros's younger brother, Vasili. They exchanged flirtatious smiles as they had for many weeks, but when I caught him winking at her as our dance line wrapped around the *platia*, her secret was revealed. The song ended, as did my turn at lead position, so I left the front of the line to join Rania at the end. Squeezing her hand, I said, "Someone's falling for someone." We continued around in the circle of folk dancing.

"He's cute, isn't he?" she replied.

"Where was I when *this* started?" I asked as we rounded the corner by Brikakis' café for the hundredth time.

"Probably off with Ari. It's no big deal, I *swear!*" she promised.

"I thought you hated all of the Antonopoulos boys," I said as I sarcastically laughed.

"Not all of them. Just Stavros," she said, laughing.

"So, are we 'in like' with Vasili?" I inquired.

"I think so," Rania confessed.

"Isn't he younger than you?" I had to press.

"Only two years. He's old for his age," she defended.

I laughed. Then I stopped for a second. "Oh, my God," I said to Rania after a quick calculation in my head. "That makes Vasili almost twenty years younger than Ari!" We exploded in hysterics.

Meanwhile, innocent and love-stricken, Vasili looked on at us nervously, unable to make out what we were saying as the music blared over everyone's ears. Despina led the line as we continued with the music late into the night. Each of our friends took a turn leading to a new song, which kept the band playing on and on. After many more hours of partying, the masses of festival visitors finally began their exodus. Most of the adults left, as well, and by 2:00 am, only our group of kids remained. No one dared say good night, as we knew—like dominoes—the rest would follow, and the following day would be nothing but suitcases, packed cars, and farewells.

Something else made us want to keep the festival going as long as possible that evening besides our vacations' inevitable end. We knew time was changing us. Loukas and Kosma, along with a few older boys from Boston, wouldn't be back the following year, as college and jobs came into play. No longer a youthful body of grade school and high school kids living carefree lives, we were slowly but steadily showing signs of change. One by one, our count lessened each year. Some local boys went into the army. Others didn't return because of jobs. A few American kids cut short their stays in order to prepare for college, and some stopped coming completely. Without warning, responsibility arrived, and as much as we tried to ignore the inevitable truth, the day was approaching when most of us would move on with our lives. We became like a band of Peter Pans that night, not wanting the festival to end, resisting the idea of growing up, fearing removal from the nursery of our village. As maturity loomed, our golden days unavoidably neared their end.

Sometime around 3:00 am, the musicians packed up and headed home. Mihali Brikaki, ever the hard-core partier, moved a few of us to tables outside his store and popped cassette tapes into a large boom box. To continue with an after-party, we sat in front of the café with the late-evening breeze blowing. We listened to old, sing-along Greek tunes, exhausted from the party. Our feet throbbed from pounding on the *platia's* hard, cobblestone streets. Most of the girls had kicked off their shoes and sat barefooted in their summer party dresses on the Brikakis' wicker chairs. Eventually, even Rania and I became overwhelmed by fatigue, too tired to keep our eyes open. One by one, we finally said our good nights, as well as *Kalo Ximona*, and left the town square as empty as a ghost town, waiting for a rebirth the following June.

When I got to my house, I quietly walked up the stairs to the upper-level balcony, not wanting to wake up Mom. I stopped for a minute and sat on a creaky, old wooden chair on the terrace, staring at a black velvet sky full of stars, reflecting on the night and the summer. So much had happened. Rania had become the other half of me. My relationship with Despina grew stronger than ever, as well as my friendship with Demetri. I had the love of a Greek god like Ari, and I relished the freedom from Mom throughout the season. A new sense of happiness energized my spirit as I finally put Stavros out of my head. I even thought I had my relationship with Ari under control. Vassara was my village now, and I loved this utopia more than any place in the world.

I took a deep breath while gazing up at the flickering sky, thinking about the winter ahead. What would life hold for me when I returned to the States for senior year? Anxious to wrap up my high school education, I eagerly anticipated the challenges of college. I wasn't sure how or where Vassara would have a role in my future, but I knew I wasn't ready to put an end to my days in the village. I had to return again.

The next morning, we said our final good-byes. Rania and I agreed to get together back in Chicago as soon as we both developed our photos. Packed up and ready to return to Magoula and then to travel to Athens for our flight home, Mom and I began our end-of-summer ritual with relatives—exchanging kisses, lots of hugs, and of course, promises to write, return, and remember. Despina and I parted again with tears.

Watching the church of Agia Triatha disappear behind the mountains, I stared out of the Audi's back window while Pappou drove the twisted road, taking us farther and farther away from the village. My heart was heavy, and I had a sick feeling in my stomach, probably from the beer the night before. Nevertheless, leaving Vassara was always sad.

Two days later at the Athens airport, I had one last moment to enjoy. Seeing Ari to say good-bye was always bittersweet, as I knew our visit would be short-lived and that we would soon say good-bye for another year.

"I thought I'd find you in the store looking at American magazines." He came up around a corner as I shopped at an airport newsstand.

"Ari!" I jumped with joy.

"*Koukla mou.*" Ari planted a big kiss on my lips.

"How I will miss his kisses," I thought. I exclaimed, "You said you were going to meet me at my gate at 3:00. It's only 1:30!"

"I had a feeling you'd be here early, so I came early, too. Thought we could spend more time together. Have you had lunch? Where's your mother?" he asked.

"She's at the counter trying to upgrade our tickets. I can't eat. My stomach is bothering me. I guess I'm nervous about the flight," I said.

"Why? You make this same flight every year," he questioned.

"It's not that. I'm just upset about leaving this year. It's been the best summer ever, and I don't want it to end," I said sadly. Ari smiled and put his arm around me. He looked down at the September issue of *Glamour* I was about to purchase for the flight and took it out of my hand.

"*This?* This is what you're going to read for eight hours? Why don't you write me a long love letter instead?" he suggested. I laughed. He pulled out some drachmas and gave it to the girl behind the counter. "Anything else, sweetheart?" he asked as he took out his wallet to pay the clerk for my magazine.

"No, thank you," I replied.

Mom came over with a frustrated look that she didn't conceal for Ari. After greeting him, she threw her hands up in the air and said, "Sometimes this country is so backward!" She was completely disgusted.

"What happened?" I asked.

"Oh, I'm fighting with the ticket agent over there, who upgraded the tickets to first class but now has the connecting flight in Amsterdam all screwed up. I have to get back there to talk with the manager." She pointed to the restaurant across from the ticket counters. "Why don't you have a Coke or something, and I'll meet you over there," Mom suggested.

"What can I order for you?" Ari asked Mom.

"Nothing yet. It depends on what happens with the tickets. I may need a drink!" she complained.

We laughed as Mom stormed off to do battle with the airline manager. Ari picked up my carry-on bag, and we headed over to the café. We sat at an end table facing the aisle so Mom could find us easily.

The waiter came over with a typical Greek, tired, 'I'm- too-good-to-be-here' look and muttered, "*Ti thelete*" (What do you want)?

Ari ordered a Greek coffee for himself and a Sprite Lite to settle my stomach. "You really should eat something before you go. How about a *toast*?" he offered.

Toast was the American equivalent of a grilled ham and cheese panini. I'm not sure where it got the name *toast*, but the sandwich had been one of my staples during years of travel to Greece.

"No, I'm okay with Sprite," I answered.

Ari stood up in his chair and reached into the front pocket of his jeans. "Well, maybe this will make you feel better."

I froze, not knowing what he was going to pull out of his jeans. For a second, I had the crazy thought that a ring might appear, but instead, Ari slowly pulled out a shiny, thick, gold bracelet.

"This is for you," he said as he wrapped the chain around my wrist. I looked up at him with wide eyes, speechless. He clasped the bracelet closed. "To remember me by," he said.

"Ari … it's beautiful." I was so surprised.

"No, *you're* beautiful. Think of me when you look at it, okay?" He smiled.

I had never received anything of value from a boy before, and Ari seemed utterly sincere, even serious when he gave the bracelet to me.

"I love it. Thank you, thank you, thank you." I put my arms around his neck and kissed him. I could tell by the smile that spread across his face how glad he was that I liked his gift, but then he pulled back and looked me in the eyes and said, "Whoever you meet this year, just remember that I love you, and I'll wait for you." His solemn tone caught me off guard.

Suddenly, the joy in his face disappeared, and he seemed desperately calculated about something, uncommon to his typical, easygoing personality. I grew uncomfortable watching this new behavior unfold, dreading the idea of him waiting for me while I went on with my life in Chicago. Ari made a grimacing face when he referred to our future, an expression that took all the happiness out of his normally upbeat grin. Did he want me to make a promise not to date? Was I not supposed to go to my senior prom? I unexpectedly felt as if I owed him something, although I found it hard to believe Ari would remain alone all winter. Surely, he wasn't shy with all of the beautiful Greek girls that crowded the city of Athens.

I loved what he bought me, and I really loved him, but his comments were unlike him and confusing. I stared at the gold on my wrist throughout the plane ride back to Chicago. Ari's generosity was charming, but we were never the same thereafter. Grasping the significance of the bracelet was something I thought I'd have an entire year to figure out. However, the true meaning of my gift was revealed sooner than expected.

Chapter 16
Vassara Is Burning

HAVING BECOME AN EXPERT at assimilating back and forth to each country, that fall was no exception. Although at times I felt I had deserted life in one country for time in the other, both worlds pulled at my heart. I loved Greece with my entire soul and missed the village every day when we left, but when I was home in Chicago, I was truly *home*. Easily falling back into a routine with my friends and school, I refused to let myself sulk while missing everyone in Vassara. Besides, I told myself, all of my Vassarean friends had returned to their real lives, as well. Feeling sorry for myself would get me nowhere.

Coming home from school one brisk September day, pom-poms in hand, I was caught off guard when Mom handed me a letter from Ari. My mind had already been absorbed by football games, practices, and the upcoming homecoming dance. Throwing my school books and cheerleading things aside, I rushed upstairs to my room, praying I'd be able to read what Ari wrote, as he only wrote in Greek. I plopped down on my daybed and started to read his letter. The beginning was typical, filled with thoughts about missing me and recalling our great summer together. But further along in the letter, he introduced intentions of moving to the United States to live, and I almost fell off of my daybed. I wasn't sure I was getting the translation correctly, but Ari wrote something about work permits and visas, a topic I knew little about.

I didn't say anything to my mother about his plan because I knew I'd get a heavy load of "I told you so." Instead, I left the topic alone. In fact, I left the letter alone, too. I didn't know how to answer Ari, so I just didn't. Bad choice. A few weeks later, I got another, slightly angry letter, asking again about visas and whether he should question my feelings for him. Suddenly, I felt that I had done something wrong. I wrote back, apologizing for not responding, making up an excuse about schoolwork keeping me busy day and night. I also confessed to him that I didn't know much about the green card process and that I wasn't familiar with what it would take for him to work in the United States. I told him that I would much rather we discuss this topic in person when I came to Greece that following June. He wrote back that he understood and that he wanted me to do well in school, keeping my concentration on my studies. He said he'd take care of everything and not to worry—that we would talk about it over the summer.

Call it immaturity, but I didn't take him seriously. Wrapped up in practicing for the homecoming parade, I gave Ari's intentions little thought. Never did I imagine he was serious about coming to Chicago. I put the whole situation to the back of my mind. *Besides,* I thought, *how could a gorgeous, single guy like Ari, who lived in a city as big as Athens, possibly go without a girlfriend all winter?* Surely he dated someone when I returned to America. I would be fooling myself to believe that Ari stayed home every Friday night thinking of his little American teenaged girlfriend.

As the last of the snow melted and graduation neared, Mom and I began to talk about returning to Greece. I had picked a local college about an hour away but would live on campus. Since I needed time to pack for school, we would only travel for five weeks instead of the usual seven. By then, my sister and brother were both out of college and consumed with their careers. Mom and I would travel alone once more.

Looking back on that late spring and early summer of 1988, I remember how invincible I felt. Senior year of high school had passed so quickly. I happily anticipated another trip to Greece and life at college when I returned. Rania and her mom planned their trip to Greece, as well. The future appeared bright. After the prom, graduation, and a huge party with all of my friends, I was ready to head back to Greece for the summer of 1988.

One night, while packing for the trip, I was watching the news when a story about Greece came on as the leading story. I stopped and looked at the screen. The newscaster mentioned something about wildfires.

"What's *that* all about?" I asked Mom.

"Oh, they happen all the time. It's because of the high temperatures—nothing to worry about," she said dismissively.

"I never remember any fires," I said.

"Yeah, they happen. We're too busy having a good time to pay attention," she responded.

I watched the television that showed villagers throwing buckets of water onto burning olive fields. "Wow. Looks serious. Where's the fire department?" I asked my mother, pointing at the scene.

"Honey, when do you *ever* remember seeing a fire truck in Sparta? There are none," she said as a matter of fact, without taking her eyes off of the stacks of clothes she folded.

"How comforting." I shut my suitcase and dragged it into the hallway.

That was the last I thought about fires until a week later when Ari showed up at passport control. His first words hit me like a brick wall.

"Vassara is burning." He solemnly looked at me with sad eyes.

Those words will haunt me for a lifetime. More than twenty years later, I still get chills remembering how Ari greeted me upon arrival with such horrible news. This was our third summer together, and I was so excited to see him. Mom and I had just landed in Athens, and there he stood, holding a bouquet of pink roses. Ari's otherwise cheerful expression held concern.

What?" I asked, breaking apart from our embrace. A sense of fear and disappointment enveloped me like a thick blanket. My intention for our romantic reunion shattered instantly.

"It's on fire," he repeated. "It has been for days."

"What are you talking about?" I asked anxiously.

Ari explained how wildfires developed in the region surrounding our village due to record-breaking heat. His parents' nearby village of Tsintzina was vulnerable, as well. The fires came about suddenly, he said, without warning. Ari described how damaging flames raged through olive groves in the Taygetos Mountains, burning the orchards of the local villagers. He said the devastation was unreal, and that at any moment, the fires could gain momentum and burn homes. Mom and I stood in disbelief. We knew Greece's hot, dry climate made the country vulnerable to such disasters. However, in all the years we traveled to Mom's birthplace, we never experienced a wildfire firsthand.

"What do we do now?" I turned to Mom.

"We'll just have to wait and see after we get to Sparta," Mom replied.

Ari put his arm around me. "Don't worry. Stay in Magoula for now. You're safe there. I'm sorry to burden you with unhappy news." He paused and then said, "It's good to see you, sweetheart." He kissed my forehead, showing discretion in front of my mother. I held his hand as we walked through the airport.

"When are you coming to Peloponnese from Athens? You said in your last letter that you weren't sure."

Ari shook his head. "I still don't know. I was there briefly to see the damage, but I had to return to Eurobank right away. I'll be back to see you as soon as I can."

"Will you take long? You know I'm only here five weeks this year."

"Don't worry, *koukla*, we'll have time together. You look great, by the way—more beautiful each year."

I laid my hand on his cheek. "Thanks, old man." I had to tease him, reminding him that he was ten years my senior.

He held my wrist and rubbed his finger across the gold bracelet he had given me a year earlier. "You wear it all the time?" he asked me.

"I never take it off," I answered, smiling at him. He returned my grin with a concentrated look that made me uneasy.

The threat of fires only added to my apprehension for the trip. Although I was ecstatic to be in Greece again, Ari's recent letters had me uneasy about seeing him, as he was intently more serious about our relationship. I could tell by his expression that keeping our relationship at a comfortable pace for me was going to be a challenge. I knew the discussion regarding his green card was coming, but it would have to be put off for a while. The last thing I was ready for was to plan our future together. "There will be time for that a few years from now," I thought innocently.

We stepped away briefly at baggage claim and kissed before he went back to work. I smiled into his eyes, which seemed a little older, his hair showing the first signs of gray. Even the lines around his smile were deeper than last year. I didn't mind. He was still as handsome and sweet as ever. Ari escorted me to customs, where Mom and I met up with Spiro, our ever-faithful cab driver. The look on his face was ominous, as well.

"Peloponnese is on fire," Spiro warned, waving his arms in the air.

"Here we go again," I thought, irritated with his dramatics. The news was bad enough coming from someone I adored, let alone Spiro, who was over the top about everything. I told this to Mom in English so that he wouldn't understand. Spiro's English was terrible. Mom agreed, and we both laughed.

But as Spiro's cab made its way down to Sparta, we saw smoke in the distance and discerned for ourselves that the fires were no dramatic exaggeration. They were real. The exact proximity to the village was hard to tell, but the faint smell of burning brushwood put me on edge.

We stayed in Magoula a few days more than usual, making sure the roads were safe. A day or so later, the winds shifted, and the fires left the area. Despina kept calling me on the phone in Magoula, yelling, "When are you coming? It's fine. C'mon!"

Rania was still in Chicago, as her arrival to Greece was later than mine that year. Despina was anxious for company. After a few days of unpacking and shopping at the bazaars of Sparta, we decided to make our way to Vassara. Nothing, not even fires, could keep us from seeing our beloved village.

"If it's bad, we can always turn back," Mom offered optimistically.

Thankfully, we never needed to turn back. The fires were gone, but the devastation along the countryside was heartbreaking. Roads out of Sparta were green for a while, but as soon as we hit the fork in the road, making our turnoff to enter the hills of Parnonas, everything turned black. Hundreds upon hundreds of olive trees were destroyed. The hills that once took my breath away with their beauty and luscious green now left me speechless in concern. A horrible and still unforgettable smell of burned brush lingered in the air that entire summer, a smell that has never left my senses. Only the immediate area on the outskirts of Vassara showed live vegetation. As we neared the village, we realized how close the fires had come to our beloved village. Vassara stood unharmed, even by this latest tragedy.

Approaching the *platia*, the expressions of the villagers proved that the flames had left their marks on everyone's spirits, as well. Gone was the typical summer smile on Vassarean faces. Although the town had swelled with visitors for the season, the *kefi*, or mood, of the place was low. Many families from Vassara lost their fields of olive trees, almond trees, and even livestock. This would mean hard economic times to come without crops to sell in the coming winter. Their faces were full of pain. My heart broke for them. The old men and women sitting at Brikakis' café tables outside the store looked puzzled and worrisome, with eyes bloodshot as if they had been crying for days. Uncle Georgo, Aunt Vivi, and Kiki greeted us. Even though we knew they were glad to see us, we didn't receive the same overwhelming outpouring of joy as in years past.

"*Kaikane olla*" (Everything has burned), Aunt Vivi cried to Mom, who embraced her with tears and then held her face with her hands as she sobbed.

"*Kala, oxi olla, to xorio einai entaxi*" (Okay, not everything, the village is okay), Kiki corrected her in a toughened tone.

"*Tha xana fitepsoume*" (We will rebuilt and replant the trees), Stathi defiantly declared as he held up his fist.

"*Emeis na eimaste kala*" (As long as we're okay), Uncle Georgo reminded everyone.

I flashed back in my mind to our 1984 arrival, just after my aunt died. Like then, we once again shared the sadness with our relatives but looked to the future with optimism.

After settling in, Despina and I escaped the obligatory family dinner as soon as possible and went up to Koulouri. I was anxious to get a better view of the fire's damage. Across the edge of the cliff stood the same breathtaking sight of luscious, green cypress trees towering to the sky. Yet, to the right, threatening patches of black, charred earth were a grim display of the tragedy and loss over recent weeks.

"It must have been so scary," I gasped as I looked across the scorched area.

"It still is," she glumly replied. "I don't want to worry you, but the wildfires are really bad this year. We won't be totally free from them until this heat wave ends. That won't be until early September."

I stood silently for while, taking in her words. Despina wasn't the pessimistic type, so I knew the situation had to be serious if my cousin was concerned. After a moment, I asked, "How's Stavros?" Despina looked at me in surprise and didn't answer. "Oh, c'mon," I said as I smiled at her. "When have I ever *not* asked about him?"

"Isn't your mind on Ari?" She looked confused.

"Sure it is, but with the fires … I don't know, I just couldn't help but wonder about him," I confessed.

"Honestly, he's been working day and night organizing fire relief, even scheduling us girls to pull shifts as watchers, looking for flames headed toward the village after the sun goes down."

"Of course he's in charge," I said sarcastically. She laughed.

I saw Stavros for the first time that night down at the *platia*, sitting with Demetri and Grigori and Niko, all of whom I was eager to greet. I gave Demetri a big hug and greeted the others, not caring what any of them thought as I handed my good friend a Chicago Bulls T-shirt. Our local team had just won the NBA World Championship Series, and since Demetri was a basketball fanatic, I knew he'd enjoy this gift. The guys teased him for a while, but he ignored them. Everyone knew what good friends we had become.

Stavros looked me up and down in my floral tank dress. He smiled, saying,

"You are a young woman now, aren't you?" I just smiled, but I didn't say anything in return. I couldn't.

Although the kids were affected by the fires, as well, we tried as a group to regain some of our summer joy despite the tragedy. We hung out in the *platia* late that night, singing songs and drinking in the moonlight. Although the fires were still in the back of everyone's mind, the golden days shone on, and over time, we returned, even if not completely, to our typical routine with caution. Looming in the back of everyone's mind was the thought that at any moment, wildfires could kick up again, and danger would return.

Still, sitting around and feeling sorry for ourselves wouldn't make for a fun vacation. While more fire-free days passed, we found ourselves enjoying daily water fights and soccer games, trying to make the most of the long, hot summer days. The real party got into swing after Rania's arrival. By the time she arrived, little was mentioned of the fires. Rania brought Stavros's little brother Vasili a Bulls T-shirt, as well. I waited for her to get to the village before we gave Panteli his Chicago T-shirt. He loved his gift from "the Chicago Girls" that showed the Sears Tower and had the word Chicago written boldly across the front in yellow. He laughed when he tried the shirt on for the first time, and he wore it every day.

Two weeks later, Mom and I decided to have a big party for the feast day of August 15. Called simply *Panayia's* in Greek, this day commemorates the falling asleep of the Virgin Mary and her ascension into heaven. This is also the name's day of anyone named Maria or Mary. August 15 is one of the most celebrated days in Greece and throughout most of Europe. Everything shuts down in countries like Italy and France. Greece is no exception. Since Eurobank and all of the other banks would be closed for the holiday, Ari planned to return from Athens in order to lend a helping hand at his father's restaurant. I looked forward to seeing him.

Mom and I planned a big get-together with all of our relatives, complete with cocktails at our house, followed by dinner at Moustokotou's taverna. Mom and I cleaned for days and made American-style appetizers to entertain our Vassara relatives as well as my father's relatives from nearby Tripoli, who would be joining us, as well. My mother was close to my dad's cousins, Uncle Ted and Aunt Thora, and their two kids, Melania and Prokopi. They also were bringing Ted's sister, Aunt Gia, and her husband, Uncle Petros. These relatives rarely left Tripoli and often waited for Mom and me to visit Tripoli to see them. Tripoli was about forty-five minutes away. Needless to say, I never wanted to leave Vassara to visit our Tripoli relatives. Quite often, Mom left me in Vassara with Yiayia so that she could see them in their nearby city while I stayed with my friends in the village. Both Uncle Ted and Uncle Petros were following each other in their cars to the village for the party.

While Mom put on her fancy white dress with a ruffle at the bottom and a big black silk flower in her hair, I headed down to the *platia* to hang with Rania before company arrived. I complained to my cousin about how much party preparation I endured while we played backgammon outside Brikakis' cafe. That's when we heard some old men talking at the next table about another wildfire in the area. We asked Panteli. He said it was nothing to worry about yet. But around five o'clock that day, just as Mom and I finished setting up tables downstairs, the unmistakable sound of clanging bells rang loud and fast throughout the town. Their rapid banging meant only one thing—a warning.

I looked at Mom inquisitively. "What is that for?" I asked, knowing the answer.

"I'm not sure. We'd better see what's up," she said.

My heart raced as I grew nervous, quickening my pace alongside Mom down the cobblestone roads, anxious to get to the town square where someone would know something. I scanned the hills in the distance but didn't see any smoke. We turned a corner leading into the *platia,* where we were suddenly stopped by an old lady. She flung open the shutters of her kitchen window and asked us who we were. This was not the time for genealogy questioning. I wanted to keep walking, but Mom was more polite.

"Eimai tis Thiamanto's I kori" (I am the daughter of Diamanto), Mom dutifully answered.

"Oh, my child, please come in," the old lady insisted.

"Mom!" I interrupted. "C'mon. We have to go see what's going on!"

"What does the child say?" asked the old lady.

"The bells—they are ringing," Mom informed the old lady.

"Yes, yes, I know. The wildfires have returned," she said ever so calmly, as if there was nothing to fear.

"Isn't she worried?" I asked Mom in amazement. The old lady looked at me as if *I* were the illogical person for being alarmed. My face must have registered the heightened sense of worry I felt in my heart, fearing we were all in grave danger. The old lady came toward me and put her hand on my shoulder, saying something I didn't understand. Mom translated, "If God wants to take us, He will. There is nothing we can do," and that we should "come in and sit for a cool drink because we looked thirsty." Clearly, we needed to get away as soon as possible.

"Mom, can we *please* go?" I begged.

"We'll just come in for a moment." Mom gave in to the old lady for what reason I shall never know. Mom continued, "We can't stay long. We have guests coming."

"You do? From where?" the old lady asked.

Mom went on to explain our plans to the old lady, shouting her answers back as I grew increasingly nervous about the bell that rang louder and louder, ominously warning all villagers. Out of the old lady's window, we heard a few people run past, shouting, *"Fotia"*(Fire)!

I glared at Mom, who seemed unable to break away from this seemingly hospitable old lady, while pandemonium broke out around us. I sat in disbelief that my mother was unable to escape from this old lady so we could run or do something to get us out of this clearly urgent situation.

The old lady came out of her kitchen, shuffling across her dining room floor, barely able to carry a tray that shook in her hands, holding small glass dishes filled with orange Jell-O. She handed each plate to Mom and me as if we were attending a garden tea party without a care in the world. I couldn't take the pressure and started to tear up. I didn't know what was happening around us, but I knew it was something bad. Were we trapped? Where was the fire? What should we do?

Mom saw my tears and finally ended our visit. We left as quickly and politely as we could and headed straight to the *platia,* where many of the villagers were gathered in a large group, most of them yelling. We stood back and listened as the men organized themselves into firefighting shifts. Apparently, our worst fears had come to fruition. The fires were back, and they were headed our way. Calls were made to the local authorities to send fire relief planes to the Parnonas hills, but their response time was anyone's guess. Soon, our phone service would be in jeopardy, as well as the power lines, the first victims to the flames after the orchards of trees.

Stavros, Maki, and some others gave direction to men of all ages, even the old men who surely saw themselves as viable contributors. They were given shifts of duty and instructions. American men and boys prepared themselves, as well, ready to work right alongside their Greek counterparts. Women had jobs, too. Some were lookouts. Others helped bring livestock in from the fields. Most of the women gathered water. The old ladies in black, however, gave themselves the job of praying in the village church. Surely God would listen to their prayers. Rania and I stood frozen in shock, not quite knowing what to do.

That's when my uncle Ted's car came barreling across the *platia's* cobblestone street, screeching to a halt in front of us. Their dramatic entrance would normally have caused a huge reaction by the locals, but everyone was distracted. Even when Uncle Ted and Aunt Thora came screaming out of the car, yelling at us to grab our things and come with them as soon as possible because the village would burn, no one paid any attention to their antics. They reminded me of a scene from Barnum and Bailey's Circus, where a small clown car pulls up and a hundred clowns come out of the small vehicle, all shouting and making crazy gestures. Even though the villagers were too distracted to notice their behavior, I still flushed in embarrassment.

Uncle Foti, Aunt Thora, and my cousins Melania and Prokopi each began shouting their own story of what they had seen on the road from Tripoli to Vassara and how they begged the driver, my uncle Ted, to turn around. They described the intensity of the fires, one comment more drastic and scary than the next. No one told us not to worry; no one said to stay calm. They were in complete hysteria and pleaded with us to leave with them for Tripoli.

We had only minutes to decide, but we declined their offer. There was clearly no room for us in their small, jam-packed cars. Additionally, we couldn't follow them in our own car because Pappou and Yiayia left with the Audi a few days earlier to take mineral baths in the oceanside town of Methena. Lastly, I think that Mom's instincts served her well, as she must have determined that we were better off staying where we were for the time being.

Mom and I returned home to a house set up for a party that would not be. We were scared, and we were sad. I desperately wanted to get on a plane and leave Greece altogether. As the smell of fire grew stronger, we could see a bright orange glow, as well as smoke in the far-off hills, and we knew somewhere out there, our loved ones were battling life-threatening flames. Rania eventually came over, and without knowing what to do, we packed our suitcases in case we decided to make a quick exit. Tatzaforo warned that, as a last resort, we could escape the fires from the back roads of Vassara, leading through Tsintzina and out toward the back side of the Parnonas Mountain region. This was an old, treacherous road, he explained, one much less traveled. Surely the ride wouldn't be easy, but at least we had a way out. I was relieved that we had an option. My heart ached for those fighting the flames, wondering what would become of them and all that they had.

Chapter 17
The Miracle

A FEW HOURS WENT by, and Rania and I became stir-crazy. Aunt Vivi was at our house helping Mom put food away. I couldn't stand to sit still, but I didn't know where else to go. The *platia* was no longer our desired destination, as the square had become a panic-stricken command center where the villagers discussed fire strategy. The first few shifts of men started to return from firefighting. Many were injured. Brikakis' café instantly turned into a makeshift first-aid station headed by Mrs. Brikaki and a few other women. Together, they worked in sync to bandage cuts and handle burns on exhausted firefighting volunteers. I wanted to avoid the nonsense talk heard throughout the *platia* as the elderly discussed what might happen, what could happen, and what they believed surely would happen to all of us. Rania and I decided to leave the *platia* when we heard one lady yell out, "The village will burn for sure!" Another old man insisted, "The winds are picking up and will soon destroy our power lines. Get ready for another blackout!" Their opinions were stated as fact, and one assumption was worse than the next. We kept walking, unsure of where to go.

As we passed along the long road leading toward the tavern and Koulouri, we noticed a small crowd of young boys gathered at Moustokotou's place. It must have been around ten o'clock in the evening. The music was off, but there were tables set up, and my cousin and I decided to join them. This was no party. The mood was grim. We sat together in this separate place, away from the dramatics of the *platia*. We wanted to be with each other, to grieve, to talk, and get through this difficult night together.

One by one, the firefighting groups came in from their shifts, making their way down the tavern steps to rest before being called back to the front lines. Moustokotou's tavern was like a secret safe house, away from the town panic. Instead of sitting at one large table, we sat in smaller groups, our eyes watching the doorway as each new group of boys came back from the fires. With every new arrival, the weary volunteers explained the location of the flames and the status of fires. Then they sat for a meal. Likewise, as one group returned, another table of boys stood up to leave and got ready to return to the fires again. The exchange of boys was hard to watch, especially as the groups returned with injuries. Many stopped at Brikakis' café to have their bandaged limbs looked at by the women. My stomach hurt as I worried about my friends.

Despina was not there to console me. She, along with Kosma's sister, Panayiota, was placed at Agio Sotira's Church as a lookout. They kept their eyes peeled as winds shifted throughout the night, on alert to the town if flames came from a new direction. Should that occur, they would ring the church's bell as a signal. I was scared for my cousin, as well. The whole night was surreal. Midnight quickly approached. We were tired, but no one could sleep. Determined to stay awake for safety reasons, I feared the fires might get too close to the village, and Mom and I would have to make our escape with Tatzaforo through the rugged back roads.

My heart stopped when Stavros came through the tavern doorway just before 1:00 am. Covered in dirt and soot from head to toe, he limped down the stairs, blood staining the leg of his pants. A bandage wrapped around his left hand. He seemed okay, but he was hurt. Several from his group were injured, as well. They trailed behind, still at Brikakis' café getting bandaged up. I'll never forget the grave look on Stavros's face. He was truly distraught. Instead of joining his friends or greeting anyone, he discreetly walked to the corner of the tavern and sat at a lone table beneath the darkness of a tree. Mr. Moustokotou went over to him with a small glass and poured a shot of whiskey. Stavros downed the alcohol in one fast swig, and the owner poured him another. He drank the second as quickly as the first and sat back in the shadows of the branches above him.

In the darkness, I was unable to see his face, but I knew Stavros didn't drink whiskey. He would never sit alone, either. Whatever he experienced fighting the wildfires must have shaken him, as he retreated inward. When the rest of the boys from his shift made their way down the tavern steps, we could see this shift was hit the hardest. Each volunteer was badly wounded, not one of them without a bloody bandage on more than one limb. Some boys couldn't make it to the tavern and were carried home from Brikakis'.

My insides felt like they were caving in as I watched the whole scene from the chair in which I had spent so many joyous nights, partying until dawn in the happy tavern. Fear of the unknown and what would become of our village hung in the air like a thick fog, and the more injured men that arrived, the deeper my mood fell. I sat in my chair, trying to hide my face as tears silently flowed down my cheeks. I was scared. I was sad. I wanted to go home. I felt sorry for my friends. Seeing them in physical pain, cut and bruised, was more than I could bear. Images of the smoke and flames and the sound of the church bell ringing played over and over in my head. I just wept, hoping no one would notice.

Stavros called a young boy over to his table. The boy, about ten, stood in front of Stavros like a little soldier. He said something to the boy, who then came to me. The boy whispered in my ear that Stavros wanted to see me. I didn't know Stavros noticed my presence and dreaded talking to him, as I was still a crying mess. Wiping the tears from my face and forcing a smile, I stood up from the table with the weight of everyone's eyes on my back. My face flushed as I walked across the tavern to his table in the corner. Like the attentive boy, I, too, stood in front of Stavros. Before he said a word, I exchanged looks with Rania. That's when I noticed that while I couldn't make out Stavros's face in the shadows, he was able to see all of us quite clearly from where he was sitting. "Isn't that just like him," I thought, "always able to read my emotions while I am consistently blinded in understanding anything about his feelings."

"*Yiati cles*" (Why are you crying)? he asked.

"Don't you know?" I sniffled.

"You're okay, aren't you?" He looked me up and down as if I had a cut or bruise on my skin.

"Yeah, but—"

He interrupted, saying, "It's going to be okay." His forced smile was little comfort.

"How badly are you hurt?" I looked at his bleeding leg.

"I'll be fine—just a few cuts from the branches." He disregarded his wounds to downplay his injury, but I knew better. I knew where he had been, and I knew what he saw was horrific. His tone was almost patronizing, as if I were a fool to worry. I knew I had reason to worry. He knew it, too, but did his best to downplay the situation.

Suddenly, a tidal wave of emotions erupted within me. With eyes clouded, the air seemed to weigh a thousand pounds. The moment held still in silence. I desperately wanted to lay my emotions on the table next to his empty whiskey glass. I longed for Stavros to know I was concerned about him, and that after all this time, despite everything, my feelings for him remained strong. I wanted him to know that I wished things had worked out differently between us. I wanted him to know that no one, not even Ari, ever captured my heart as much as he did. I couldn't say the words but somehow wished he knew. I just stood there, speechless, hoping my eyes would convey what my mouth could not.

"Don't be afraid," he said. "Everything will be all right." He looked right through me with his insightful eyes, challenging my fears with faith.

"Promise?" I said with a half smile.

"*Sigoura*" (For sure), he said as he grinned sweetly.

"Can I get you anything?" I asked, looking at his empty whiskey glass, still surprised that he drank the first.

"No, I'm fine. You should get some sleep. Try not to be upset, okay?"

I nodded, slowly backing out of his shadows. I glanced up at him one last time, and he held my look sincerely. Walking back to be with the girls, my heart broke for him all over again.

"What'd he say?" Rania anxiously asked before I could sit down at my table.

"Nothing important," I replied artificially, unable to explain an eternity of emotions.

Eventually, all of the guys went back to the line of fires that night. There were shifts throughout the evening, but for Americans like Rania and I, we had little to do but wait and pray. Sleeping was out of the question, but by 2:30 am, exhaustion took its toll, and we left the tavern. When we reached our houses, Rania suggested we sit up atop her balcony together. She brought blankets out to the terrace, and we sat with our feet up on two white plastic chairs. I needed to be with her that night, and she needed to be with me. We anxiously waited for sunrise. But as the final moments of the Virgin Mary's feast day elapsed, smoke in the evening's air permeated our senses, and we fell asleep.

That's when the miracle happened. I suppose it only makes sense that the Mother of God's blessing took place during the early morning hours as the countryside held itself in a moment of solace. There, in that instant, and certainly not for the first time, the Virgin Mary saved her people. Out of nowhere, the fervent winds shifted, and the flames from the wildfires that ravaged the landscape all night, destroying hundreds of olive groves throughout the Parnonas hills, were stopped cold in their tracks. The flames reached no closer than the front gate of the monastery, with its large, golden icon of the Virgin Mary. Perhaps the quiet, little nun, Ourania, having obeyed the vision from her dreams to build these churches less than a decade earlier, was the greatest firefighter of all.

Some say the evening breeze caused the flames to change direction. Others credit the men and boys who fought the flames throughout the night. Surely their efforts don't go unnoticed, but most of the people who where there that night believe it was the Virgin Mary that kept the fires from burning village homes down to the ground.

Even as the night unfolded, I was certain the experience would live on in my memory for the rest of my life. As I look back years later, I am astonished at the miraculous event we experienced. How blessed we were to have been saved, along with our town. "What is it about this place that makes Vassara so blessed by God and so endeared by the Virgin Mary to be saved?" I ask myself repeatedly, although I know the answer is far beyond any human comprehension. Is Vassara's survival because of its ability to change the people who go there? Perhaps so. Whether our burden is due to war or death or famine or fire, this village manages to calm, love, and heal the pain. Over again through time like the Virgin Mary herself, Vassara accepts our suffering and ingests our afflictions into its loving heart. What is given back to us in return is a healing peace, that we might reenter the world outside the boundaries of Parnonas and share our joy to enlighten others. This is what I've come to understand and believe about my village.

The following day was obviously a day of celebration. Everyone was grateful that the threat of fire was over. Many villagers gathered their families at tables in the *platia* to break bread in honor of the simple fact that we were all alive and had survived a horrific night. With the wildfires diminished, Vassara was finally clear of any imminent danger, and everyone seemed to dismiss the threat as if we were guaranteed safety.

I, however, was unable to relax like the rest of the villagers. I was horrified. The panic and fear Stavros saw on my face remained, and all I wanted to do was leave. Mom didn't disagree. We seemed to be the only two who wanted to escape. I invited Rania to come with us to Sparta, but she wanted to stay. Mom and I packed our things and said good-bye to the relatives and Rania and left for Magoula before dinner that day. Our departure angered our relatives, especially Tatz. They didn't understand. In their minds, the threat was over, so our leaving didn't make sense. For us, we felt lucky to escape near tragedy, and we weren't about to wait around for another wildfire. We wanted out of Vassara.

I was never so happy to see the house in Magoula. Even the bee-infested, green gate didn't bother me as I did my duck and run to enter into the courtyard and put my suitcase upstairs. Yiayia and Pappou had returned from Methena and waited for us at a table near Yiayia's roses. Yiayia was so glad to see us, although I really don't think she grasped the whole idea of how dangerous our situation truly was. We didn't want to burden her with all of the scary details, so we put our bags away and sat in her garden, listening to their news of Methena and updates regarding their mineral bath treatments. Yiayia said she felt like a new woman. She looked great. Magoula looked great. Everything out of the scorched Parnonas hills looked great. Life was green again, and I wasn't sure I ever wanted to enter that area again.

The few days in Sparta felt like a vacation from Vassara. For the first time, I enjoyed the solitude our house provided. The isolation didn't bother me one bit. I spent the next couple of days with nothing else to do except sunbathe atop our balcony alone.

"You'd better be careful in the sun up here!" Mom warned me as I spread out on a beach towel over our hot, white marble terrace with a bottle of Coppertone and my beloved boom box. Basking in the Mediterranean sun, I tried to soak up the last rays of summer as the inevitable time to return to Chicago approached. I woke myself up early enough each day to go with Mom into Sparta for the bazaar, and I helped bring back fruit and vegetables with Yiayia, while occasionally assisting in the cooking of our afternoon meal.

Life in Magoula was without drama. As the lazy days of summer lingered on slowly, I finished reading *The Sun Also Rises* by Hemmingway and began to write poems. Feeling a bit lonely and overcome with emotion, I had a lot of feelings to express on paper about what we experienced in the village. I stayed up late almost every night, alone under the star-studded sky above the Magoula terrace, writing pages and pages of love and fear, anticipation, and introspection. Slowly, I came to the realization that Vassara wasn't the only place in which I could happily live out my tomorrows and that I was indeed an American at heart who may one day need to return home for good.

Each afternoon, usually before dinner, Despina or Rania would call, complaining on the other end of the line that I had deserted them and asking when I was coming back to Vassara.

"I don't know," was my standard answer, and truthfully, I had no idea.

"Demetri's been asking about you," Rania would say.

"Tell him I'm just too freaked out still. I'm not ready to come back," I said.

In the meantime, Ari called, as well, apologizing for not being able to get down to the village to see me. He was just as upset about the fires, and he was glad that we had moved ourselves back to the Magoula house for the remainder of our trip. He apologized a hundred times for not spending more time with me during my vacation, explaining how the fires affected his time off and that his boss called him back to work unexpectedly. I could tell he felt horrible.

"I'll for sure see you in Athens," he said sadly over the phone. He added, "Can you come earlier?" I couldn't. There was no way Mom was going to go for that. "I checked into the paperwork," he mentioned.

"Paperwork for what?" I had no idea what he was talking about.

"The papers … for a green card." My heart stopped.

"You do want me to come to the States, right?" he asked.

"Of course," I said, not knowing what else to say.

"Well, I'll talk to you more about it at the airport," he said.

The words "visa" and "green card" stuck in my head for the rest of that day. Again, I didn't dare mention it to Mom, but Ari's plan to move to Chicago seemed to be picking up steam. I couldn't deal with the concept. My head was still spinning from the fires.

The next day, Mom asked me if I wanted to go back to Vassara. Both of us realized that we had to see everyone one last time, even if it was just to say good-bye for the summer. With the wildfires totally gone and the weather changing to rain, taming the heat wave, we decided to return for the last two days of our trip in Greece and then head to Tripoli to see my father's relatives. From there, we would go directly to Athens and leave for Chicago. I was glad the trip was coming to an end. That summer had been such a letdown compared to the previous summer. I had barely seen Ari, and as it appeared, we'd only share airport moments this year.

That night when the phone rang upstairs, I was certain it was going to be Rania again, but the voice on the other end of the line was deep.

"*Pou eisai*" (Where are you)? a man asked.

"Demetri!" I answered with joy, taking the receiver and stretching the long cord into my Magoula bedroom for privacy. Clothes and suitcases were scattered all over the room in preparation for our trip home. I cleared a place on the bed to lay while I spoke with my friend.

"You're wasting your days away in Magoula! What's wrong with you?" he persisted.

"Oh, Demetri." I started to cry. "Are you guys okay?"

"We're *fine*. Don't be afraid. The fires are over. You *know* that." He let out a sigh on his end. "You Americans! You're not used to such excitement, are you? Vassara isn't the same here without you. Get back before you leave, okay?"

"I will. We're coming up tomorrow." I looked around at the mess, hand on my forehead, knowing I'd be up all night packing.

"That's a good thing, because we're going to party at Moustokotou's one last time, okay? I can't believe you're missing the festival again."

"I know, but I have to move into my dorm next week. Sorry," I explained as I let out a big sigh.

"Just get back here. I can't function without my *kolite*," he said. There was affection in his voice that seemed uninhibited for the first time, as if the fires had brought out the truth in everyone's heart.

I sat up and held the receiver with both hands, saying quietly, "I know. Me, either. See you tomorrow."

I stood to hang up the phone, but he added, "One more thing."

"What?" I asked.

He paused and then said, "Vassara is *still* your special place. I know you're

scared, but it's over. You can't stop loving the village because of the fires, okay?"
I looked out the window as he said those words, watching the late afternoon
sun stream a white ray of light across Mount Taygetos, offering a stark contrast
to the already shaded crevices deep in the mountain's shape. Evening was
coming, and Taygetos basked in one last shine before nightfall.

"You always read me, don't you?" There was an awkward silence. Neither
of us knew what to say.

Then he cheerfully added, "That's my job. I'm your *kolite!*"

"I'm glad you called." I took the receiver back to the base and hung up
the phone, and then I returned to my bedroom to figure out what to wear for
our farewell trip to the village.

Chapter 18
Under a Broken Streetlight

OUR FAREWELL VISIT TO Vassara would only last one night, so I packed a small bag. The plan was to make a quick visit, say good-bye to the family, and head to Tripoli, where we would do the same with my father's cousins. Their tiny town of Steno was located just outside Tripoli. Although my mother was excited to spend time with them, I dreaded the detour. I figured we would have to endure a lot of criticism for not leaving the village with them the night of the fires. Our relatives from Tripoli were overly dramatic about everything, so certainly our refusal would be seen as a big deal. At least we were going to Vassara first.

When our car turned off the main road at the fork, I prepared myself to see a changed topography from the fire's damage. With the devastation of the second fire, the hillside's destruction was much more extensive. Entire olive fields were completely scorched; not one of them showed any sign of life. Turn after turn revealed devastated countryside, and an unforgettable smell of burned trees lingered in the air. So sad. Mom and I were astonished by the charred, black path that reached the village. We witnessed for ourselves how close the flames had come to Vassara's doorstep, ending at the entrance of the Virgin Mary's church, named *Panayia Eleftherosa*, or The Virgin Mary, the Liberator. Indeed profound. The Mother of God gave us life that night. Beyond the charcoaled earth stood her village, ever protected, ever alive, and surviving.

When our car pulled into the *platia*, I was a bit apprehensive, still feeling guilty about leaving town after the fires. I didn't want anyone to think I had abandoned our village, even though I had. However, my true hesitation came from a fear that another wildfire might develop and trap us again.

Demetri and his brother Grigori shot baskets near Brikakis' as we pulled up, and I asked Pappou to let me out of the car. Rania was waiting on a bench nearby.

"What took you so long?" she shouted as I got out of the car nervously.

"My Pappou had to stop for gas," I explained.

"*Kalosorisate*" (Welcome)! Grigori shouted over to me. Demetri winked. "That was weird," I thought. Maybe not. Rania didn't catch it. I just smiled. The boys stopped playing ball, and we made our way over to some tables outside Brikakis' and sat under a shaded tree.

"So, what are we doing tonight, guys?" Rania asked the ball players.

"We're having a party at the town hall building," Grigori said. That's when Stavros's little brother, Vasili, came over to us. The kids welcomed me back wholeheartedly, which put my mind at ease. Vasili didn't look at Rania. She ignored him, too. I snickered, realizing their flirting had finally materialized. The two of them were trying so hard to act indifferent. When the boys resumed their game and left our bench, I pushed my cousin away with both arms.

"You are *so* busted!" I said to Rania.

"Stop it!" she said as she smiled back. "It was really boring here without you."

"Uh-huh!" I laughed.

Now I knew why Rania asked about the plans for the evening. She wanted to spend quality time with Vasili as summer came to a close. A dance was a good idea. I was happy to spend my last night in Vassara with friends, absorbing all I could of the place before we flew home. Jaded as I was after the fires, I couldn't help but love the place and the people in it.

"Stavros is gone," Rania said suddenly when she saw me looking around the courtyard.

"Why?" I looked at her, surprised.

"Something about registering for classes in Athens. He won't be back until the festival, after you've left. I can't believe you're missing the party *again*!"

"Did he say to say 'bye'?" I asked. Vasili looked up at me. I don't think he ever understood my feelings for his older brother.

"Yeah, actually, he did. He said to tell you that you're a crazy American for missing the *panigiri* again and to have a *Kalo Ximona*," Rania answered. I was disappointed that I wouldn't see him again, especially after our exchange at Moustokotou's tavern.

Demetri picked up the ball he and Grigori were playing with and walked toward their home. "We're going to grab a bite to eat. See you tonight," he said as they walked away. Vasili got the hint that Rania and I wanted to talk and went home, as well.

Seconds after he walked away, I turned to my cousin. "I want *details!*" I looked right at her guilty face.

"Nah, there's nothing to tell. He's actually a nice guy. I'll tell you all about it tonight," she said.

"Yes, you will," I demanded. Then I thought about Demetri, the phone call, the wink. "Okay, what is up with Demetri? Is it just me, or is he acting strange?" I asked her, hoping she'd have some kind of insight.

"Oh, someone's friendship feelings are about to bust at the seams, I'm guessing," she offered.

I took a deep breath. As Demetri and I had been friends for years, both of us fared our share of teasing from everyone that our relationship was more than platonic. But we were just that. Although he was nice, funny, good looking, and more caring than most of the other guys, we simply remained each other's *kolite*. Even if Demetri liked me at some point, I never imagined he would act on those feelings, especially with Stavros around. I assumed Demetri had written me off years ago as a helpless girl, unable to shake her first love. But then came Ari. Maybe seeing me begin a relationship with someone new changed Demetri's mind. I thought about Ari and how weird he was acting lately, expecting me to arrange his move to Chicago. I was almost glad I hadn't seen him yet, able to avoid uncomfortable conversations about his green card. As for Demetri, I didn't dare risk ruining my bond with him. Our friendship meant too much to me. I shook my head to get rid of the whirlwind of thoughts and asked Rania if she wanted to take a walk up to the cliff before we headed home to grab dinner. I would finally have a chance to ask her privately about Vasili. While we walked up to Koulouri, she gave me the scoop.

"He's actually a really nice guy," she explained.

"Rania, I know. I've known him since he was twelve. He is nice. I'm just freaked out that he's Stavros's brother."

"*Trust* me." She threw her hands up in the air. "He's *nothing* like his brother! No offense."

"None taken. I don't know what my problem is. I think I'm still a little jittery about being here after the fires. You know, I vowed never to return to this place when I was in Magoula. My mind is so screwed up right now. Ari is starting to talk about green cards. *Green cards*, Rania! What is *that*?"

"Does he want to move to the States?" Rania asked.

"I have no idea, but that's the last thing I need right now. My mind should be on joining a sorority, not commiting myself for the rest of my life," I explained.

We walked on and reached Koulouri, making our way to the flattened surface that overlooked Vassara. This was always the place to come and contemplate the future, wonder about life, and reflect on the past. Somehow, the air up on Koulouri's cliff always seemed to bring answers to life's questions. I loved to stand at the edge of the rock, look out onto the vast, green mountainscape, and breathe in the cool air that swept across the hills no matter what time of day. The quiet that existed in this serene place had a lasting effect, and every problem became minimized atop this glorious viewpoint. Looking toward the mountains of Parnonas and the surrounding village from up high helped me to put everything into perspective. I knew something wasn't right with Ari, and I couldn't be pushed into making permanent plans for my future. Demetri, on the other had, was someone I adored in every sense. Our bond was undeniable, but I didn't want to sacrifice that friendship.

Rania let me alone at the edge while she smoked her cigarette on a rock behind me. A few minutes later, I sat down on the other side of the rock while she shared all the juicy details of her love affair with Vasili. I listened attentively. Being alone with her at Koulouri was like taking a time-out from Vassara. Time stood still. We gathered our thoughts and gave each other advice. Feeling the peacefulness of an approaching sunset, I could have had stayed up at the cliff all night, but when Rania told me we had to meet Despina, our time to contemplate the universe was over. Despina, who had taken the bus into Sparta earlier that morning, was due to return in the *platia* any moment. Both of us were anxious to meet her and make our girl power complete.

Walking down from Koulouri, Rania and I discussed what we'd wear to the dance that night. I had a teal blue minidress, saved for my last night in the village. It had a tank top with buttons that led down to a layered skirt. Vassara had already swelled with festival visitors for the following week. The energy in the streets was high. Villagers were especially anxious to celebrate the feast day of the Virgin Mary after being saved from the fire. I imagined our grotto-styled church up in the mountain would be packed with worshipers.

We met Despina's bus and returned home to change. When we headed back down to the *platia*, the music was already pumping out of loud speakers from the town hall building next door to Brikakis' café. Cleared out of inside furniture, the large, rectangle-shaped building had benches along each wall in a large room that had small, white lights strung across the ceiling, giving off a cool glow. The room looked like Vassara's version of prom, and I smiled at the hall's charm. Behind a table at one end, the guys were busy trying to figure out the stereo since their DJ, Stavros, was absent. Eventually, the boys got the music in sync, and young people gathered inside. Dancing to Madonna's "Vogue," Rania and I hogged the dance floor as if we owned it. Rania performed styled moves from the video, mastering a perfect performance of the song. Everyone watched her, impressed with her skill.

When the pop music finished and the songs slowed down, Vasili danced with Rania. My cousin and her Vassarean boyfriend swayed the dance floor while "Take My Breath Away" turned the air romantic. Demetri held out his hand to dance with me as he had done a million times before. That night, however, things seemed different—his body was a little closer than usual … his looks lingered a bit longer. After our dance, Demetri said little while we talked with the other kids.

Later, Kosma and Niko switched the slow American songs over to loud Greek music, and once again, the town hall building became alive with energetic lines of *sirto* dancers. More and more kids joined in, and before long, the air grew hot and stuffy. Rania, Despina, and I decided to take a break from the party and sit outside at Brikakis' tables to cool off in the evening breeze.

Countless stars illuminated the dark sky. Most of the adults in the *platia* had gone home, leaving only our group of partiers in the town square. While the traditional tunes pumped a muffled beat behind the building's walls, my cousins and I were glad to be out of the overcrowded building to enjoy the *platia's* serenity. Our peace and quiet didn't last long. Soon, friends inside had the same idea, and our secret place of solitude was discovered. Demetri came out with Grigori, Vasili, and Anastasia. They filtered themselves into our area, creating a sort of quiet party outside the dance hall.

Grigori leaned against an olive tree opposite a bench, while Demetri sat in between Despina and I. Next to Rania was Vasili and Cat-man, who we nicknamed because of his jet-black hair and bright green eyes. Cat-man had been in the army for the last two summers, so we hadn't seen him in a while, but we were thrilled when he returned to the village for the party. Cat-man was Demetri's best friend. His real name was Vasili, but Rania and I decided that there was too many Vasilis in our crowd and called him by his nickname all summer.

The streetlight next to our bench had gone out, keeping it especially dark where we sat and making us feel as if we were hiding out from the rest of the kids inside the dance. Demetri remained quieter than usual. We sat silently for a while until Rania broke the stillness.

"Okay. What is going on with you, Demetri? You've been acting weird all night." My face flushed as I felt Demetri's embarrassment.

"*Tipota*" (Nothing), he answered.

"Nope. Something's up." She turned away.

I looked at Demetri, feeling bad that Rania called attention to him, but he just smiled back at me. I tried to read his puzzling expression. Sitting beside me, Demetri had his arm on the back of the park bench. He moved his hand to the back of my shoulders, underneath my long hair, touching my neck. I smiled. He smiled. I started laughing. He started laughing. We sat that way for a while, fooling everyone around us as they went on talking.

Under the broken light, our friendship took its inevitable turn. While others kept busy with their conversation, Demetri turned toward me as if to tell a secret and kissed me. His was a short and sweet kiss, gently pressing his lips to mine. He quickly pulled back and looked at me, testing the boundaries. I smiled into his eyes. Rania left with Vasili, and no one paid attention to us, but when Demetri kissed me again, we heard Grigori say, "Oh, boy!" We knew he knew.

That was my simple, sweet moment of romance with Demetri. In some ways, our kiss was years in the making. Like Ari, he was honest and good, but he was also pure-hearted and innocent in his youth. He wasn't rushing my future. We were both at the same stage in life, still hanging onto our freedom, enjoying all that our young years had to offer. Demetri wasn't out for a green card or a move to the United States. He didn't want anything from me. All he cared about was enjoying his summer before returning to college.

Chapter 19
"See that Barrel?"

We left early the next morning for Tripoli, offering little time to dwell on Demetri's kiss. I was glad to avoid any awkwardness with my *kolite*. Were things going to be different now? What about Ari? What will everyone in Vassara think if Demetri and I become more than friends? As our cab neared the large city, my mind traveled the many twists and turns of questions and insecurities, but it inevitably drifted back to remembering Demetri's endearing good-bye the night before.

Rania had disappeared with Vasili after our group left the *platia*, and Demetri took me home late, just as he had done a thousand times before. Our walk in the pitch dark was silent. We didn't say much. We didn't have to. We reached my doorstep after 2:00 AM. He looked down at his feet, and I knew he felt as awkward as I did.

"I wish I hadn't waited until the last day of your trip to kiss you," he said.

"Yeah." I looked down, too, not knowing what to say.

Then Demetri's face showed a sudden look of relief. He looked up at me optimistically and said, "Look, we don't have to figure this out right now. Let's just say good night and *Kalo Ximona* and leave it at that." He smiled.

"Okay," I said, glad to be free from pressure. I couldn't begin to make sense of my feelings for Demetri, let alone explain them to anyone else. So much had happened that summer—the fires, Ari, and even seeing Stavros wounded and vulnerable put my head into a whirl. The last thing I needed was another situation to challenge my thoughts. I was thankful Demetri knew when to give space. In his honesty, he wasn't a puzzle to figure out like Stavros, and he didn't expect anything back in return for his affection like Ari. He was real, and he was my friend. The simple fact remained that we just liked being together. After spending some time in silence outside my gate, he gave me one more kiss to last all winter. His affection was warm and tender, and—most of all—felt true. I wasn't intimidated in Demetri's arms. I was at ease. He was honest with his emotions, and the bond that grew between us came about naturally, as if our feelings were predestined in this already close relationship. Despite Stavros's perfection and Ari's gorgeous looks, my connection with Demetri was the most real. Our friendship over the years laid the foundation for a deeper connection. Aside from being each other's *kolite*, Demetri's sincerity was unmatched, and a part of my heart will be his forever.

We said good night and good-bye for the winter. He promised to write, and I knew he would, as we had been pen pals for years between summers. When I got inside, Mom came out of the bathroom with a sleepy face.

"What are you doing up so late?" I asked her.

"Oh, I couldn't sleep. I think I drank too much Greek coffee over at Kiki's tonight. Ari called while you were out," she said, her eyes half shut.

"He did?" I was surprised. I didn't intend to talk to him again until the airport the day after next.

"Yeah, he called about an hour after you left with the girls. He wanted to know if it was okay with *me* if he stopped by the hotel in Tripoli. He said something about not being in Athens when we leave."

"Why not? He was supposed to meet me at the airport next week," I protested.

"He said he had a special meeting at the bank that he couldn't miss, but he asked if I would mind him coming to Tripoli." Mom seemed as surprised as I was.

"If *you* wouldn't mind?" I asked, confused.

Mom smiled. "Yeah. Always checking with me." She laughed. I knew the last thing Mom wanted to explain to Dad's relatives in Tripoli was why my Greek summer boyfriend was following us to Tripoli. "I told him that it was fine and that he could stop by the hotel in the afternoon. Maybe you guys can escape Dad's relatives for a while," she added. I stood there sort of shocked for a moment, feeling totally unprepared to face Ari. "You're okay with him coming, right?" Mom looked at me.

"Yeah. It's fine. Sorry … just a late night, you know." I threw my keys on the side table by the green rotary telephone. Looking at it made me flash back to the conversations with Ari the summer we first met. "Things were so much easier then," I thought. We didn't talk about the future. We didn't make big plans. We simply lived in the moment.

"He said he had something important to talk to you about—something that couldn't wait," Mom added.

I felt a knot in my stomach. "Really?" I knew exactly what he wanted to talk to me again about—green cards and working permits. I also suspected he purposely called the house in Vassara late, knowing I'd be out with Rania and Despina so that he could speak with Mom about seeing me in Tripoli. Maybe he suspected I would make up an excuse not to meet him. The idea that Ari tried to get to me through my mother only added to my frustration.

Mom turned and shuffled back to her bed. I lay down on my Vassara bed, staring at the same ceiling I did back in 1984 as a naïve, fourteen-year-old, boy-crazy in love with Stavros Antonopoulos. Now I was faced with a man in his thirties, wanting a future in America. Then there was Demetri—my best friend—where did *that* come from? I was too tired to make sense of anything and closed my eyes to sleep.

Pappou's obnoxious horn woke me up only a handful of hours later. Both my grandparents were dressed, fed, packed, and standing in the street next to the Audi. They looked at me as if I were from an alien planet, unable to understand my constant fatigue. While they averaged at least ten hours of sleep each night, not including the three to four hours of sleep they took during afternoon *mesimeri*, I was lucky to get any sleep at all, not wanting to waste a moment of vacation. Stumbling out of bed, I went to the window to see why they were ready for Tripoli this early, as we said we weren't going until the late afternoon.

"Where are Yiayia and Pappou going so early?" I mumbled to my mother.

"Oh, my goodness! I forgot to tell you, didn't I?" Mom asked, surprised.

"What's going on?" I looked at a lineup of packed bags by the balcony door.

"I am so sorry! I must have forgotten to mention it last night. I was so tired. We have to make a quick stop in Tsintzina before we go to Tripoli," Mom said as she went out the door with her carry-on. Then she yelled back, "Which means we'll be leaving a little earlier than we planned. No big rush, but try to get ready so we can leave in a little bit."

"What? When did you guys decide this? Tsintzina is totally out of the way! Why do we have to go *there*?" I followed her out to the balcony. Even though I enjoyed a lot of freedom on our vacations, there were times I still felt like a trapped teenager. Aggravated that my grandparents and mother changed plans at a moment's notice, I let out a loud groan.

Mom shot me an irritated look as she set her bag down outside on the terrace. "Pappou is interested in a car that his friend's brother is selling. The man lives in Tsintzina, and Pappou wants to go see it before we leave." She stopped and smiled, taking a deep breath. "I'm sorry I forgot to tell you. We'll make a quick stop there this morning, see the car, have lunch, and be in Tripoli by late afternoon. If you're concerned about Ari, don't worry. He's not getting to the hotel until late afternoon. We'll be there by then." My sympathetic mother was always trying to keep everyone happy.

"So am I to assume we're going to Kyriakos's to eat?" I sarcastically asked.

"Well, where else would we have lunch? It's the only restaurant in town!"

"But I thought we were shopping in Tripoli for the day?" I continued to protest. The last thing I wanted to deal with was Ari's parents. I wondered if they knew about their son's plan to move to Chicago. I tried unsuccessfully to undo the change in our plans. "Lunch will take forever, and the stores will be closed by the time we get there," I complained.

"No, they won't. Today is Thursday, remember? They're open late tonight." I could never keep Greece's crazy retail hours straight, closing everyday at 1:00 in the afternoon and then opening again at 6:00 pm, but only on Thursdays. None of it made sense.

I took a deep breath and looked at my mother. "So let me get this straight. We're going to Tsintzina where Ari *won't* be, but we'll see his family and have lunch with them. Then we're going to Tripoli to see Dad's family, where Ari is meeting me?" This was nuts.

Mom started laughing. "Yep. You got it. Never a dull moment, huh?" She walked down the balcony stairs, seeming not to have a care in the world, and set her bag in the Audi's front seat. Pappou was already sitting in his parked car, waiting for us to leave, and I hadn't even gotten in the shower yet. There was no stopping my mental tornado. Considering everything that had happened only hours ago with Demetri, the last thing I wanted was to see Ari's parents. As usual, I had no choice in the matter.

Pappou said he was going down to the *platia* to buy cigarettes and that he would be back in twenty minutes, which meant at least a half hour, as all of his old friends would be gathered for morning coffees and discussing the politics of the day. Relieved to have more time, I called Rania as soon as I got out of the shower. With dripping wet hair and a short, pink terrycloth robe wrapped around my body, I went to green rotary phone by the balcony doors to wake my cousin. She would help me make sense of everything. Standing outside with our telephones and looking at each other across the street, I described the details from the night before with Demetri, as well as my plans to meet Ari later that day.

"That's crazy! *You're* crazy!" she said as she laughed, looking at me from across the street. I had my hand on my throbbing head, asking my cousin what to do.

"Okay, okay," she said, laughing. "You'll be fine. Just go with the flow. See what the old man wants. If it's another visa discussion, you're gonna have to level with him, and better sooner than later." She paused. "As far as Demetri is concerned, my beloved cousin, I knew this was coming. Don't question what feels natural. He's cool. You're cool. Summer's over, anyway. Just go home, and you guys will figure it all out next year."

"I know. You're right." I paused and said, "Thanks." Smiling at her, I said, "Don't leave yet. I'll be down in a few to say good-bye." We hung up, and I went inside to get dressed as quickly as I could, popping a Nuprin to relieve my blasting headache.

Forty minutes later, Pappou returned from the *platia*. Despina came down the street to say our final, final good-bye, along with Rania. The two of them had their sad faces on as the three of us hugged farewell. Aunt Vivi came up behind us, crying at our packed car.

"Tou xronou" (Until next year)! Uncle Stavros said to Mom as they embraced. Kiki handed me a bag of fresh chamomile tea, harvested from Mount Taygetos, to bring back to the States. She knew the herbal tea was my favorite.

"Say hello to everyone in Tsintzina!" she said as she smirked at me. I forced a smile and got into the car. We loaded into the Audi and pulled out of Vassara.

The forty-five minute ride to Tsintzina took us almost an hour and a half because Pappou was behind the wheel. Hungry and tired, head still throbbing, I stared out the window, observing the region between Vassara, Verroia, and Tsintzina for the first time in daylight. Ari's village was much higher in the Parnonas hills than Vassara. Even though the hot August sun shone, the air was cool enough for a jacket. Pappou met his friend with his car for sale in the Tsintzina *platia,* while Yiayia, Mom, and I walked through the town to Kyriakos's restaurant. We were a little early for lunch, but the tavern doors were open.

Heading down the steps into the restaurant filled with empty tables, I flashed back to the night of the power outage when our group took over half of the restaurant, and I surprised Ari. Now the place was still, void of crowds or music. Ari's parents were inside the kitchen, preparing the midday meal. Yiayia called out to her longtime friends and went inside to order coffees. Mom shot me a look when we heard Kyriakos's welcoming yell as he greeted my grandmother loudly. Within minutes, we were seated at a table and served hot coffee, Greek salad, and freshly baked bread. I wondered if the loaves came from the same bakery Ari and I had visited years back on our way to Gythion.

"What a tragic twist that you're here, and he's not!" Kyriakos put his arm on my shoulder. "But don't fret, my dear. I hear he's meeting you in Tripoli later today. He can't wait to see you."

I just smiled at the man as he went on and on to my mother at how wonderful he thought I was and how happy Ari had been since we first met. Sitting at the end of our table, my eyes repeatedly glanced up at the staircase leading to Ari's bedroom, recalling the night we retreated to the upstairs apartment. He seemed so different back then—no hidden agenda. Now I had my doubts about his real intentions. At the same time, I hated myself for being suspicious.

Kyriakos served us a delicious lunch of *yemista*—stuffed ripened beefsteak tomatoes filled with sautéed rice, onions, and vegetables. Pappou returned from the *platia* a little disappointed that his friend's car wasn't in the condition he anticipated. Yiayia, who had until then remained relatively silent about my relationship with Ari, asked me to walk her to the bathrooms, which were outside and behind the tavern's kitchen. We walked together behind the building toward the glorified outhouse and past another door that revealed a small courtyard in back of the restaurant.

Across from the outdoor bathroom stalls sat Ari's mother and grandmother, parked atop two short barrels, with a third empty barrel beside them. At their feet rested a large tub of water filled with peeled potatoes, and next to each of them was a burlap bag of the unpeeled vegetable. Yiayia and I smiled and waved to them as they sat with their legs spread apart, making a hammock out of their calico skirts, which held a few potatoes and their paring knives. They waved back to us in return and then put their heads down and resumed peeling.

Yiayia squeezed my arm. "See that over there?" she asked, pointing to the empty third barrel.

"Yeah." I looked over to the ladies. "What, Yiayia?"

"That empty barrel in between Ari's mother and grandmother. See it?" She pointed with her eyes.

"What about it?" I asked.

"It's waiting for you!" She smiled and shook her head as she went into one of the stalls. I sort of laughed, not completely understanding her joke, but when Yiayia came out, I realized she wasn't joking. As we returned to our table, she continued, "What do you think? You won't be expected to help out around here? After all, this is his family's restaurant. This is where you would spend your free time, working with your in-laws for the summer, not partying with your friends in Vassara!" She paused and then added as we neared the table, "Go on! Go on and be with him! Forget about your life in America, the education your parents want for you, the career you've waited for. Go ahead and throw your life away, marry the good-looking village boy and peel potatoes with his mother and grandmother for the rest of your life!" She was half laughing, but completely serious. I sat down, speechless.

"What's wrong with *her*?" Mom asked Yiayia about me.

"*Tipota*," replied Yiayia. "*I alithia*" (The truth).

Yiayia's words felt like a stinging slap. For the first time, I pondered the "what ifs" of Ari's intentions and wondered what my life might actually be like if we stayed together. From the beginning of our relationship, I had only considered our fun times, never realizing that our connection had a real impact on Ari's future plans. Despite all warnings from Mom and even Ari's claim of wanting a green card, I had yet to take his intentions seriously. Somewhere in my immature mind, marrying Ari seemed like a funny joke, a topic to talk about over coffee along with winning the Lotto or sailing a boat around the Greek islands. None if it was real. Now I comprehended the consequences of dating Ari, a man more than ten years older than I, and certainly one who was ready for the next step in his adult life. I knew at that moment that although my feelings for Ari were genuine, I was the only one not taking our relationship in earnest.

Stronger than any of Aunt Potoula's words, Yiayia's comments were impactful. Although I put Chicago out of my mind for many weeks, thoughts of home flooded back. I thought about starting college, my friends, my family. Despite many years of fitting into Greece's culture, I knew I eventually belonged in the country of my birth. Facing this reality was difficult. College was the next milestone in my life, not a husband. Ari's plans weren't mine. I needed my future to unfold my way. Disappointment filled my heart as I understood we were going in separate directions, something I could ignore no longer. Fearing our next meeting, I sat quietly for the rest of our lunch.

Chapter 20
A Stop in Tripoli

WHEN WE CHECKED INTO the Artemis Hotel a few hours later, Ari was not there. I was relieved. "Maybe he got called away again for work," I thought. But then I looked at the clock above the check-in desk and realized that we were an hour ahead of the scheduled rendezvous time. In an instant, I was at the mercy of Dad's relatives. Uncle Ted was already at our hotel and waiting for us in the lobby when we arrived. He sat in a chair across from the check-in desk, hurriedly finishing a cigarette he must have lit as he waited. Uncle Ted's green Nova was parked outside our hotel, right in front, disregarding the No Parking/Loading Zone sign. His car always seemed ready to whisk us away somewhere I never wanted to go.

"Ela! Ela!" He stood up when we walked into the lobby and pointed to his Nova while we attempted to check in at the front desk. The young girl behind the counter handed Mom a large, metal key. She held up her hand to Uncle Ted to wait a moment while we signed for our room. Uncle Ted's frantic behavior was the same as the last time we saw him—the night of Vassara's fire. He acted as if the world would explode if we didn't leave the hotel immediately. Mom patiently ignored his pestering.

"He's just excited to bring us to his house." She tried to excuse his behavior. "You know Aunt Thora—she's probably cooking up a huge farewell feast for us. That's just how they are!"

"Please tell him to wait, Mom." I nudged her. "The last thing I want to do is rush off to Steno. I really want to go up to our room and change clothes. Why do we always have to rush off to Uncle Ted's village and sit around their house all day? I want to walk in the Tripoli *platia*! I want to have a Coke and relax for a minute before we do anything else!" I raised my voice, upset and overtired.

"Coke? Does the child want Coke?" Ted intruded on our conversation. "We have liters of Coke back in our village of Steno. *Ela*, Aunt Thora awaits you with a big feast she's been preparing especially for you." He stood shouting in the lobby with his arms spread wide, making a big scene, as always. I was utterly embarrassed.

"Please, Mom, please let's just relax a bit. I'm exhausted!" Mom looked at me with wide eyes, and I knew she hated the horribly difficult job of appeasing Uncle Ted as well as keeping to our own schedule first and foremost. This was no easy task given my uncle's persistence.

"I had no intention of going to Steno this soon. I wanted to hit a few of the shops around here before they close for afternoon siesta and get your father, sister, and brother some gifts to bring home. Relax. I'll handle it." She winked.

I smiled in victory. Mom turned to Ted and gently explained our conflicting agendas while I walked away, knowing he'd be upset that we were once again refusing his plan. I always sensed he blamed me for not complying with his wishes, assuming that my mother supported his every idea and that any disruption to his plan must be coming from the bratty teenager. He always wanted us in Tripoli, and I always begged Mom to stay in Vassara. Uncle Ted couldn't comprehend why I would "waste" our summer there.

Mom told my uncle to come back after siesta to get us. He wasn't happy. I waved good-bye and headed up the stairs to our hotel room. Dragging my bag into our fresh room, I plopped down on the newly white-sheeted twin bed. As I stared up at the ceiling, I smiled, grateful that soon I'd be back in my own room, with my own mattress, soft bedding, stereo, air-conditioning, and yes, Walgreens.

Within seconds, the phone rang. Mom was calling from the lobby.

"Ari's here!" she said with tension in her voice. She paused. "Uncle Ted is talking to him."

"What? Uncle Ted hasn't left yet?" I answered back.

"Uh-uh," said Mom, echoing my reaction. "So here's another plan change.

Uncle Ted says he'd like to get to know your *friend* better, and maybe the four of us can get a coffee at the *platia* for a while." My heart sank. Mom continued, "Then you and Ari can spend some time together while Uncle Ted helps me shop for the family. Then he'll take us back to Steno with him." Mom was saying all of this with that "I-hate-this-idea-but-don't-know-how-to-get-out-of-it" voice.

"He always gets what he wants," I barked back.

"That's not true," Mom defended herself pitifully.

"I'll be down in a minute. Tell Ari to wait for me in the lobby. I'll be right down. *Please* don't let Uncle Ted say anything stupid to him," I instructed.

"Yeah, right! I'd get down here fast if I were you!" Mom laughed.

I quickly threw on my red tank dress, wishing I had something else to wear. There was no time to fuss, however, as I put on the only thing left in my suitcase that was clean besides my outfit for the plane.

Ari was leaning against the check-in counter when I made my way down the stairs.

"Hi, there!" I said cheerfully, hoping our visit would go better than I anticipated and that he couldn't see the guilt over Demetri behind my eyes. Even though Ari was smiling, he looked different to me as I approached him, but I couldn't figure out how or why.

"Did your mother give you my message? I hope you don't mind," he said as he kissed me hello. The hotel clerk looked us up and down.

"Let's get out of here. How much time do you have?" I asked.

"Just a few hours. I have to be back in Tsintzina for the dinner rush. I heard you saw my folks this afternoon," he said.

"Yeah, lunch was great. Weird with you not there, though." I looked over at Mom and Uncle Ted. "Sorry about my uncle. He follows us everywhere when we're in this city," I explained.

"No, it's okay. Actually, I think it's kind of nice that he wants to get to know me. After all ..."

We walked out of the hotel, Uncle Ted's shouted greeting from across the café cutting off Ari's words. Mom and Uncle Ted were at a small, round table with four chairs. I could hear Mom giving Uncle Ted Ari's bio as we approached. My uncle had a critical look on his face that made me want to vomit. "Give me a break," I thought. "You are *not* my father, and it is *not* up to you to approve or disapprove of anyone for me." I wished I could have said that aloud.

"Would you *kids* like some ice cream?" Uncle Ted asked as our waiter approached.

"What are we, twelve?" I thought. I wanted to say, "Yeah, Uncle Ted, my thirty-something boyfriend wants ice cream." Instead, I said, "Nothing for me."

Ari pulled out a cigarette that Uncle Ted lit, and he ordered a coffee. I kicked him under the table. Couldn't he have just had water and we could leave? Instead, Ari morphed into a never before seen "I'm-trying-to-impress-the-family" routine, answering all of Uncle Ted's questions as if he were applying for a job. Mom and I rolled our eyes back and forth across the table. Uncle Ted and Ari went on with their banter in some sort of male-approval ritual while they pretended to be interested in what the other person was saying.

Finally, I had to put an end to this back and forth, and I broke the line of questioning. "Okay, well, Ari doesn't have a lot of time in Tripoli, so we're going to go now." I stood up and grabbed a room key, shooting Ari a look to get up, as well.

Mom jumped in to help. "Yeah, I really want to get to these stores before they close." She got her purse off of the back of her chair and pulled out a gift-shopping list from her wallet.

Ari shook Uncle Ted's hand and said good-bye. Within minutes, Ari and I walked across the street. He put his arm around me as we walked away from the hotel toward the Tripoli *platia*. The town square was famous for its rose gardens, a perfect place to have a completely uncomfortable conversation. Happy to see Ari, I was still uneasy knowing it was a matter of time before the green card conversation came up again.

As we walked off, a vision of Ari's mother and grandmother sitting on two barrels with an empty one next to them kept popping up in my head. I tried to stop recalling Yiayia's words, but over and over, I remembered her warning, "*See that empty barrel? It's waiting for you!*" I squeezed his hand that held mine in an effort to dismiss the memory. Ari stopped to look at me now that we were finally alone. He was different. In many ways, I didn't recognize the man in front of me. This was not the Ari I knew. He leaned forward to kiss me, but instead of butterflies in my stomach, I heard Potoula in my head saying, *"Don't do anything stupid. Go back to America and get your college degree. Forget about marrying a guy from here— it will never work."*

After our awkward kiss, we continued on toward the garden path. Before we saw our first rose, he asked if I had given the subject of him coming to America any thought. I didn't know what to tell him. I beat around the bush for a while until finally he said to me, "Don't you want me to come?"

"Of course I do," I answered. "But I have to finish school."

"There's nothing stopping you from finishing school. You'll study, I'll get a job, and we'll be together." As he said this to me, I didn't feel a bit of sincerity in his voice. I got the sense that his focus was more about coming over to the States than being with me.

The idea of Ari in Chicago was terrifying. Even if his intentions were real, the last thing I needed was a visitor hovering over me while I tried to thrive in a collegiate setting. My thoughts were on having fun with my sorority, trying out for the collegiate cheerleading squad, and enjoying campus life, not betrothing myself for all of eternity. I couldn't help but hear the warnings screaming in my head that Ari's real plan was to establish residency in America by engaging himself to a U.S. citizen. The pushier Ari became about the green card, the more apprehensive I grew. I figured any guy that loved me would want to wait for me, not back me into corner and suggest that if I truly loved him, I'd bring him to the States as his sponsor.

In the past, our good-byes were spent reminiscing over our time together while dreading the inevitable separation over another winter. Now, due to the fires and Ari's work, we had no time to go to the beach or see each other like we had in the past. Instead, what remained what merely a lot of talk about the future through questioning phone calls about whether or not I had talked with my parents regarding his visa.

Time wasn't going by fast enough as we walked the pathways of flowers and statues that adorned Tripoli's public buildings. Since Ari wouldn't be in Athens at the airport to see me off, this was our last good-bye. He let me change the subject for a little while as we proceeded to an outdoor café and sat down for something to eat. Ari was agitated; I could see it on his face. I didn't know how to answer his questions about "our" future. Truth be told, I didn't know if we had one.

After a lunch of few words, Ari walked me past some museums, and we both agreed that Tripoli was not even remotely as beautiful as Sparta. Near a statue of an ancient Tripoli warrior that stood across the street from my hotel, we said a tear-free good-bye for the first time ever.

"I leave it up to you," he said defeatedly.

"I just don't know, Ari. I don't know if my father will sign for you."

"Well," he said as his hands fell at his sides, "you know I love you, and I want the best for you. Right now, it comes down to what *you* want."

I kissed him softly and told him I'd call when I landed in Chicago. He didn't smile. Gone was the twinkle in his eyes. He looked distraught. I walked away unsatisfied and uncertain. Disappointment settled in my heart over our less-than-romantic farewell that was void of any real passion or love. Now I was on the hot seat, left to make a final decision regarding our relationship.

After an unbearable night of getting my cheeks squeezed by my father's cousins at Uncle Ted and Aunt Thora's house and avoiding the many questions about my "friend" at the hotel, Mom and I returned to the Artemis Hotel and slept.

The next day, we left for Athens. Glad to get out of Tripoli, my heart was heavy with regret that a once beautiful and exciting love affair had soured. In addition to Vassara's wildfires and Ari's pressure to come to America, I wondered if my days of gold were coming to an end. That summer was disappointing on many fronts, and I wasn't sure I wanted to return. I knew my days in Vassara wouldn't last forever. I also knew I wouldn't find true happiness in a land where I would always be a foreigner. For the first time, I was glad to get on a plane and return the United States of America.

Chapter 21
A Final Farewell

WITHIN A WEEK OF returning from Greece, I was off on my own for the first time in my life. I loved living on campus, and I soon made friends in the dorm as well as with the girls on my collegiate cheerleading squad and in my new sorority. College was more than I imagined. With the distractions of campus life, thoughts of Greece were temporarily put aside. Like our group of friends in Vassara, I adored spending time with a large group of friends that spent their days and nights together. My older sorority sisters took me under their wings, and along with other freshman classmates, I once again celebrated being a part of something bigger than myself.

A few weeks into the school year, I received my first envelope from Demetri in my college mailbox. He sent a beautiful card with a photo on the front of a man and woman embracing next to an airplane. The man in the photo resembled Demetri, and the woman had long, dark hair. In the card, he wrote:

"To my Koliti,

Thank you for the beautiful letter you sent. Congratulations on making the cheerleading squad of your college. I knew you would do well. How is college life? I'm glad you like your roommate. I think you will also like the photo on the front of this card. Last week, a few of us went out to the dance clubs in Sparta. The night wasn't the same without you. We had a good time and gathered a good amount of the kids before everyone returned to school. We partied all night. Don't worry, we made a special toast to you and Rania! Can you believe the holidays are almost here? I hope this new decade of the '90s brings us all together just like we were in the '80s. I'm playing a lot of basketball here in Athens at school and am studying hard, but I miss you. Can't believe we're all back to our real lives again. Summer went by so fast. That's really all my news. I am anxious to hear back from you. Write me right away. I kiss you with love, Demetri. P. S. What do you think of the couple on the front of the card?????

Your Kolite,
Demetri"

I answered Demetri's letter quickly and didn't hesitate to express anxiety over returning to Greece. I knew Demetri would understand. He did, and he wrote that he felt I'd eventually let the good of the village outweigh the bad and desire once more to spend summers in Vassara. Ever the friend, Demetri advised gently, without criticism or judgment, and over time, he dispelled my pessimistic apprehension of the village. In another letter the following month, he wrote:

"Don't remember the bad—remember the good. Remember staying up late under Koulouri's stars and singing along with Kosma's guitar. Remember drunken Panteli attempting to learn your American songs and believing he sounded like Madonna. Remember how we laughed with Rania. Remember all of these good times. There are more memories for us to make. Our village and all those who live there wait for you to return. Vassara will never hurt you. She loves you as much as you love her.

You are in my heart. Demetri."

On cold winter nights, I stayed up late into the night in my dorm room, windows iced over from winter's frost, with a stack of English literature books on my desk or a term paper to write. With dorm walls covered by posters of Sade, U2, and Greece, I read and reread Demetri's cards and letters, looking at photos from the summer of Rania and I and the gang. There in my dorm, I escaped back to the village I loved. I wrote him back long, detailed letters describing my new college life, while at the same time recalling our fun summer memories with Rania and the rest of the gang. He told me of his life in Athens, as well, and always about getting together with other kids from the village for holidays or long weekends. Our exchange was relaxed—never overwhelmed with themes of love or romance. We were friends first.

Throughout the school year, Demetri was a constant supply of encouragement and love, but never in a way that I found threatening. I was grateful for our connection that helped me get through the many ups and downs that any college freshman experiences. Our communication was a constant reassurance that someone out there understood me—someone out there knew the "other" me that longed to be in the mountains of Parnonas, gazing at Mount Taygetos and tall cypress trees.

Eventually, after many exchanges of thoughts and memories, Demetri helped me fall back in love with Vassara. I let go of bad memories about the fires and quite consciously chose to keep only positive thought regarding Vassara foremost in my mind.

While this was occurring with Demetri, something very opposite developed with Ari. For a long time after my first arrival on campus, I didn't hear from him. I knew Ari's feelings were hurt that I wasn't able to promise sponsorship before leaving Greece. Close to Christmas break, one early Saturday morning, my dorm room phone rang, and I heard his familiar voice on the other end. At first, I was excited that he'd called. I hoped that in talking to him, we could mend whatever went wrong months earlier. Ari didn't waste any time asking for help getting to America. I tried to explain how busy life was on campus and that I had yet to make sense out of anything regarding his visa. I tried to ask him how his parents were doing and how his job at Eurobank was going, but he was angry and refused to talk about anything else. He didn't ask about my studies. He didn't ask me what I thought of college life. The multitude of Ari's charming traits evaporated as he remained obsessed with moving to the States. I felt an increasing distance between us but told him that I'd look into the situation. He said he'd stay in touch to find out my progress. The time had come to tell my mother. Since I wasn't twenty-one, and sponsorship papers required a legal signature, I had no choice but to involve my parents. When I finally confessed Ari's plan to Mom, she reacted just as I'd imagined she would.

"Are you *crazy*?" Her anger came through the phone. I didn't have the nerve to bring up the subject with her in person. "I'm not asking your father to sign anything!" Mom exclaimed.

"I don't even understand why he needs it. Why can't he just come on a plane and visit the U.S. like we do when we go there?" I naively asked.

"Because he wants to stay for an extended time," Mom explained. "They can't just come here and stay indefinitely like we do when we go to Greece. It's different for foreigners. He needs a signature from a legal-aged citizen if he wants to work here. That signature is a voucher for his conduct in the United States. If he does anything illegal while he's here or gets into any trouble ..."

"Dad is responsible. I get it," I interrupted. Mom softened her tone, and she sensed I finally understood the impossibilities.

"Look, honey, I know you really like this guy, but there's no way Dad would sign anything like that, number one. Number two, I don't even want to imagine your father's reaction if you asked him about it. You need to tell Ari this is not going to happen."

After months of denial, I concluded that Ari would not come to America on my watch, and I knew that the time had come to tell him. Certainly this would end things between us, I thought, although our relationship had already drastically changed. Later that day, I finally picked up the phone and explained that I couldn't ask my father to sponsor him. Ari was, as I'd expected, furious. Our conversation was brief at best. As soon as I stated my position, he hung up the phone with barely a good-bye. He said he'd call back later, but he never did. I tried to call him back the next day, and the day after that, but he didn't take my calls.

A month passed, and with no phone calls returned, I was happy to discover a card from him in the mail. Curious to see if he had gotten over his anger, I opened the envelope optimistically. Perhaps he realized what an enormous amount of pressure he was putting on me and finally accepted the idea of coming to the States on his own. The card was a cut-out of a dozen red roses, as if Ari was sending me another bouquet like the day he greeted me at the airport. I smiled, relieved that at long last, he understood.

I was mistaken. Instead of words of love or friendship, Ari wrote an angry note inside the paper roses expressing his resentment over my refusal to help him, and he called my feelings for him insincere and untrue. He blasted me for leading him on, and he cursed the day he met me. I sat for a while, dumbfounded, and then I picked up the phone and dialed my mother. I read his words over the phone to her. She was just as shocked.

Tearing the card into pieces, I threw the scraps in the garbage, refusing to believe Ari thought I was insincere. We had known each other for years, and surely he knew how much I cared for him. The more Ari displayed his anger, the more I wondered if I was the one who had been mistaken all along. Perhaps all he wanted from the beginning was a way into the United States. I had heard plenty of stories of other girls who had been fooled by citizen-seeking men. I was not about to destroy my future by bringing over a Greek boyfriend to Chicago, only to be betrayed the minute he settled in America.

Reflecting on our relationship, I realized in recent years that most of our time together was spent discussing his immigration to the States. Our relationship had become more about his visa than about our feelings for one another. "Forget it," I thought. "Forget Ari. He didn't talk about *our* future; he talked about *his* future in Chicago." My initial anger quickly became a sense of self-awareness and relief. At long last, I saw my love affair with Ari for what it really was—a summer fling. In the end, I was thankful to avoid potential disaster.

Several weeks after the rose card arrived, I received a voicemail from Ari apologizing for sending angry words. He said he wrote it out of frustration and that he didn't mean what he said. He said he knew my feelings for him were true but that he was overwhelmed with disappointment. He also said that he'd find another way to get to America. He hoped when he arrived, I'd agree to see him. Despite his apology, I couldn't get over the shock I felt that a man who supposedly loved me could turn into an angry, mean person so easily. This side of Ari was one I never knew and didn't care to see again.

While I gained interest in returning to Greece through Demetri's letters, Ari's actions only reinforced my feelings to leave Greece behind. The timing of their letters was ironic, as I corresponded with both of them at the same time. While one pulled me toward Greece, the other pushed me further away. As a result, I grew ambivalent about the approaching summer, unsure of what to do in the months that lay ahead until I spoke with my mother.

Ever the wise woman, she gave me great advice. "Well, you don't *have* to tell Ari that we're coming."

What a great idea. I could enjoy my last summers in the village without Ari knowing I was in the country. As far as Kiki outing me, I wasn't worried. Besides, I thought, the time had obviously come to let my relatives know that my betrothal to Ari wasn't going to happen. I hadn't thought of going to Greece without telling Ari, but that's exactly what I planned. Ari never came to America of his own accord, and I never informed him of my subsequent trips to Greece.

1989 and 1990 were my two last summers in Greece before I graduated college, got a job, and met my husband. They were fun summers, spent without an emotional agenda. No one waited for me at the airport when we arrived the following July. Thankfully, the wildfires didn't rekindle in Peloponnese. These last two trips were enjoyably uneventful. Perhaps as I matured, simply being in Greece became enough.

I never had any sort of resolution with Stavros. The big *"tell him you'll always love him"* scene that I had played out in my mind so many times never happened. He treated me politely and distantly as always. Rania remained involved with his little brother Vasili. But she kept her Greek summer loves in perspective like I did.

Demetri was all smiles when he saw my taxi pull into the *platia* that next July, and we spent many nights in each other's arms under Vassara's sky of stars. I got to know his parents, who were very kind, gentle people. His mother liked me especially. Rania and I even went to their house for lunch one day. Demetri's mom made us tuna salad sandwiches and french fries that were outstanding. She always smiled at me warmly, knowing her son and I had a special bond. After all, we were each other's *kolite*. In the end, Demetri was good and true and honest about defining our relationship. Both of us knew eventually we would move on with our lives, apart from each other.

When I arrived to Greece the following year, I learned that Demetri was seeing one of the Boston girls. She was as beautiful as a supermodel, and I knew I couldn't compete. In many ways, I didn't want to try. Knowing we weren't overly serious about one another, I was relieved to return to our "best friend" status. That was my last consecutive summer in Vassara. No one really said it, but we knew the golden days were over. Our group diminished almost completely through the demands of school, the army, or jobs. Left as only a few diehard Vassara summer lovers, we desperately attempted to hold on to the last magic sparks of an era that will live on in our memories forever.

I spent many afternoons that final summer taking long walks alone through the village streets, nostalgically recalling all that the village meant to me through my teenaged years. Almost a decade earlier, I had come to Vassara like a wounded animal, too sad and weak to heal myself while grieving for my aunt. After she died, my whole world died, too, and I never thought there would be a reason to be happy again. But, through time, I did heal, and I grew. My heart opened up like a flower to the places and people around me, and once again, I found joy in this hidden town halfway across the globe.

On one of my final walks through the village during a warm afternoon siesta when most everyone was asleep, I walked past the school and the *Yipetho*. No one was practicing soccer. The area was quiet and still. Only the soft, warm breeze hitting the grapevines growing from balconies broke the otherwise silent afternoon.

As I reached the outskirts of Vassara and came upon the monastery, I thought about the wildfires and Ourania's churches. Did she ever imagine her quest would save the village? Did she know her vision of *Panayia* would impact everyone around her?

I stood at the steps of the Virgin Mary's monastery, looking up at a circular mosaic icon of the Mother of God that overhangs the front brass gate and pondered these thoughts. The church buildings behind the gates stood strong, as if they had been there for a hundred years. Yet leading up to the monastery from the left was a small plot of land with newly planted olive trees already flourishing in the summer sun. That's when I realized she was there. She came to our rescue. She came to my rescue, as well. Her presence was always there, even when we weren't looking. In that moment, I knew just as the Virgin Mary's church spared this town from raging wildfires, the Mother of God also saved me from the moment I arrived in 1984. Perhaps the only way I'd get over the pain of losing my aunt was to fall in love and find life in another place. Somehow, I was brought to this village for a reason.

In later years, I came to know more stories of the Virgin Mary in relation to our village. Yiayia explained that the Mother of God has been protecting the village for centuries. But as recently as my lifetime, Vassara was spared before my own eyes. I wondered how many other lives were saved by coming to this enchanted village over the centuries, hearts full of pain, troubles overwhelming. How many souls were healed by the *Panayia* in this ancient town through its beauty and uniqueness?

As I now know, Vassara is and will always be a miracle village, remembered by the Mother of God herself. Vassara is a sacred place to all its descendants. As *Panayia* protects Vassara, we know that she is alive today, working miracles in a miraculous village. Perhaps this is God's purpose for a little, hidden community in the mountains of Parnonas. Perhaps this is his will. Through Vassara, we see the Mother of God, and through Vassara, the Mother of God loves us.

When we made our final farewells that summer, I had a sinking feeling I wouldn't be back for a long time. Despina echoed my suspicions, as well. We cried together up at Koulouri, promising to stay a part of each other's world as much as possible despite the distance. We planned optimistically for the far-off future, hoping that someday the golden days would return in a new form or likeness. In the meantime, they would live on in our memories forever.

Chapter 22
Never Did I Imagine

SITTING SHOTGUN IN OUR tiny, rented Fiat driven by my American husband, I passed a bag of fruit snacks to my four-and-a-half-year-old son. I couldn't help but find the whole experience surreal. Without realizing it, over the years since my consecutive visits to Greece, I built up my memories to the point where I started to question my own experience. Was it all real? As soon as I saw the view of the village break through the mountains, I knew the golden days were indeed true. Although a decade had passed, I felt as if I never left. Even seeing Stavros wasn't weird. Afterward, my heart beat little faster—but perhaps only because I thought it should. He seemed shorter, less grand.

Kiki's face was the same—a little more aged, eyes slightly glassier from age or illness or both, but she still held her fiery personality. The same went for Uncle Tatzaforo. Uncle Georgo and Aunt Vivi were timeless. The great, green door is now painted a muted grayish blue, but it still stands high to those that enter their welcoming home. Despina, God bless her, lives a happy life in Athens as an artist with an adorable son and loving husband. She is a beautiful mother.

The faces of the kids of yesteryear are older, but their spirits remain the same. Thanasi is still Thanasi. Grigori is still Grigori. Even Vasili had his same crooked smile as though he was thinking something sly. Who knows what they said about me after I left, but hopefully they understood that despite my many years away from the village, their home is still my home in my heart and in my soul. I leave a part of myself behind, waiting for the rest of me to return, so that only when I am there am I complete.

I felt the spirit of our house in Vassara still in the walls and floors, although decrepit and old. The rooms spoke to me. They echoed laughter of the 1980s and '90s. They reminded me of my teenaged heartaches. Full of voices from the past, I could almost hear Rania's laughter, feel Yiayia's happiness, and sense my mother's friendship as I recalled how much I tried to make the golden days live on forever. Surely something permanent would come of these years in the village. Surely he would realize his mistake and marry me. Surely I would move to the village and never look back at the United States again. Surely I would have Vassara forever.

Never did I imagine a decade would pass before I returned. Never did I imagine Yiayia would be gone from us. Never did I imagine that my life's partner would not only not be from Vassara but not even be Greek.

How the previous decade laid out didn't matter anymore. The truth was that 1984–1992 still defined me, and it will forever. Vassara lives. Vassara is a plane ride away. Vassara waits for me and for anyone who wants to touch the magic. Vassara is for believers. Vassara makes the nonbelievers believe again. Vassara is life. Vassara is love. Vassara is a miracle. Vassara is a story worth telling.

The End

FOL

MAY 2 9 2024

LaVergne, TN USA
19 October 2010

201375LV00006B/75/P